surrender

Also by Lisa Renee Jones

The Inside Out Series
If I Were You
Being Me
Revealing Us
*His Secrets**
Rebecca's Lost Journals
*The Master Undone**
*My Hunger**
No In Between
*My Control**
I Belong to You
*All of Me**

A Standalone Inside Out Novel
*Inside Out: Behind Closed Doors**

The Secret Life of Amy Bensen
Escaping Reality
Infinite Possibilities
Forsaken
*Unbroken**

The Careless Whispers Series
Denial
Demand
Surrender

---

*Ebook only

surrender

LISA RENEE JONES

G

GALLERY BOOKS

New York London Toronto Sydney New Delhi

G

Gallery Books
An Imprint of Simon & Schuster, Inc.
1230 Avenue of the Americas
New York, NY 10020

First Gallery Books trade paperback edition July 2017

GALLERY BOOKS and colophon are registered trademarks of Simon & Schuster, Inc.

The Simon & Schuster Speakers Bureau can bring authors to your live event. For more information or to book an event contact the Simon & Schuster Speakers Bureau at 1-866-248-3049 or visit our website at www.simonspeakers.com.

Library of Congress Cataloging-in-Publication Data

Names: Jones, Lisa Renee, author.
Title: Surrender / Lisa Renee Jones.
Description: New York : Gallery Books, 2017. | Series: Careless whispers ; [3]
Identifiers: LCCN 2017016438
Subjects: | BISAC: FICTION / Romance / Suspense. | FICTION / Romance / Contemporary. | FICTION / Contemporary Women. | GSAFD: Romantic suspense | fiction. | Erotic fiction.
Classification: LCC PS3610.O627 S87 2017 | DDC 813/.6—dc23
LC record available at https://lccn.loc.gov/2017016438

Interior design by Davina Mock-Maniscalco

ISBN 978-1-5011-2288-0
ISBN 978-1-5011-2294-1 (ebook)

Dear Readers:

I can't believe we are finally about to *Surrender*, after all that denial and demand ☺. For the many of you who have written me, so very eager for this book, thank you for your patience and excitement. I hope it lives up to your expectations and makes the wait worthwhile. I am excited about this one for many reasons. Ella's such a survivor, and as she takes on her own life, she inspires me to be one, as well. And I wouldn't mind kicking ass the way she does, too!

Many of you started Ella's story with the Inside Out series, and for those of you who know that series, guess what? Chris and Sara are back in *Surrender*! And oh, how surreal it was to write about them again, if only a little bit. For new readers, Chris and Sara will offer you some small glimpses into Ella's life from the Inside Out series. So let's recap before we start *Surrender*. Spoiler warning! If you have not read *Denial* and *Demand*, do not read forward!

We all remember where this story started in *Denial*. Ella wakes up in a hospital bed with amnesia, having been saved by Kayden Wilkens. As they wade through the dangers of her memory loss and his Treasure Hunting world (The Underground), their passion and connection become something they can no longer ignore. And what comes of their weakness for one another is a lasting emotional bond and the ultimate exchange of trust.

Kayden and Ella began book two, *Demand*, by testing
the strength of their relationship with the weight of their
secrets and lies. What eventually comes of that is a stronger
and deeper connection in the face of both Neuville's
impending threat and Niccolo's deception. The two warring
stepbrothers, who run the French and Italian mobs, are at
odds over each other, Ella, and the butterfly necklace that she
once held in her hands. But her memory still refuses to allow
her access to why she had it and where she left it.

We left Ella and Kayden right after their confrontation
with Blake Walker, one of the founding brothers of Walker
Security, who was sent by Ella's best friend, Sara, and Chris
Merit to find Ella. After Blake finally found her, he helped
shed some light on who she is. Yet with more of the truth
came more uncertainty. Ella has just dropped the bomb that
she believes she has a connection to the CIA. She's unsure of
what kind of connection it is—but what will this mean for her
and Kayden's relationship? And who does this make her in the
grand scheme of the terrifying web of danger they still find
themselves in?

There is so much more to explore in *Surrender*, and I hope
you'll enjoy the final installment of Ella's story . . .

xoxo,
Lisa

characters

Ella Ferguson (25)—Heroine in the series. Woke alone in Italy, saved by our hero, Kayden Wilkens. Best friend to Sara McMillan from the Inside Out series.

Kayden Wilkens (32)—Our hero in the series. Leader of the Italian branch of The Underground (a treasure-hunting operation). Saves Ella and brings her to live in his castle while she recovers.

Niccolo—Very dangerous Italian mobster. Ella has some sense of unease and knowledge of this man that she can't quite grasp.

Matteo—Works for Kayden and The Underground as a hacker. He helps create Ella's new identity as Rae Eleana Ward, and continues to try to find out who Ella is.

Adriel Santaro—Both lives and works for Kayden running a high-end collectibles store from the castle. Kayden fired him from The Underground after Adriel's father was killed on a hunt.

Giada Santaro—Adriel's sister. Also works in the collectibles store. Has a very hard time coping with her mother and father's deaths. Blames Kayden and The Underground for her father's murder.

Marabella—Kayden's housekeeper, lives on the premises. Very close to Kayden, Adriel, and Giada. Is considered a mother figure by them all.

Detective Gallo—Kayden's greatest adversary. Very intent on making trouble for Kayden, and on finding out who Ella really is.

Chief Donati—The chief of police; Detective Gallo's boss. Friendly with Kayden, yet hiding secrets of his own.

Sasha—A Hunter. Her family is made up of Hunters and Hawks that used to run the French branch of The Underground, before Kayden took over for them. She befriends Ella and has quite the personality.

Blake Walker—A transplant from both the Tall, Dark and Deadly series (you can read his and Kara's story in *Beneath the Secrets*) and the Inside Out series. Chris Merit (Inside Out) hired Blake to help him and Sara find Ella after she ran off to elope with David and disappeared. At the end of the Inside Out series, Blake was still searching for her.

Enzo—One of The Underground's newest and youngest members, killed during a dangerous mission.

Elizabeth—Kayden's deceased fiancée. She was murdered in the castle five years ago.

Nathan—Physician for The Underground who helps Ella as she recovers from her severe concussion. While very charismatic, he is also tough and implacable.

David—Ella's ex-fiancé (mentioned in the Inside Out series). He swept Ella off to Paris to elope. Very vivid and shocking memories return to Ella of her time with David, involving lot of arguing and anguish. At the end of *Denial* Ella still cannot remember all that transpired between her and David, but she does know she didn't love him.

Kevin—Kayden's adoptive father. He was the original owner of the castle and the previous leader of the Italian branch of The Underground. After he was murdered along with Elizabeth five years ago, Kayden took over his post in The Underground and ownership of the castle. Best friend to Kayden's father.

Sara McMillan—Ella's best friend from San Francisco. Readers might know her as the heroine from the Inside Out series. She is married to Chris Merit.

Chris Merit—Famous billionaire artist married to Ella's best friend, Sara. They are currently residing in Paris. Read Chris and Sara's full story in the Inside Out series.

The Jackals—A highly corrupt group of "pirates" who will do any dirty work and double-cross anyone they see fit.

Alessandro—Leader of The Jackals.

Garner Neuville—Head of the French Mob. "Saved" Ella after David abandoned her in Paris, but soon turned out to be her worst nightmare. He is the cause of her most horrific memories as they slowly return. Stepbrother to Niccolo.

Carlo—One of Kayden's hunters. Former Jackal.

prologue

sara

*E*lla's alive!

It is the news I have hoped and prayed to receive for months on end. It doesn't feel real until I hear her voice on the phone, and suddenly all the pieces of my heart, which I was certain would end up shattered, are healed. But too soon, she ends the connection. I hold the phone to my ear, not ready to let go of her, haunted by her secrecy and reliving the past thirty minutes that got me to this moment. I was in Chris's studio, reveling in the fact that this famous, sexy artist has been my husband for almost two weeks—and then it happened, the moment I'd been anticipating for months. I shut my eyes and live it again, because how can I not want to live it again?

A Matchbox Twenty song fills the air, fuel for his creative juices; a canvas is in front of him, a brush in his hand. He's only a few feet away from me, focused on his work, his longish blond hair sexily mussed up, his feet bare, his jeans slung low. He wears no shirt, of course. He never paints with a shirt on, which is quite all right with me, considering I have a delicious view of a well-defined chest, and his multicolored dragon tattoo that speaks of a jagged-edged past and a soul that is dark and light in equal parts—much like the paint he marks on his canvas.

There is something special about watching him work here in Paris, in the city where he first picked up a brush that would turn him into a rock star of the art world. Especially since he is painting me. I am naked and exposed in every way with this man, sitting in the alcove of a massive arched window, my legs pulled to my chest. There was a time when I swore I'd never let him paint me. When I knew he'd see things I didn't want him to see, because I didn't want to see them myself. But that was then, and this is now. And while I am still damaged, still fighting old wounds, no one understands better about the cuts that never heal than Chris Merit. No one understands the damage that can never be repaired, but simply caressed. We are two lost souls that were found in the fog of pain and heartache, able to see again, to breathe again, as one.

I am lost in that spell when Chris's cell phone rings and he digs it from his pocket. The instant he gives me his back, I know something is wrong. It's in the sharp way he turns and the knotting of his shoulders. I'm on my feet in an instant, darting for his T-shirt on the chair next to his easel and canvas. I've just pulled it over me when I watch him drag his fingers through his hair, an act of emotion he'd show no one but me. Ella, I think, fearing that this is the news we've waited for from Blake Walker, the PI we'd hired to find her, and that it must not be good. I hug myself, preparing for the worst. She's dead. She must be dead.

"Now?" Chris asks the caller, turning to look at me, his green eyes lighter than I expect, no tragedy in their depths. "Yes. Give me sixty seconds to fill her in."

"What is it?"

"Ella's alive."

"What?! You're sure?"

"She's with Blake, and he's going to let you talk to her."

"Yes," I say, rushing forward and reaching for the phone.

"Easy, baby," he says, his fingers catching my hip as he pulls me to him. "There are things going on that we don't know about, and she won't tell us. You can't push her for anything she doesn't feel ready to tell you."

"Oh my God," I say. "Ella! It's really Ella?"

"It's really her."

"Is she in danger? What happened to her?"

"Just talk to her and be glad she's alive. We'll figure out the rest later."

I put the phone to my ear and her voice radiates through it with joy. And then we are talking, about me and Chris, and she won't talk about herself. But I talk. I walk to the ledge and sit down and I hold onto to every word she speaks, because she's alive. But then we say goodbye, she hangs up, and I have no way to reach her again. And that joy I felt while talking to her begins to transform to worry. To fear.

∽∽∽∾∾

"Talk to me, baby."

At the sound of Chris's voice, and the feel of his hands on my naked leg, I return to the present, blinking him into view and setting the phone down on the ledge.

"She's not okay, Chris," I say, covering his hand with mine. "I sensed it. She's different. She's changed, or . . . I don't know what. But she only wanted to talk about us getting married. She wouldn't tell me anything about where she's been, and she says the man she's with is wonderful, but she'd also said that about David. Where is she?"

"Blake said he can't tell us that."

"Why?" I don't give him time to answer. "She's in danger."

"Yes," Chris agrees. "She's hiding from something."

"Is it Garner Neuville?" I ask, aware that he'd had an affair with her and has been looking for her too.

"We don't know anything, Sara."

"We know he's dangerous, and I wanted to ask her about him so badly. Can we call Blake and find out what's going on?"

"Let him focus on taking care of her. He'll call us the minute he can." His phone starts ringing again. "And that's going to be him."

"Oh, thank God," I breathe out, while Chris picks up the phone off the ledge and then gives me a nod, telling me it's Blake.

"I'll put him on speaker," he says, and I quickly scoot over, giving him room to sit next to me, both of us leaning against the alcove surrounding the window.

"Blake, Sara and I are both on the line," Chris says, setting the phone on the ledge between us.

"I can't believe you found her!" I say. "Thank you so much."

"I'm glad we found her, too," he says. "But here is where things get complicated. She's hiding, and when you uncover someone who's hiding, you either save them or destroy them."

"Who is she hiding from?" Chris asks.

"I don't know," he says. "But the man she's with is protective as hell."

"Is she his prisoner?" I ask. "And who is he?"

"She's not a prisoner," Blake says. "I'm sure of it. Now, does that mean she's aware of the many sides of the man she's with? That, I cannot say."

"What sides?" I ask.

"He's a powerful man," Blake says. "And while he's known to have a moral compass, he's also known to be a person you don't cross."

"You're not making me feel good here," I say. "Who is he, exactly? Powerful in what way?"

"I'd like to know those answers, as well," Chris adds.

"He's the leader over France and Italy for an organization called The Underground. They're Treasure Hunters by their own definition. They will find anything, from people, to things, to data—you name it—for a price. I did some digging around when I found out who he was with, and he's known to have offered aid to a few U.S. government agencies."

"So he's not a bad guy," I say, relieved.

"Sweetheart," Blake says, "I've known agents who were bad. I'm not willing to define him as good quite yet. The problem for me is that he doesn't seem to feel that the group we hired to help find Ella is trustworthy. He's concerned they'll sell her out to whoever she's running from."

"Is he right?" Chris asks, an edge to his voice.

"They're European-based, and there's no record of them with any U.S. agency. I'm digging deeper."

"Do they know who we are?"

"I never used your names," Blake says, "and we have no reason to believe they'd connect the dots or even bother trying, but—"

"That's as far as you need to go," Chris says. "I'm taking Sara back to the States tonight and I need your men there waiting for us."

My objection is instant. "You have a huge charity event at the Louvre in a couple of days, Chris. People paid big money to meet you."

"Your safety is first," he says. "The end. We aren't talking about it."

"Actually," Blake says, "pulling out would get attention you don't want. At this point, we don't know who Ella is running from, why she's running, or even if we have a problem at all."

"We don't know that we don't, either," Chris counters.

"This event is important to you, to us," I say. "And to the Children's Hospital."

"Your bodyguard, Rey, is excellent," Blake says. "So is his brother. I'll coordinate with them and cover you now."

"Rey's already on duty," Chris says, "and so is his brother."

"I'll update him on the situation, then," Blake says. "And I'll get my men on a plane to you to cover the event. If you want to leave right after the event, we'll take you straight to the airport."

Chris's lips thin, the lines of his body are tight, and I can almost feel his fear for me clawing at him, taking him to a private hell I'll visit with him when this is over.

"Or," Blake says, clearly uncomfortable with the silence, "they can escort you back to San Francisco."

"When do we get an update?"

"Twelve hours."

"We'll let you know our plans then."

"Understood," Blake replies.

Chris ends the call, sucking in air and lifting his face to the ceiling. And I know what's going on in his head. Paris is where he lost his mother and father. And it's where street robbers killed his ex-girlfriend's parents and he was forced to kill a teenage boy before he shot her, as well. And it's where that same ex killed herself only weeks ago. Paris is the hotbed of his torment, yet it's also the place that put a paintbrush in his hand and began to heal him. But he doesn't need me to tell him I know these things. He knows I know. He knows I understand.

I stand up and walk to the easel he was working at in the center of the otherwise nearly empty room, stopping at the table next to it. I flip on the radio and find the angst-filled Hozier song he's been listening to recently while working on one of his charity projects featuring the catacombs of Paris. The music fills the air: *"Take me to church, I'll worship like a dog at the shrine of your lies."* But there are no lies between Chris and me—and I don't want anything else between us right now. I pull off his shirt and turn to find him standing in front of me. And when my eyes meet his, the punch of emotion I see in them weakens my knees.

"Nothing is going to happen to me," I promise, and before the words are out, his fingers are tangling roughly, erotically, in my hair and he's dragging me against him. And when he kisses me, it's laced with torment and pain. I just pray that the only enemies we have to face in our future, or Ella's, are the ones inside us right now.

one

ella

Minutes after I've ended my call with Sara, Kayden and I are standing in the break room of the shooting range and Kayden is kissing me, drinking me in, his hands possessively on my waist and at my neck, as if he's afraid to let me go. As if he's afraid somehow I will be lost, and the truth is, so am I. *So am I.* It doesn't matter that he is my next breath, and that I believe I am his. It matters that exposing my past might steal everything we think we are and want to be together. It matters that while reconnecting with Sara was welcome and wonderful, there was other news that came with finding her again. News that I may really be a CIA operative, as I've suspected, perhaps here in Italy for reasons that don't suit The Underground—an organization where Kayden is The Hawk, the leader.

"We are *not* enemies," Kayden declares, tearing his mouth from mine, repeating the words he'd spoken before the kiss as if he's tasted the doubt on my lips, as if he's willing me to let it go, when I have tasted it on his as well. But I have never wanted to surrender to anyone else's will—or to anyone—more than I do to his and him, right now. But it isn't that simple and we both know it, no matter how we might reject that fact.

"In this moment," I say, "and in every moment since you found me in that alleyway, no. But if I am CIA—"

"You were never my enemy, Ella." He turns over his arm, exposing the hawk tattoo on his wrist, the mark of a leader in The Underground, in his case over all of France and Italy. "This represents me having the right to make choices for my organization that will never put me at odds with you or the CIA."

"Not by choice," I say, my hand flattening on the hard wall of his T-shirt-covered chest, knowing everything about him is strength and power. "But sometimes you're forced into situations."

"That I manage, and manage well."

"Yes," I agree, recognizing not arrogance in his words but rather confidence and character. "I know that. I've seen it. And I feel it when I'm with you."

"But you're not convinced that doesn't leave us at odds."

"I want to be convinced. I do."

He takes my hand and turns it over to reveal the newly inked hawk on my wrist, a perfect match for his except for the pink-etched wings. "This says that I will always put you first. It says you will *never* be my enemy." He joins our hands and connects our wrists, our hawks. "You are a part of me now."

"As you are of me," I say, my voice raspy with love for this man who has seen my worst and barely knows my best, and yet I know he would die for me. That thought brings worries to mind that he doesn't give me time to express, lacing his fingers with mine.

"Let's get out of here."

"What about Blake Walker and his wife?" I ask, reminded of Walker Security, the team Sara had hired to find me. "Did they disappear as quickly as they showed up?"

"They know you're safe now," he says. "And at this point, any further conversation needs to come after I've had time to check them out. Your friend might trust him, but I also need to trust him, and so do you."

"Agreed," I say, and I do not miss the way he makes this about us, not him, never throwing his role of Hawk in my face unless it concerns someone's safety. "How did he react to you questioning him?"

"He offered me references that he's sending by email, but what I care about most is what he won't willingly hand over."

"The stuff Matteo can find by hacking."

"Exactly," he confirms. "I've already called him, but my gut feeling is that Blake Walker is legit, right along with Sara's new husband, Chris Merit."

"Please tell me you don't think he's after the necklace? That can't be. It can't. He came into her life after I left." Yet as surely as I say the words, I know that might not matter.

"I'm just being safe, sweetheart."

"Right. That's good. And Blake Walker hiring The Jackals to help find me? How bad is their involvement?"

"It's not good," he says, holding nothing back, which I

appreciate. "Their leader, Alessandro, is a low-life scum who has no loyalty to any client. He'll pass the same information he gave Blake on to another paying client if he becomes aware you're being looked for."

"As in Garner Neuville," I supply, now knowing exactly who the man in my flashbacks is. No. The *monster* in my flashbacks. He is no man. "You can say his name," I add. "He won't make me cower, Kayden. I won't give him that power."

His eyes warm with obvious pride and he cups my head, kissing my forehead. "Of that, sweetheart, I have no doubt." He inches back to look at me, his hands settling at my waist. "I'll handle Alessandro. You have my word."

"Handle him how?"

"Depends on how dirty he plays—which means I have plans to make, and we need to get out of here." He folds my arm at the elbow and settles our joined hands between us. "I sent Giada home," he says, reminding me I was playing big sister to Adriel's sister when all this happened.

"I'm going to have to make this up to her," I say, "but getting out of here and forming a plan both sound good to me."

"Giada will get over it," he assures me. "I have a car waiting for us."

I nod, and eagerly let him guide me into the hallway and down the stairs. I want a plan. I want control. I want all these holes in my memories filled in and I need to do whatever is necessary to ensure that happens, and standing in place isn't the answer. We exit into the hallway and Kayden leads me down the stairs, and while the way our hands meld together so easily speaks of how connected we are, I can't help but feel that we could be ripped apart at any given moment. And he feels it, too. It's in the hard lines of his body, in the slight tightening of his grip on mine, as he leads me through the retail area of the shooting range, where he gives several people waves but doesn't stop walking.

We pause at the exit, where a man hands Kayden his gray and black biker jacket, which he slips on before helping me with my black Chanel trench coat I don't even remember removing. *How very non-CIA of me*, I think. But the amnesia and flashbacks of my past seem to remove me from the present, a problem I'm hopeful that I'm close to removing from my life, and Kayden's. I'm so close to having *me* back, minus my red hair that will remain dark brown as long as Garner Neuville lives. I want to kill him. Another very non-CIA feeling. But if I *am* CIA, where were they when I was lying in that alleyway where Kayden saved me? Where were they when I was tied between two poles, being beaten by a whip? But then, maybe I didn't want to be saved. Maybe I just wanted that monster behind bars. And yet . . . why would the CIA be involved with the mob? The FBI prefers to take the lead on mob activity, despite some crossover. And how do I know *that* if I'm *not* CIA?

Kayden grabs the door for me and I exit into the chilly February air of Rome, still trying to make sense of where I fit into that picture. Kayden's next to me in an instant, his arm draping my shoulders, his big body sheltering me from an early-evening wind, while tourists bustle in the shopping area neighboring the Spanish Steps. He motions forward and to the cobblestone street to our left, where I spot a black Mercedes. Adriel exits the driver's door facing us, running fingers through his dark hair, and I'd bet he's hiding a weapon under his sleek, fitted brown leather jacket and another at his ankle.

We're almost to the car when a limo pulls to the curb in front of the Mercedes, and I immediately know who it is. "Niccolo," I say as two goons in trench coats exit from either side of the car, a chill of foreboding running down my spine.

"Yes," Kayden agrees, his hand slipping away from my shoulder, no doubt to free it for his weapon. "He uses impromptu meetings as a way to ensure he's in control, and that everyone else is unsteady."

In turn, my hand has settled under my coat where my purse rests at my hip, my fingers tugging the zipper open, then discreetly finding the cold steel handle of "Annie." Adriel steps to my opposite side from Kayden at the same moment, and one of the men stops a foot in front of us and center, which means directly in line with me, but he looks at Kayden.

"Niccolo would like to talk with you a moment," he says, but his gaze then flicks to me. "And you."

"Come with me, Ella," Adriel orders, his hand going to my arm.

"Ella stays with me," Kayden says, and I can feel the instant, silent resistance in Adriel. He knows nothing of my involvement with the necklace they all hunt, and Niccolo wants to find it before anyone else. But Niccolo knows, and should I avoid him now, it will look as if I have remembered where it is but wish to hide it from him. The reality is that I have *not* remembered. And while I would never hand it over to Niccolo, at present I am not hiding it from him, and at least for now, that message is one I can look him in the eye and deliver. A message that this meeting allows me to deliver—and, in fact, buys us time to find the necklace and ensure he never gets his criminal hands on it.

I step forward, aligning my boots with Kayden's, silently offering my agreement, though it's not needed. Niccolo's goon has already taken Kayden's word as gold, and is now walking back toward the limo. Kayden doesn't look at me, nor me at him, both of us focused on the back door of the limo. We step forward in unison, connected in ways that go beyond our personal bond that I understand now, but hadn't before; nor, I suspect, had he. We both know danger. We both know the importance of keeping our eyes on the danger ahead, along with who and what awaits us is in this limo. We both don't intend to be the ones who fall, if someone has to take a hit.

One of the goons opens the back door and I start to get in, but Kayden gently shackles my arm. "Wait here with Adriel until I set ground rules," he orders softly. Fully in his role as Hawk, he doesn't await confirmation from me, assuming it and already stepping toward the car, and I do not question him. Not when Niccolo is watching. Instead, I stand my ground, Adriel appearing at my side like a guard dog ready to snarl and bite, while my gun is ready to snarl and bite right along with whatever weapon he chooses.

I sense his dedication to doing whatever is necessary to protect not just Kayden, but me, another reason for me to warm to him when I'd once thought that impossible. Kayden enters the car, and less than a minute later he leans out and offers me his hand. I do not hesitate to press my palm to his, and while his touch is always welcome, it serves a purpose now. It's a message to Niccolo that we are united and that I'm not only under Kayden's protection, but that of The Underground. Yet there is no fear in me, not even of Niccolo. I am instead appropriately on edge about a powerful man who plays games, with me the one holding the card, or rather the location of the necklace that he wants to hold himself.

I move forward, and the instant I'm inside the car, sitting next to Kayden, my mind quickly ticks through observations—a process I instinctively know started with my father's training. Everything is in slow motion. It's like an out-of-body experience. In a matter of seconds, I register Kayden's leg next to mine while his hand slides away from me, then the door shutting and fine leather cradling my body. The spicy, masculine scent of Kayden merging with Niccolo's, which is somehow soapy and clean in a sterile kind of way, like a hospital you want to escape but cannot. There is also a window sealed between us and the driver at Kayden's and my back. Last, I focus on Niccolo sitting in the center of the seat across from us, looking gaunt, his scalp freshly shaved, his expensive blue suit too large yet he manages to own it, like he intends to own us. He will fail.

"Ella," he greets me, those cold eyes still hollow of emotion and laden with sickness, with the death haunting him, landing on me.

"Niccolo," I say, ensuring he knows that I will meet him tit for tat at every turn.

"Let's skip the dinner party greetings," Kayden says, no doubt purposely, and successfully, pulling Niccolo's attention to him.

"Police Chief Donati has been dealt with," Niccolo states. "Should he give either of you trouble again, I'll want to know."

"Dealt with how?" Kayden asks.

"Effectively," he states, offering nothing more. "And he'll ensure your Detective Gallo is also dealt with, as I understand he's a nuisance."

"Please tell me that's not code for killing him," I say, incapable of keeping my mouth shut at this point.

"But my brother is a more complicated situation," he says, ignoring my words, as he cuts his gaze to me again. "Have you remembered where my necklace is?"

His necklace. It is *not* his necklace, but the property of the British government, an artifact long ago stolen that he will never possess.

But instead of correcting him, I speak the only truth he needs to hear. "I only remember what it looks like, and that at some point I had it."

"Do you remember promising it to me for safe passage from Paris to Italy, as well as my protection from my brother?"

"I do not."

"But you remembered him?"

"Flashbacks of a monster," I say willingly, not hiding my hate for Garner. Niccolo needs to know I have no distorted memories of his brother that would suddenly make me hand him the necklace.

"Who will pay for his sins," Kayden adds, his voice etched with hard promise.

Niccolo's gaze swings to Kayden. "And me? Will I pay for *my sins*, Hawk?"

He's goading Kayden with the murder of his family, which Niccolo has all but admitted to. I turn my back to the door to read both men's expressions, preparing to react to any problem, and doing so with the sureness that Adriel will not allow me any surprises from behind. But if Kayden is agitated, his energy doesn't darken, his expression doesn't harden. In fact, his lips quirk, his eyes filling with amusement that I swear is genuine, his elbows settling on his legs as he leans closer to Niccolo and goads him right back. "I don't need to make you pay, now do I?" he asks softly. "That bitch Karma already found you for me, and we both know it."

Niccolo's gaze sharpens with the implication that Kayden knows of his illness. "Karma's my sister, Hawk. And she might be a bitch, but it turns out we're getting pretty damn friendly, so watch yourself. She might find you, too."

"Is that a threat, Niccolo?" Kayden asks. "Because I don't respond well to threats, especially when they come from someone I know will act on them. It makes me turn an Evil Eye on them. Not that it would matter to you. You just said that Karma's your sister, and we all know how you regard family—seeing as you'd like nothing more than to take out your own brother."

"Enough with the word games," Niccolo snaps. "We have a common cause now. We both want my brother destroyed." He flicks a look at me and then back at Kayden. "And she's the key you seem to want to protect."

Kayden goes still, his mood darkening, easily read by the crackle of energy around him, before he shocks me by pulling me closer and shoving back the sleeves of my coat and sweater to reveal my newly inked skin. "I am, and I will, protect her, Niccolo," he declares, his voice soft and yet somehow intense, fierce, and I can barely breathe from the unnamed emotions stirred by his complete, utter devotion to protecting me.

For his part, Niccolo shows no emotion or immediate reaction, his expression remains unchanged, his gaze fixing on my hawk tattoo, lingering there for what feels like an eternity but is only seconds, before he looks at Kayden. "Is that a claim for the woman, or for a necklace worth three hundred million dollars?" he asks, his voice cold, calculated, and etched with accusation, and I'm not sure if it's meant to rattle Kayden, me, or both of us, but there is no time for me to react.

Kayden's response is instant, something about Niccolo's response is more than the word games I take them as. He moves and in a blink, draws his gun and points it, not at Niccolo's head but at his groin. "It would be a lethal mistake to underestimate what she means to me," he says, his voice etched with the same cold calculation as Niccolo's question.

But there is more. Kayden didn't pull that gun as a threat or a bluff. This is the man who killed the woman Kayden loved and the man who raised him, so he knows it's the wrong choice. And Kayden knows all the reasons he can't kill Niccolo now. He needs to ensure the new leader is of his choice, but that doesn't change one fact: He wants a reason to justify killing Niccolo. And he wants that reason here and now.

two

The glass window behind us starts to lower. Adrenaline surges through me, and it takes me all of ten seconds to reach into my purse for my trusty gun, good ol' "Annie," and point it at the driver, who has clearly been watching us. "Don't even think about it," I warn before he even lifts the weapon I know he's holding, counting on Adriel to have our backs from outside the car.

"Tell him to get out of the car," Kayden orders Niccolo, "or I'll shoot you in the leg."

Niccolo laughs, low and deep. "Temper, temper, Hawk." He flicks a look over Kayden's shoulder. "Giorgio, leave us so The Hawk can regain his control."

It's an obvious attempt to downplay Kayden's control, but whatever the case, it works. Giorgio hesitates, then backs away from the window. Kayden seems to know. "Tell him to raise the glass again."

Niccolo doesn't comply, and while I don't dare look at him, I sense the challenge in his stare, as if he really believes

Kayden's focus on the business side of his role as Hawk dictates his actions right now.

"He'll do it," I say, not daring to look away from Giorgio. "And he'll just clean up the mess the way he cleaned up all of the others before you, no matter how bloody."

"Should I do it?" Kayden taunts Niccolo.

Another few beats ticks by before Niccolo says, "Do as he says, Giorgio."

Giorgio's compliance is instant, the glass rising, and I slowly lower my gun, turning to find Niccolo looking at me, not Kayden, despite the weapon at his groin. "It's quite the powerful reaction you create in men, now, isn't it? First my brother, and now The Hawk, ruler of two countries." He flicks a look at my gun, then at me. "There is more to you than meets the eye, isn't there, *bellissima*?"

I have about three seconds to worry that I've shown my hand, or our hand, before Kayden says, "What she is is the one and only reason that I'm willing to team up with you to destroy your brother, rather than doing it on my own. And I did that to offer her the protection we both give her."

Niccolo's gaze snaps to Kayden's. "You might want to protect her, but you also want to avoid the war that shooting me, or stealing my necklace, would create. Put down the gun we both know you won't use."

Kayden doesn't comply, instead leaning closer to Niccolo. "There won't be a war if anything happens to her," he says, his voice tight, hard. "There will only be the moment I look you in the eyes before I kill you."

"You want to kill me," Niccolo says, no question in his voice.

Kayden's reply is slow; an edgy, dark power rises off him before he says, "No." His gun slides back into his holster before he leans back, his tone absolute as he adds, "Death is too kind for you and your brother, Niccolo. But luckily for you, we are one regarding his destruction. And for that reason, and that reason alone, I'm going to find that necklace for you. And then watch with amusement as you try to figure out how to take it to the grave with you."

Kayden makes this declaration with such cold intent, I almost believe him, while Niccolo seems to make his own assumptions. "You do not fool me, Hawk. You're thinking that when he's dethroned and I'm gone, you'll gain the kind of power no Hawk has ever had before. You'll own our two countries. The problem is, whatever you think you know about me, you don't."

"I think and know a lot of things," Kayden replies dryly, "none of which I plan to share with you. And on that note, I have a necklace to locate. We're done here."

He starts to move, and following his lead, I reach for the door, my hand freezing as Niccolo announces, "The men I sent to retrieve Ella the night in the alleyway disappeared that same night."

"When were you going to tell me this?" Kayden demands, shifting back to face him, playing this game oh so well, acting as if there is no chance this is an accusation aimed at him or Adriel, considering Adriel killed those men right after they attacked me.

"I'm telling you now," Niccolo replies, while I discreetly settle Annie back in my purse, my hand resting on the soft leather, ready to draw her again should this turn nasty.

"Why now?" Kayden asks. "Why not last week when I told you about Ella?"

"Aside from the fact that I had yet to conclude my internal investigations, until now, you hadn't committed to finding the necklace for me."

"But you committed to protecting her." Continuing to act as if he didn't know the men are dead, Kayden adds, "And if they took the necklace, the attention turns from her to them. Where are they now?"

"They've yet to reappear, and no one I've persuasively given incentive to find them has any clue where they are—which leaves me with one of two assumptions. Either they were attacked when Ella was attacked, and they're now dead, or they've betrayed me, and they're as good as dead."

"In other words, they mugged Ella and took the necklace," Kayden concludes.

"Negative," Niccolo says. "They didn't know about the necklace. They knew about the woman."

"I intercepted internet chatter about that necklace and that location," Kayden says, protecting his inside source. "Don't tell me they didn't know about it too. You have a leak, Niccolo."

"And yet, the necklace hasn't gone on the auction block. Obviously"—he flicks me a look—"Ella didn't have it with her that night."

"Or," I say, "the two men who worked for you attacked me, took it, and disappeared with it."

His gaze sharpens. "I don't remember saying 'two men.'"

"I don't remember referencing anything you said," I

counter. "I simply stated a fact: two men attacked me in that alleyway that night."

"You remember your attackers?"

"Not their faces," I say. "Just two men in suits. It's sounding like they were yours."

Irritation flickers over his hard features. "You seem to have missed the part where I said it's not gone up on the auction block."

"That means nothing," Kayden interjects. "Whoever mugged her, be it your men or otherwise, could be holding the necklace and biding their time."

"Three hundred million dollars says they won't hold it," Niccolo snaps back.

"A price tag that could get them killed if they don't have the right broker says that they would," Kayden counters. "And you'd better hope it's not The Jackals they go to for help, because I promise you: Alessandro will own that necklace, not your men."

"Assuming they took it," he states, "which I still doubt."

"And yet they're missing, and so is it," Kayden reminds him.

"Yes," he says keenly. "They *are* missing—and it seems to me that aside from Ella, you're the only other person who's been placed at that scene that night."

"Murder isn't my style," Kayden says, never missing a beat, "and you know it."

"But you will kill, if necessary," Niccolo states matter-of-factly.

"Yes, I will," Kayden replies, equally matter-of-factly. "But I didn't have the pleasure that night."

"As you say," Niccolo remarks, his lips twisting. "Whatever the case, Alessandro's not a problem."

"In other words, he's on your payroll."

"Of course he's on my payroll," Niccolo says. "Anyone and everyone I was able to eliminate as competition to get that necklace, I did, and I will continue to do so."

"Alessandro's the redheaded stepchild that wants to be us. He wants to be *you*. He *will* take that necklace and sell it out from under you."

"You underestimate me, Hawk, if you think I don't know these things about him and don't have the leverage to ensure that he does exactly what I say."

"What leverage?" Kayden asks.

"You also underestimate me if you believe I'll tell you that."

"How do you know it wasn't he who attacked Ella in the alleyway, intending to double-cross you? How do you know he's not double-dipping and also working for your brother? Or even for Raul?"

"The kingpin of the drug cartel?" I ask.

"Yes," Kayden confirms, answering me but focusing on Niccolo. "He knows about the necklace. He wants it."

"Of course he wants it," Niccolo states, "and as you keep forgetting, I know Rome. I know my business. And he's not a problem."

"Raul is not a man who can be threatened."

"But he can be bought," Niccolo replies. "And he does bleed. He's contained, as is Alessandro. End of topic."

"Nothing is done until I say it's done, when it comes to the safety of those I protect," Kayden states. "Raul will turn on you if he gets even a sniff of weakness, which we know you have right now. And Alessandro is not just a Jackal. He's *the* Jackal, and my enemy."

"Thankfully you've made your Evil Eye apparent where Ella's concerned."

"And should I have to invoke it on him, consider yourself part of that for bringing him into this."

"Relax, Hawk," he says, his eyes flecked with amusement. "I've ensured he knows that should my brother get anything he wants, including her, he will pay a price worse than death."

"Then why," Kayden says, "is Alessandro handing out her location to the private investigator her friend hired to find her?"

"Perhaps he felt that the more questions this investigator was asking, the more attention it brought in unnecessary places," Niccolo states.

"In other words, you thought the investigator was asking too many questions," Kayden surmises, the timing of this visit suddenly far from coincidental.

"Or perhaps," Niccolo continues, homing in on me, "Alessandro thinks your past is where he'll find the necklace."

"My past has nothing to do with that necklace," I say firmly. But there is this odd, uncomfortable niggle of something in my mind that I can't explain, and a flickering image that I can't quite materialize. "And your Jackal made a misstep," I add, now worried about Sara's safety and desperate to get her out of the picture. "What if this man Chris Merit, who's funding Sara's hunt for me, is after the necklace?"

"I myself own several Chris Merit works," he says. "He's well known and highly respected. He's also far more concerned about curing children's cancer than finding that necklace."

"Maybe he wants the necklace to fund research," I counter.

"He'd have to explain all that money, and even he, a billionaire in his own right, wouldn't be able to do that without joining the likes of me and my methods. And he will not. But we're certainly watching him and your friend, Sara. But tell me. How does someone with amnesia selectively have such certainty?"

I blink at the odd question. "What certainty are you talking about?"

"You said that your past has nothing to do with the necklace. You seem quite sure about that, but not a great many other things."

"I can't snap my fingers and get every piece of my memory back, any more than you can snap your fingers and—" I stop myself before I say more, actually feeling bad for what I was about to say, despite the inkiness blotting his soul.

"And what?" he bites out, his dark eyes flashing with irritation.

"Nothing you don't know."

"Say it anyway," he insists, his voice hard with command, and it hits me that I've cast a net, perhaps luring him to a confession he's dodged and weaved, handing us knowledge we can use against him.

I nod. "Any more than you can snap your fingers and beat cancer." The harshness in my voice has nothing to do with him, and everything to do with the past I'm slowly threading together.

His eyes darken, pupils fading into black. "What do you know of cancer?"

"Enough to know that even the mob, even *you*, Niccolo, cannot buy, threaten, or beg its mercy," I say, and unbidden, an image of my mother in a hospital bed, brittle and aged beyond her years, knots my belly. "If it decides to take you, it takes you."

There is a spike of some unnamed emotion in his stare, there and gone in an instant, right along with any hope he might make an admission. "You remember its viciousness, but not the location of the necklace," he says, casting a net of his own.

"It seems that its brutal nature transcends all else, including amnesia," I say, my answer giving him nothing, while cancer takes everything, before I add, "much like your desire for that necklace."

"What I desire," he says tightly, "is to protect my legacy. It will live on when I'm gone, but my enemies will not."

"And that's why you want the necklace," Kayden says. "One last big bang." He doesn't wait for an answer. "Well, what legacy do you have if a Jackal outsmarts you?"

"I have him *contained*, Hawk," Niccolo states irritably, and then shifts to Italian before returning to English. "Do you understand it in my native tongue better than your own?"

"If I were Alessandro," Kayden states as if he hadn't spoken, "I'd have taken that necklace from Ella, hid it, and then done my best to destroy whatever evidence you have on me before I sold it."

"You continue to underestimate me," Niccolo replies dryly. "When I own someone, Hawk, I own them. I layer the many ways I control them, in ways they know they cannot escape."

"You underestimate *me* if you think I couldn't find a way to shove whatever you had on me right up your pompous—"

"Alessandro is not you," Niccolo says, cutting him off. "On that, I think we are all quite clear."

"If he took that necklace he can simply wait for your death," Kayden points out.

"Those layers I've explained extend beyond my death, a fact on which he's quite clear," Niccolo replies.

"A caged man has nothing to lose, and no choice but to try to escape," Kayden retorts.

Niccolo's jaw tics. "Then it's a good thing that I now have The Hawk and the best Hunter in two countries, if not more, aligned with me."

"Only if you hand me whatever ammunition you have on Alessandro. All of it. Every last detail."

"That would be control I'm not willing to give you."

"Well then," Kayden states, "as of this moment, Ella remembers the necklace being in her pocket before she was attacked. When she woke up it was gone, and the two men in suits who mugged her, who I suspect are working for Alessandro, took it. If you want her to look at photos of your men, send them to us. Otherwise, our deal is complete. She is done with you, as am I."

Niccolo's eyes flash with agitation, that tic in his jaw more distinct. "What happened to destroying my brother?"

"See, this is where the fun starts for me," Kayden says. "Now Alessandro is working for you, most likely playing you and your brother, on both payrolls. I get to sit back, order popcorn the way we Americans do, and watch you all destroy each other. And as a bonus, Raul is hovering, sniffing out blood. Oh yeah. It's going to be a good show."

He shifts in my direction again, and Niccolo must know he means business this time because he quickly states, "I'll give you the information you want."

Kayden reaches over me and opens the door, giving Niccolo a dismissive half glance. "When and how?"

"Delivered to your castle, by sunset. Then we take down my brother and Alessandro together. Four men now standing that we turn into two."

"Five," Kayden says. "Dismissing Raul would be a mistake I won't make. I want what you have on him as well."

"If I agree to that," he says, "you agree right here and now that we fight this war together."

It's a command, and Kayden doesn't take commands, this I know, even before he says, "I'll let you know where we stand when I see that delivery," and with that, we exit the vehicle.

I'm the first to the street, with Adriel stepping directly into my path, waiting on us. Kayden joins me, and the three of us move in unison toward the Mercedes, where Kayden and I climb into the backseat and Adriel into the front.

The instant the doors are shut, I turn to Kayden. "I'm trying to be comforted by the fact that it sounds like Chris Merit is safe for Sara, but I can't be. Not with Alessandro and Niccolo watching her. Not when they can use her to convince me to give them . . ." It's all I can do to stop myself from saying "the necklace," since Adriel has no clue it's connected to me in any way. "I tried to play Sara off as unimportant to me, but clearly that isn't going to work."

"I'll get our people protecting them by nightfall," he says, glancing toward Adriel. "Why aren't we moving?"

"Niccolo has us blocked in," he says. "Am I clear in the rear? Because if I sit here another minute, someone is going to tell me what the fuck is going on."

Kayden gives a look over his shoulder that I mimic and says, "We're clear in the rear, and we'll talk at the castle when we know we're one hundred percent secure and uninterrupted."

Adriel doesn't argue, pulling us onto the road, and I don't even want to think about how furious he's going to be when he finds out everything we've kept from him. Or about why I have a knot in my belly at the idea of him being brought into the circle of trust. As Adriel drives, all eyes go to the windows, the energy between and around us jagged and weaving, with sharp edges that promise more trouble. But seconds tick by, then minutes, and that trouble doesn't seem to plan to follow.

I know the moment Kayden decides the same thing; his hand settles on my knee and he pulls me to him, a silent reminder that he is my partner in this. But he also is The Hawk, and Adriel is his hunter, his friend—his family. He can't keep this from Adriel much longer. I'm not sure he will agree to keep it from him any longer at all. I have a sense of being cornered, an awareness that we can't just shut Adriel down. We damn sure can't just shut Niccolo down, and unbidden, and seemingly without a trigger besides Niccolo's name, my declaration to him replays in my mind: *My past has nothing to do with that necklace.* I said those words because I was right. My past *isn't* a part of this. This started with David giving me the necklace as a gift. It's unrelated to anything else. But if that is true, why did I have that funny feeling in my belly when I'd declared the separation of past and present to Niccolo? Why am I hyper-focused on the past here and now? What am I missing?

As if in answer, my mind jerks to the past, to a memory of me pulling into the driveway of my old family home in North Carolina, after my parents were gone. *I exit my Ford Focus as a black sedan pulls up and stops. I stand by the car door, watching as two men get out, both in dark suits, one blond and in his thirties and the other dark-haired and in his fifties. I don't know who they are, but I know what they are. And I have a bad feeling about why they're here.*

Which is what? I ask myself.

The answer is unexpected, my mind thrusting me back into the moment in time when David died. I'm leaning over him on a cold Paris street, his body lifeless, hearing his warning about not giving the necklace to "him," whoever he is. Then the memory fades into what feels like reality. I'm there . . .

∞

David's hand falls away from mine, his body now lifeless. Survival instincts kick in and I don't give myself time to process the blood or his death. I stand up, the darker-than-dark night offering me the façade of shelter, my hand closing around the necklace in the pocket of my coat, which I have only because Garner Neuville paid for my hotel room for two weeks. That, after my credit cards were oddly cancelled and I started putting together the bigger picture, of something nefarious going on. It was then, the moment after I'd called credit card company number four, that I set aside the façade of the schoolteacher, which I'd adopted to get the wrong people to stop looking at me, and became the woman beneath that façade. Then I tracked down David to this location, looking for answers. Right now, though, I need to make decisions, and quickly.

First and foremost, David is dead and I don't want to end up that way. And since I have the necklace, and I'm 99.999 percent sure that's what got him killed, I'm now a target. If I call the police, whoever is looking for it and me will find me.

I start walking, cutting left into a quiet neighborhood only blocks from the craziness of the busy Champs-Élysées Boulevard, where I don't plan to return. My mind begins ticking through options. There are people I could call right now, but I've burned bridges and I don't know who I can trust. Hell. For all I know, those burned bridges have something to do with why I'm involved in this. Knowing I need answers and shelter until I can get them, I cut into a chocolate shop, pull my phone out of my pocket, and punch in the only number in Paris I have. Garner Neuville's.

"Ah, ma belle," he answers in one ring. "I am pleased you have called."

I'm no damsel in distress, but right now this sexy Frenchman makes me feel a little less alone, and I've been alone for a very long time. I hate that I feel this. I hate that it's a sign of weakness I cannot afford, but it's a living, breathing sensation—I'm alive, in the way I intend to stay.

"I'm in trouble and need help," I say, forced to this admission to ensure he helps me avoid the police. And for reasons I can't understand, I am certain he will.

"Where are you?" is all he asks.

I give him my location and end the call, intending to tell him David is dead and I fear for my safety, but nothing more. The question now is, what do I do with the necklace?

∽∞∾

The memory fades, and I know those people I wanted to call but didn't are connected to the men in the black sedan. They were CIA, and I didn't trust them enough to call them for help. It's an answer. Finally an answer.

"I know why I was with Neuville," I whisper, my lashes snapping open to find us already pulling up to the front of the castle, already sealed inside the gated front yard. It's then that my gaze lands on the rearview mirror, Adriel's gaze meeting mine, and when his instantly darkens with anger, I know that I've done something that's not as simple as opening up a can of worms. I've angered a beast who now wants blood in the form of answers.

That beast, I realize in that moment, with astounding clarity, was also the last one to see Niccolo's men alive. The same men who we believe mugged me and who may well have had the necklace they'd taken from me.

three

For several more beats, Adriel and I stare at each other, our gazes locked in a collision course of questions and accusations thrown in both directions. He obviously wants to know why we've kept him in the dark, while I want to know if he ever really has been at all.

"Obviously," Kayden states, his fingers flexing at my knee, "there are conversations to be had."

"After we talk," I say, ensuring Kayden understands I'm not ready to be forced into this here and now. And I don't give either of them time to challenge that declaration, or to try to bypass that order with a question. I exit the vehicle before my statement can become a discussion. I don't even bother to shut the door behind me, assuming Kayden's exit as well. But also afraid he might snag my hand or arm, and press the conversation, I am quick to dart toward the concrete steps.

Starting the upward climb, I can feel Kayden behind me but don't turn, since I know he has questions about my statement regarding Neuville, which I'm not ready to answer with

Adriel present. Almost at the porch I reach for my purse, digging for my electronic key, but by the time I'm at the security panel Kayden is behind me, his big body framing mine. His hands rest on the wall on either side of me.

"He lives here, Ella," he says softly, his breath warm near my ear. "It's time to bring him into the loop."

"I know how close he is to us," I say, quickly swiping my card and keying in my code before turning to face him. "Which is exactly why—"

"A private word, if you will, Kayden," Adriel says from behind us.

"It's time," Kayden repeats.

"*After* you hear me out," I say, and to drive home how important I believe that is, I add, "*Hawk*."

His eyes darken, his stare probing, seconds ticking by before he gives a barely perceivable nod, steps to the left to open the heavy, arched wooden door, and waves me forward. "I'll meet you inside."

I don't wait for my reprieve to somehow expire, nor do I let myself process or dissect what I've remembered just yet. Distance and time between me and Adriel is my goal, and I enter the oval foyer, two arched wooden doors framing me left and right, East and West. And while I fully intend to hurry toward the West Tower that Kayden and I call home, somehow I've stopped walking, and I'm staring down at the stone floor, remembering Kayden's young hunter Enzo lying on the rug that was once there, bleeding out. Almost instantly, that image transforms into David lying on a Paris sidewalk, also bleeding to death. Then another shift, and it's my father, his long, powerful body stretched out on the kitchen floor, limp in a pool of his own blood. So strong, so amazingly strong, and then just . . . dead.

Emotions well in my chest, and while I know these images connect by way of death and me as common denominators, there's more to what my mind is telling me. Something I don't understand. But when I would shut my eyes and reach for that "more," instead I find a prickling sensation of not being alone, of being watched. My eyes open and my gaze jerks toward the massive stairwell leading to the Center Tower, but find no one there. Not Marabella or Giada, who live with us, or anyone who might be visiting. Uneasy, I scan the second-floor balcony left and right before focusing on the center again, still finding no one.

Trying to shake off the sensation, I walk to the security panel by our door, punch in the code, and watch the door begin to rise, but the prickling doesn't fade. Impatient to find out if it's gone once I'm in the tower, I duck under the half-open door into the mini-foyer, punching the button there to shut myself inside. I watch the dungeon-style door begin lowering and glance up at the stairwell leading to the main living space, before turning my attention to the arched entryway to an office den. I wait for the prickling sensation, but it doesn't follow me here, and I know without a doubt that someone had been watching me out there. Giada maybe, hiding in some corner and trying to figure out what was happening? But . . . it didn't feel like her energy.

Walking forward, I enter the den, the motion detectors triggering the lights to a dull glow, while I flip on the fireplace in the corner, hanging my coat and purse on the rack to my left. Continuing onward into the room, I bypass the leather couches framed by bookshelves loaded with books I pray a calmer time will allow me to explore soon. Instead, I make a beeline to a massive mahogany desk, where I step between the two high-backed chairs sitting in front of it and press my hands to the shiny surface. "My past has nothing to do with that necklace," I say out loud, my voice firm. But the way my mind is connecting past and present, and the sensation I had when I'd said the same to Niccolo, declares otherwise.

The sound of the entry door beginning to rise again has me turning and watching it lift. Kayden ducks under it as I had, obviously impatient to find out what I've remembered, his leather jacket and his shoulder holster missing, his navy T-shirt hugging his broad, hard chest. It is then that I am reminded of what made me request that we talk alone. It's not something he wants to hear, but has to. I need him to listen. And I need to stay focused on my memories, and what they're telling me—not what he makes me think and feel, or what the past tells him about Adriel.

He strides toward me, his energy predatory in this moment. Actually, there is always something rather predatory about him, which is far too sexy to ensure conversation, especially after today's shift in events. I could be CIA. I could be his enemy, no matter what he says otherwise, and really, truly, right now, I just want to feel him close, to get lost with him in the way he makes me get lost. But there are things bigger than us at stake, things that are far too complicated and dangerous to indulge in such desires, even if they feel like needs.

Determined to stay focused, I round the desk, placing the massive wooden surface between us. By the time I've shoved back the desk chair, claimed the spot in front of it, and pressed my hands to the surface again, Kayden is doing the same opposite me.

His gaze meets mine, his probing, intelligent eyes those of a Hawk who sees the past clawing at me, while I fight to contain it and control it. "Why are you running from me?" he asks.

"I don't run," I say, and I can almost hear my father say, "*Running makes you a victim. Never be a victim.*"

"Then why are you over there while I'm over here, when we'd both much rather you be here or me there?"

"I'm giving us space to have the conversation I need to have with The Hawk—not with the man who loves me."

The predatory gleam in those pale, too blue eyes of his softens, right along with his voice. "He's the same person. I will always be The Hawk *and* the man who loves you."

"And therein lies a problem. When you operate as The Hawk, you can't be the man who loves me or you'll make decisions you might not otherwise. And that could put you and other people at risk. I won't be that person in your life."

"You make me more cautious, sweetheart, and believe me, that's not a bad thing."

"You were always cautious. I've seen that in everything you do from the moment we met."

"Then what's the problem?"

"Nothing's wrong with caution," I say, deciding to use the opportunity presented, "and that's exactly what I'm going to ask you to have with Adriel."

"You helped him return to hunting," he reminds me, "and he'd die for you, Ella, just like he would for me."

"He was the last person to see Niccolo's men alive. And while I can't fathom how I'd actually have brought that necklace with me and given it to Niccolo, maybe I had a plan to get it back. Or maybe I knew it was a decoy. Maybe I had it on me and Niccolo's men took it."

Kayden straightens, his expression incredulous, his hands settling on his hips. "You actually think Adriel took it from them? He didn't know you were involved in this, any more than I did."

"You don't think he did," I say. "Or maybe he didn't and he still doesn't, but he would have searched those men. If they had it, he would have found it."

"And brought it to me."

"You can't be sure," I say. "You can't know he didn't sell you out. You cut him out of hunting, Kayden. He resented that."

"Adriel always had the power to come back, and he knew it," Kayden replies. "He didn't resent me. He resented Giada for forcing him to make the decision to get out of the hunting game. Adriel is loyal, Ella. He would die for either one of us."

"I want to trust him, Kayden."

"Do you trust me?"

"You know I do."

"Then know that he is one of the only other people on this planet that I'd trust my back or yours to, and I don't trust my back to anyone."

"Those close to us are the ones who can hurt us the easiest," I say, the words spoken from some dark part of my memory I can't yet access.

"Are you talking about Neuville? Or someone before him?"

"Don't make this about me."

"Tell me why you were with him."

"I want to talk about Adriel."

"After Neuville. You had a flashback in the car."

"I'm not letting this thing with Adriel go," I insist. "We're circling back to it." I don't give him time to argue. "And yes. I had a flashback." I sit down in the chair, crossing my arms in front of me. "It was the same moment I'd remembered previously. We were on a deserted Paris sidewalk, and David was bleeding out and warning me to protect the necklace."

"What was new about this flashback over the past ones?" Kayden asks, rounding the desk and stopping in front of me, leaning against the hard surface. "Because clearly something was, or you wouldn't have said you now know why you were with Neuville."

"It was more detailed," I say. "And I knew that I had the necklace in my pocket."

"Is that because you ripped the chain beyond repair?"

My hand goes to my neck. I'd ripped the chain from my neck. "Yes," I confirm, seeing myself leaning over it where it had landed on the floor—but another memory comes to me, as well. It plays in my mind before I speak it out loud. "But ironically, when we landed in Paris, David had warned me not to wear the necklace. He said it would attract pickpockets." I grimace. "I hate how I get these random memories, but the entire picture won't fall into place."

"There are more of those random memories now than ever, though," he reminds me. "When you first woke up, you were completely blank."

"Yes," I agree on a sigh. "There is that, and it seems now that when I talk about a memory, I suddenly know more about it."

"Well then, let's talk about that night," Kayden says. "Previously, you said that David left you at your hotel and your purse and identification disappeared. Where did you go, and what did you do?"

"I'd met Neuville in the hotel lobby right after the fight with David. I'd gone downstairs to get coffee at Starbucks, and I couldn't get my key card to work to go back upstairs. Then the desk staff told me they couldn't let me in without my identification. I was furious that David had left me in that situation, so when Neuville showed up and asked me to dinner, I accepted."

"It's a safe assumption that he ensured your key card didn't work," Kayden notes.

"I'm guessing that to be true," I agree. "And when we got back from dinner, things snowballed. I was told my room was no longer active, but they got my suitcase from housekeeping. My purse was missing."

"And Neuville was still there."

"Yes. He waited with me while I called my credit card companies and found out they were cancelled." And like a snap of fingers I am back in the hotel lobby, the moment after I've discovered my last card is as dead as the other three. Neuville steps in front of me, looking like Mr. Tall, Dark, and Prince Charming in a finely fitted suit, his dark hair slicked back:

"Your key," he says, offering me a small envelope.

I don't reach for it. "What do you mean?"

"I paid for two weeks for you. That gives you time to replace your passport, and hopefully have dinner with me at least one more time."

"I'm a stranger. Why would you do this? The room is expensive."

"The money is of no consequence to me," he says. "You being on the street, however, I find, is. Take the key, Ella."

"This doesn't mean I—"

"Of course it doesn't. There are no strings."

Only there *were* strings, I think bitterly, though I know bitterness is a dangerous emotion. "He paid for my room for two weeks and promised it came with no strings," I say, shaking myself back to the present. "Which, of course, we now know was all about building a façade of trust." The way I'd built the one where I was a schoolteacher by trade, I think before adding, "Getting back to David and my flashback—I don't know how I found him. Maybe it was the address in the necklace. Did you check it out?"

"I did," he says. "It's a large building with residential and commercial tenants. The unit in question is vacant."

"Vacant? That makes no sense."

"It sounds like a drop location for the necklace."

"Who owns the property?"

"Neuville."

"Of course. So everything that happened to me was a setup. Do you have photos of the building? Google Maps or something else that I could look at? I'm wondering if that's where David died, since that's the last place I remember having the necklace."

He opens a drawer in the desk and pulls out an iPad. I stand and lean on the desk next to him, and he hands me the Google Maps view of the building and street around it. I give a quick shake of my head. "That's not where David died." I step in front of Kayden. "If the address was a drop location, why would David leave me with the necklace and with no money or place to stay?"

"I told you. It's a decoy."

"And yet he told me not to give it to 'him' as he died. That makes no sense."

Kayden sets the iPad on the desk. "But I'd argue it as fact."

"Based on what?"

"We know that Neuville being there in that hotel, and your needing his help, wasn't an accident. And if that necklace was real, he would have taken it from you."

"Unless I'd already hidden it."

"At that point, you didn't seem to know what was going on."

"I'm smart enough to know everything wasn't as it should be, and I darn sure knew there was a note in the necklace. I also knew that wasn't normal. And you said that address was a drop location. David left the necklace with me."

"He went to negotiate a higher price, and it backfired."

"He left the necklace with me."

"And checked you out of your room."

"He also begged me not to let 'him,' whoever he is, have the necklace. Why would he do that if it was a decoy?" My stomach knots. "Unless . . . he didn't. Neuville either set all of it up or he intercepted David and whoever he was working for." I press my hands to my face, frustrated with myself. "I *have* to remember."

Kayden steps to me and lowers my hands, his covering mine, now resting between us. "You will. And talking about it seems to fill in holes for you."

"Yes. It does, actually."

"So talk to me," he encourages. "Tell me the part we both know you don't want to talk about."

"How I ended up with Neuville." I hate that just his name sends a shiver of dread down my spine.

"Yes. How did you end up with Neuville?"

I withdraw from Kayden, moving to sit in the chair, and he doesn't try to stop me. Somehow, he seems to understand that I'm not rejecting him. I'm just not capable of reaching the monster in my life when the man I love is touching me.

"I had a dying man at my feet," I say, as Kayden once again leans on the desk, "a necklace in my pocket, and people after me who would likely kill me for it."

"And you had no money or resources in Paris," he supplies, leading me to my next decision.

"Exactly. And knowing I had the necklace that seemed to be the reason David was killed, I couldn't call the police without taking the risk of alerting who knows who. I needed help, and I needed it fast."

"You called Neuville."

"Yes," I confirm. "Where else was I going to go? He was conveniently the only person I knew. The man set up to be standing in my path. He was this rich, powerful man who seduced me with any method he could including the promise of a safe place to hide that was never safe at all."

"You were drawn to him," Kayden says, and it's not a question.

My eyes meet his, and the combination of knowledge in his eyes and understanding in my belly punches me in the chest. But I don't run from it, or try to sidestep it. "Yes," I admit, self-loathing filling me. "I was. Too much in the beginning, I think, and being that bad a judge of character doesn't seem accurate. I don't understand it, yet I've had random flashbacks that tell me it's the case."

Kayden pushes off the desk and steps in front of me, offering me his hand. I flatten my palm in his, warmth radiating up my arm, across my shoulders and chest. But I don't look up and make eye contact, instead savoring the way I feel him everywhere, in places he isn't touching me but I want him to touch me. In places deep in my soul that somehow I still don't know, but he does. We linger like that a few moments, connected in ways that I know I have never felt with any other person, right in ways that I somehow know few things have been in my life before him. And this bond I share with this man only drives home how odd my pull to Neuville had been.

It is this question I'm still asking when Kayden gently urges me to my feet, but when I would search those now warm blue eyes for an answer, he simply offers me one. "We're all human," he says. "You were alone, and from what I can tell, you'd been alone a very long time."

Somehow he's hit on exactly my feelings when I'd called Neuville that night at the chocolate shop. "That's not an excuse for not seeing him for the criminal he was right away. I might not know if I was CIA or not, but I know I've had the training and experience to see through that man."

"He's the head of the French mob for a reason," he says, his hands settling on my waist. "He's a master manipulator."

"Don't make excuses for me, Kayden," I say, my fingers balling around his shirt. "Excuses equal weakness, and you can't have a weak woman by your side, any more than I want to be one."

He turns us, settling me against the desk, his hands on the desk on either side of me, mine beside his, while his big body frames mine but does not touch it. "I didn't give you an excuse, Ella," he says, his voice strong, almost hard. "I gave you a reason, a way to understand your actions and decisions, because you can't control what you don't understand. You are human—and if you forget that, it becomes a weakness. Know yourself. Know what can or cannot get to you, because your enemy always will."

Those words trigger a whisper of my father's voice in my head: *Know yourself better than anyone else knows you. Know your adversaries more than they know themselves.* That was exactly why I'd taken on the façade of a schoolteacher. To know me more than others knew me. But who were those others, and why did that matter? And why is my declaration to Niccolo, that my past has nothing to do with the necklace, feeling less and less right?

four

"Ella."

I blink at the sound of Kayden's voice and come back to the present, with me still leaning on the desk, him in front of me, his hands bracketing my body. "Where are you in your head right now?" he gently prods.

"Thinking about control," I say. "Everything is about control. I was trying to get it when I lost it completely."

His eyes narrow. "What does that mean?"

"I don't know," I say, hyperaware of my hands touching his on the desk behind me, "and that's the problem. But I am certain of this: my mind shows me things in seemingly random ways that always prove not to be random at all. I told Niccolo the past has nothing to do with the necklace, yet I keep seeing the past weave its way into the present. My father keeps coming back to me."

"He formed much of who and what you are."

"Yes," I agree. "And it could be that, but I'm not sure anymore. When I told Niccolo my past had nothing to do with the necklace, something felt off. And almost immediately when I got in the car with you and Adriel, I flashed back to something that happened at my old home in the States."

"What happened?"

"Two men visited me and I know they were CIA, but I know it somehow connected to my dad's death. I kept my gun close. What the hell does that even mean? Are they bad? Am I? Oh, God—what if I'm working for Niccolo?"

He cups my face. "You *are not* working for Niccolo."

"You can't know that. We can't know that."

"You remember when you are connected to things." His hands move to my waist. "Do you feel connected to him?"

"No. Not at all."

"Then you are not working for him. And we know you weren't working for Neuville."

"Why did I remember that day now?"

"You just found out your father was CIA this very evening. A high-level CIA operative who was murdered. Of course your mind is going there, but don't read into it. The possible reasons for that encounter are many."

"But it was important. That meeting is why I created the façade of being a schoolteacher. I needed to convince them that I wasn't a problem."

"'Them' who?"

"I don't know. The CIA, I think. Or maybe they were helping me hide. I hate this not knowing, so much! But more so, the idea that I was hiding from something that could have brought attention to Sara really worries me."

"You would never put someone in danger, especially someone you care about."

"I can't risk her or anyone else. We can't risk a mobster getting that necklace."

"What are you suggesting?"

"I need to go to Paris."

"No. Absolutely not."

"I have to go, Kayden. If conversation triggers memories, then seeing where I was will remind me—"

"No. And in case you didn't get that—no."

"You don't get to make this decision." I try to escape the cage of his body and the desk, only to have his hands come down on either side of me once more. "I'm serious, Kayden. You aren't—"

"Neuville is hunting you."

"And I have Evil Eye to protect me."

"To avenge your death," he says, "which isn't going to happen because I won't let it."

"The threat of Evil Eye—"

"Won't bring you back once you're gone, and I do not plan on losing you."

"I thought you said it protected me."

"Never assume absolute protection, or you'll let your guard down. I know you know that. Especially with people who are emotionally involved, like Neuville."

"Emotionally involved?"

"No matter what he feels for you, you sliced his pride. You escaped. You beat him. Men like him don't like to be beat."

"We haven't beat him yet, but we can. And we can't do

that if we go on like this. And I need to protect everyone. Sara is—"

"I've already told Matteo to coordinate protection for her, and she'll never know we're there."

"For how long do we do this, Kayden?"

"As long as it takes."

"I can't let her become a target."

"Blake Walker didn't share her information with Alessandro. I made sure of it, but we don't know if we can trust Blake's word. Matteo is checking them out, and I'm going to contact my people inside the U.S. government agencies about him and Chris Merit. But even if we can trust one or both of them, Alessandro's resourceful and Blake didn't have his guard up with him. We're not taking any chances with your friend."

"What about your people, Kayden? Marabella? Adriel? Giada? And you, Kayden. Being close to me means being at risk as long as I'm hunted."

"We're going to end this."

"*Exactly.* We have to end this. And I'm not missing the fact that you haven't denied the danger." I don't give him time to argue. "I remember a chocolate shop I went to when I was waiting for Neuville to pick me up that night David died. I could have hidden the necklace near there, or even in the shop itself. I need to go there and—"

"I'll send Adriel—"

"How would Adriel know anything about what I need to see and remember?"

"You send him to the places you want him to go; he'll take video. He'll—"

"This is ridiculous." I shove on his chest. "Let me off the desk." I slide to the left but he shackles my arm.

"Ella," he says, turning me to face him, our opposite hips pressed to the desk. "He's a good man."

"I don't trust him, Kayden, and you won't listen. You aren't hearing me."

"Sweetheart. I always listen to you."

"No. Not about this. And I get it. He's been with you forever."

"I'm *listening*. Tell me now."

"The day of the party," I say quickly, "I was with Giada, Adriel, and Marabella in the television room in the store. I had my journal with me to make sure I could jot down notes as I remembered things, but I walked off and left it for a few minutes. Adriel had it. He returned it to me. There were two pages missing, Kayden. A drawing of the necklace."

"Adriel's a Hunter, Ella. He would have made sure you didn't miss what he found. He would have taken a picture instead."

I feel the blood run from my face, disappointment and hurt stabbing at me. "Giada," I whisper, my hands settling on his chest. "I thought I'd gotten through to her—but the only way she knew that necklace was important was through betrayal."

Kayden shifts us, resting my backside against the desk again, his legs framing mine in a position of control. He always needs control, and that should bother me after all I've been through, but somehow it doesn't.

"Are you sure that page wasn't gone for longer than you realized?" he asks.

My brow furrows. "Well, I . . . I guess not, but I never took it out of the castle. So really, it doesn't matter when it happened. It has to be Giada. You have no idea how much that disappoints me."

"We've been watching her, sweetheart. She's had no more contact with Gallo since we called her on it. She's had no contact with anyone else of concern."

"It can't be Marabella."

"There are cameras in the store. We can look."

"You think it could be her?"

"I think it's Giada," he says. "But the good news is, whatever her reason for taking it, she hasn't acted on that reason yet. And she knows she's being watched. So she's not going to act on it anytime soon."

"There is that," I say. "But we're off track here. *Paris*, Kayden. Let's end this. Let's go and I'll—"

"No, Ella. There is nothing you can say that will convince me that we should do this."

"You don't get to decide this on your own. I'm not one of your Hunters."

He tangles his fingers into my hair and drags my gaze to his. "You're the woman I love more than life itself, and I will not, I am not, going to lose you."

"You won't," I vow. "I know how to—" His mouth closes on mine before I can say "protect myself," a hot slide of tongue that I feel in every part of me, wicked hot, passionate. Demanding.

I try to resist, to insist we talk first, but on the next caress of his tongue I taste his fear of losing me, his need to protect me, and yes, possession. He wants to possess me right now, I feel it in every part of me, and I know it's driven by a need to protect me. Because I'm a part of him, as he is of me, and those things undo me. Those things take me to a place that I can only go with him, an escape I would never dare allow myself without him. I sink into the kiss, arching into his body.

He tears his mouth from mine, our gazes colliding, and he repeats, "I love you, woman."

"I love you, too," I say, emotion welling in my throat, while his hands slip under my sweater, warm, right, and he eases it upward, pulling it over my head and tossing it away.

"Isn't Adriel waiting for us?" I ask, sounding as breathless as I feel. "We need to deal—"

He kisses me again, another deep slide of tongue against tongue that is over too soon before he declares, "Adriel can wait. I cannot." He says those words with a low rasp to his voice that leaves no question that he means them, his fingers trailing down my cheek and settling at the center clasp of my nude bra, which he unhooks.

"I can't do us halfway, sweetheart," he says. "I'm yours and I'm not going to let you get hurt. You're just going to have to deal with what that means, if I'm what you want."

My hands go to his as they cover my breasts. "I don't want halfway either," I say. "I just—"

"You just what?" he asks, leaning in to press his cheek against mine, his fingers teasing my nipple, tightening it into a hard, sensitive knot.

"I just want to . . . " He gives my nipples gentle tugs and I swallow against the sensations rolling through me, before I manage to finish with, " . . . do the right thing."

He goes still for a moment, his breath warm on my neck, his hands bracketing my waist. "Do the right thing," he repeats softly.

"Yes," I say. "Do the right thing."

He leans back to look at me, his blue eyes etched with shadows, and some emotion I cannot name. Seconds tick by that give me zero answers to what he's thinking, and without a word or a response, he reaches over and pulls open a drawer before setting something next to me that I can't see.

"What are you doing?" I ask, curious and confused.

He takes my hands and presses my palms together, never once looking at my naked breasts. "Lace your fingers," he orders softly.

There is a sudden newly sparked erotic charge in the air and my nipples tighten again of their own accord. I do as he asks, and for a moment, his hands hold mine, the look in his eyes dark, unreadable, and for reasons I cannot name that reach beyond that charge in the air, my heart begins to race.

"Do you trust me?" he asks.

"You know I do."

"I do know," he surprises me by saying. "But though you say you know, too, I'm not sure you really do."

"I do," I insist. "I absolutely do."

"Just know this. I would never betray you. I would never hurt you. I would, as I have said, and will say over and over, die for you."

"As I—"

"No," he says roughly, his voice gravelly, affected. "Do not say you would die for me, because that is not what I want from you. *Never* do I want that from you."

"I know you don't want that," I say, my voice now gravelly as well, "but you see, I feel what you feel. I can't stand the idea of living instead of you, without you."

"I don't plan to let you." His fingers flex around my hands. "Hold them right here." He waits for my reply and I give a tiny nod, before he reaches beside me and produces a roll of masking tape, already tearing a long piece.

"What are you doing?" I ask again, my heart now skipping and racing, but by the time I start to pull my hands back, he's already holding them.

"Aside from protecting your newly inked wrist by avoiding a tie that would be on top of it," he says as he attaches one side of the tape several inches up my arm, "I'm proving a point." He finishes wrapping my arms, then grabs the roll to pull off another piece.

"What point?"

He wraps more tape around my arms. "You can't get free," he says, tossing the roll over his shoulder. "I can do anything to you I want to do to you, and you can't stop me. You could fight, but I'm bigger and stronger. Does that scare you?"

"No, it doesn't scare me, but if I wanted to get free, I could fight. I'm good at fighting."

"Do you want to fight me, Ella?"

"No. Of course not."

"Because you're safe with me. I want you to *stay* safe with me. That is why we can't go to Paris. Not now. Not yet. I'm not trying to dominate you or control you. I just want you to be alive to fight with me like you just were. To change my mind. And for me to change yours, and in this case, I'm going to." He folds my hands behind my head, and orders me to keep them there while his hands slide to my back, molding me to him, his breath a warm wash on my lips. "I *can't* lose you, Ella."

"Kayden," I breathe out, emotion tightening my chest, so many emotions I cannot even begin to name them. Things I've felt in the past and present, things I know and do not know, colliding and erupting inside me. I need him and I know he needs me, and I have never felt such a thing with anyone, ever.

"Not *can't*," he amends. "I *won't* lose you. Do you understand?" He doesn't give me time to answer, or to let my fears that I will become his weakness take shape. Already he is kissing me, deeply, fiercely, kissing me and lifting me as he does. And even this, the way he holds me and I cannot hold him, not with my hands behind my head and my forearms taped. So I just savor the taste of him, of us together, and all we are here and now.

He settles me on the couch, my hands going to his chest as he comes down on top of me, lifting himself long enough to pull his shirt over his head, the sweet weight of his big, muscular body quickly returning to settle onto mine. "Lace your fingers behind your head again," he orders, helping me move my hands to rest there. "I don't want you to hurt your wrist. Keep them there."

"Are you still making a point?"

"If you have to ask, I haven't made it."

"Is that point that you have control and we aren't going to Paris?" I ask.

"No. That is not the point. At all. Now. *Don't* move your hands."

"And if I do?" I ask, challenging him to give me everything, to take everything including the memories I want to erase. To show me how he erases his. "Is this where you show me that dirty sex you say is your escape?"

"Is that what you want, or what you fear?"

"I'm not afraid of you, Kayden. Any part of you."

"Good. Then you know this isn't about control."

"Then what is it about?"

He leans in, pressing his cheek to mine, his breath warm on my neck. "What do you think I should do to you if you move your hands?"

"Un-tape me so I can touch you."

"That's not a punishment for you or me."

"Why do we need to be punished?"

"No risk, no reward," he says. "And if you move your hands, you'll pay a price." He nips my ear, a rough bite that has me yelping, and then moaning as his tongue strokes over the offended skin. "And I'll use my imagination as to what that will be." My mind conjures the memory of him promising all kinds of naughty ways that he escapes with sex, but before they run away with me he declares, "You have on too many clothes." And just like that, he is sliding down my body, leaving me breathless with my imagination, trying to decide where his will lead us. And for reasons I don't question, I really want to move my hands right now. But it's his hands that dominate, his that cover my breasts, in what becomes a tease of a caress, as he slides down my body, his tongue doing a quick stop at my nipple for a sultry swirl, which I feel everywhere he isn't touching and I hope he will be soon. But there is no time to savor his touch or hope for where it will follow next. He answers that question when his palms find the naked skin at my waist, branding me, while his lips press to the bare skin above my jeans, his fingers working down my zipper.

"I should help you," I whisper, but he dismisses that idea with actions.

I blink and he's not only pulled down my jeans, but my boots and socks are gone. Suddenly, I am naked, hands over my head, breasts thrust in the air, and he is standing over me, towering over me. Tall and broad, he is power and male dominance, while I am exposed, vulnerable. "What do you feel?" he asks.

"Naked," I answer honestly. "In every way. Can you please be naked, too?"

His lips, those sexy, sometimes brutally arousing lips, quirk on the sides, and too many seconds pass before he moves. He sits on the arm of the couch, taking his time to remove his boots, leaving me *naked*, as I have proclaimed myself in every way, thinking about that promise of a price to pay. Wondering why I want to move my hands and find out what it is. Finally, he stands, giving me his back, and suddenly I'm staring at the circle of skulls tattooed there that now includes two new ones. One for my mother and one for my father, both of whom have joined his family, including his godfather and fiancée, who were slaughtered by Niccolo.

A burn starts in my chest and I have a flashback of my father lying in his own blood. My breathing turns shallow, and I fight some place my mind wants to go, thankful when Kayden slides his pants and underwear down. Suddenly I have a view of his tight, perfect backside to focus on, and a moment later he's turned around and there is much to appreciate. His broad shoulders, light brown hair sprinkling a perfect chest that tapers to rippling abs and long, powerful thighs. A thick, jutted cock that is somehow a part of his power, and of course, so much a part of his incredible, forceful masculinity.

He returns to the end of the couch. "Now how do you feel?" he asks.

"Hot," I whisper. "I feel very, very hot."

"What if I told you I was going to spank you and clamp your nipples?"

If I was hot moments before, I am hotter now, heat gathering with slick arousal between my thighs. "I'd say you don't have any clamps."

"I'm going to spank you and clamp you."

I'm shocked at just how aroused I am in this moment, just how curious I am about what he will do to me. Just how much I want the escape that he's claimed sex can be for him. An escape chosen with him. "I've never . . . I don't . . ."

"I do. I will."

Butterflies flutter in my belly. "Can you just do it now so I don't have to be nervous?"

"Are you afraid, Ella?"

"No," I say, meaning it. "I am not afraid."

I blink and we're face to face, his back against the couch, his shaft thick and hard between my thighs. He pulls my hands between us and he cradles me, his palm on my backside. "I told you I would spank you."

"I'm quite clear on your tastes, Kayden. It's not the first time you've . . . done that."

"This is different than before," he warns. "This is a real spanking, not the pats from before."

"Those were pats?"

"Yes. Those were what I call pats. You still—"

"Yes," I say firmly.

"After all he did to you, even beat you, you'd let me do that?"

"You're not him."

"Why aren't you afraid, Ella?"

"Because *you're not him*." And then it hits me, the message he's getting across. "I trust you completely. There's your point. But I told you that I trust you. I think it's you who doubts me."

"No. I don't doubt your trust. Why do you trust me? And don't say it's because I'm me."

"You would never hurt me. Because you're . . . safe."

"Yes," he says, his free hand brushing my hair back and tilting my face to his. "Safety comes first. It allows you to keep fighting the battles that need to be fought."

Suddenly I am squeezing my eyes shut, and I'm back in time, in a gym with my father.

∽∾∽

We are facing each other, circling on the mat. "Defend yourself at all costs," he says, throwing a punch that should hit me, but he stops short.

"Damn it, child." He knocks me to the ground and stands over me. "You could be dead right now. Your mother could be dead right now."

"Don't say that," I hiss.

"Because of you, she could be dead," he says. "Defend yourself at all costs."

A growl escapes my throat and I stand back up. He throws a punch and I duck under it, kneeing him in the stomach. He catches my leg and I go down again.

He stands over me. "What do you do now?"

∞∞

"Ella."

I blink and the moment I look into Kayden's eyes, he presses inside me. I gasp, and then pant, the feel of him stretching me, of pulling me down his hard shaft, stealing any thought or worry. "Now you're with me," he says. "That's where I want you. With me and safe."

I lift my bound hands and touch my fingers to his face. "I like that I am safe with you. But you are safe with me, too. I want to be that for you. You know that, right?"

His forehead finds mine. "Ah, woman, what you do to me. Yes. I know I am safe with you, in ways only you understand." He reaches up and rips the tape, leaving it connected to my arms but freeing me. I immediately dive my fingers into the thick waves of his light brown hair.

"That means I need to be that person you can escape with," I say, tightening my grip on his hair. "I need, I want, to be the person you escape with."

"You already are."

"I mean that dirty sex you talked about."

"Ella—"

I press my lips to his, lingering there a moment, our bodies gliding just a little left and right. "I want that part of you. I want it to be a part of me. I want us to be that . . . complete."

He cups my backside, pulling me farther against him. "You really want this?"

"Yes. I want to escape too. With you."

He does a slow slide in and out of me, his lips brushing mine, his teeth nipping my lip. "Feel my hand," he says, squeezing my backside.

"Yes. I feel everything."

"I'm going to keep caressing," he says, rubbing the sensitive skin, "and fucking." He drives into me. Slow. Gently. He slides his hips back and forth, moving our bodies together. "Then, I'm going to spank you. Three times. Not hard, but not soft. And then we're going to fuck hard."

"Can you just do it now so I don't have to be nervous?"

"If I do that, there's no anticipation."

"Right," I say. "Anticipation."

He kisses me, a long swipe of his tongue, followed by another, our bodies moving, his hand caressing. "Anticipation," he murmurs, "is good."

"My heart is racing," I confess. "Really fast."

"I'm not going to hurt you."

"Promise? No. I know you won't."

"Easy, sweetheart," he says, dragging his cock slowly back

and then driving into me. "What are you thinking right now?"

I gasp. "Thinking? I'm . . . not."

He drives into me again and squeezes my cheek. "Now?"

"That felt good."

He does it again. "And that?"

"Better."

He kisses me again and then says, "Now, sweetheart. One, two, three."

"Now? I—"

He smacks my backside, with a firm, flat palm that bites sharply, and a roar of sensations erupts inside me, my sex clenching his cock, air lodging in my lungs. Already another smack comes, and then another. Then Kayden is kissing me, wild, crazy kissing me, and our bodies are melded together, the world falling away. There is this deep burn in my body, in my entire existence, that needs to be closer to him. That needs him to drive harder and faster. I have never been so lost, so explosive, and I lose everything but the sensations. Strokes. Grinds. Touches. Kisses. And then suddenly reality is spinning and fading in and out, my body stiffening. And then I am tumbling into oblivion, quaking from within. Kayden cups my head and leans into me, a low groan escaping his lips, rough and sexy, before he's shuddering, shaking.

Slowly his body eases, and so does mine, the present returning, and awareness with it. I am limp, completely, utterly sated, my leg resting on his hip, when I don't even remember it being there. Seconds tick by, our breathing all that fills the air, and everything comes back to me. The slow caresses, the sting of my backside. The absolute lust I felt in the wake of that sting.

Kayden cups my cheek, tilting my face to his. "Are you okay?"

"Yes. I am."

"Did I—"

"Hurt me? Scare me? No, you did not."

He studies me, then, "Would you—"

"Do it again? Yes, I would." My hand flattens on his chest. "I can't explain it, and I know that was barely anything, but it was intimate in ways that I couldn't be with anyone else. In ways I thought that I would never be with anyone, after Garner Neuville. You are somehow dangerous and sexy and still safe, and I don't know how that's even possible."

His eyes darken, some emotion I cannot name flashing in their depths, and then he kisses me hard and fast, before he eases my leg down and reaches over to the table. He relaxes beside me again with a tissue that he presses between us, slipping it where he had been. But already he is pulling me closer again, maneuvering to his back, with my head on his chest. We melt into the couch and each other, a blanket of warmth wrapping around us, and I can almost feel our bond growing. This is what safe feels like. But even as I try to revel in this moment, there's a nagging feeling that when we leave this room, we are no longer safe.

"Ella," Kayden says, and I wonder if he feels it too.

"Yes?"

He rolls me to my back, one arm bracketing me, light brown hair draping his forehead. Those blue eyes becoming warm in the way they do only for me. "I want you to be my wife."

I suck in air, shocked when perhaps I should not be. I love him. He loves me. And yet I can't seem to make myself say the magic word: *Yes*.

five

sara

*W*riting this entry is rather surreal considering it's only hours after I spoke to Ella, confirming she's alive. Alive! I cannot believe it. As silly as it seems as I write this now, I never said it out loud, nor put ink to paper, for fear I'd somehow jeopardize my chance of ever seeing her again. But back to why this is surreal. Well, I guess there are many reasons, but ultimately one. It was Ella who handed me a journal in the first place. Not my journal, but Rebecca's, a woman I didn't know then, but now . . . now I feel as if she is a part of me. Rebecca certainly changed my life. Her words touched my heart, my soul. Her words scared me enough for me to look for her, and while I didn't find her, I did find Chris. And Chris is most certainly a part of me.

And that all came about because Ella became obsessed with <u>Storage Wars</u>, and decided to auction hunt during last summer's break. She found Rebecca's journal in a storage unit, obsessing over it before I did, and then leaving it with me the night she abruptly left for Paris to elope with a man she barely knew. And since a journal was the last thing Ella and I *shared before our call today, somehow writing in one now that I've found her again seems profoundly well timed. That journal changed my life..*

So with all of this in mind, I'm attempting to start my own journal. Again. I always feel weird about exposing myself on the page, but this time I'm committing because Rebecca's fears, dreams, and life in general drove me to be better. And I think I've grown enough since meeting her on that first page I read to make that growth come from reading my own fears and insecurities on the page. And if I share them with Chris, because I am able to with him, who knows where that will lead us . . .

So where are we now? I am sitting in Chris's Paris studio, curled inside the nook in front of the window where he was painting me just two hours ago. He's back to painting. "Take Me to Church" is still playing on repeat in the background, while he works on one of his Underground Tom paintings, all of which have been dark, and no doubt inspired by the recent and past tragedies of his life, as well as his fear that part of his life will somehow touch me and us. He is broken in many ways, as dark as those paintings, but somehow that part of him collides with all the others and equals perfection to me and the canvas. He started by painting me, quite literally, and I'm not talking about the canvas. I'm wearing his shirt now, but beneath it, I have paint all over my body. My God, the things that man does to me!

One minute he was kissing me, the next my hands were bound and I was at the center of the studio, on the floor, his brush, hands, and mouth driving me wild. Controlling me the way certain triggers make him want to control everything around us, and yet he manages to keep those moments naked and raw. And somehow, I like it when he controls me. The control freak in me stopped fighting that months ago. I like it. I love it. He might dominate in those intimate times, but I am never as free in life as I am then, when I don't have to be anything but his woman.

But going back to how the need for control started today, or rather, why it started . . .

The minute he'd heard I might be in danger, I knew it would be a trigger for him, for which he'd need a release, which for Chris used to mean pain. I still can't believe how he'd . . . I can't write it. I just . . . can't. Now, his release is sex. Hot, amazing sex, and this time it included binding my hands, painting my body, and teasing me incessantly. Teasing both of us, because when we finally . . . it was explosive. This is how he heals now. How we heal.

We.

I like that word.

Wife.

Husband.

I like those words, too, though there are still no white picket fences for Chris and me. I'll happily take the many shades of perfect imperfection that define Chris Merit. But I really want Ella to have her version of the white picket fence. And I know she's not the simple happy schoolteacher she played at being. I saw her own shades of imperfection because they spoke to mine. It's why we connected and understood each other, beyond what we dared speak to one another. But maybe we will now. I just want the chance for us to get that close. I really need her to be okay, and my gut says she's not. The way it said Rebecca was not.

❧ *ella* ❧

"This is where you say 'yes,' sweetheart," Kayden says. "This is where you agree to be my wife."

"*Wife*," I say. "I never thought . . . but I like how that

sounds." I have recovered from the shock of his proposal enough to know why I'm hesitating to accept. "But there are so many reasons—"

"For you to say 'yes,'" he supplies, his voice rough, shadows in his eyes that weren't there moments before.

He's right; there are. But instead I say, "For us to talk. I need to sit up so we can talk."

He stares at me, his expression unreadable, his naked shoulders bunched, and I can tell that he wants to refuse to move, but he doesn't. He leans back just enough for me prop myself on the arm of the couch behind me. But he continues to bracket my hips, caging me as if he thinks I'll run away, when all I want to do is kiss him. I settle for reaching up and fingering a strand of his light brown hair. "You're The Hawk."

"And that has what to do with you marrying me?"

"Everything," I say, my hand moving to his jaw, the newly forming stubble rough beneath my fingers, while my rejection of his proposal is a weight on my shoulders and heart. "You'll make decisions to protect me."

"That's right," he says unapologetically. "I will."

"But those might not be the right decisions."

"We had this conversation thirty minutes ago. Caution is good."

"Unless it makes you afraid to act."

"Sweetheart, I get that you just saw Enzo die. But he was young and foolhardy, two things I am not. I don't let fear control me, and I don't make rash decisions. If I did, Niccolo would be dead right now. Because believe me, I wanted to kill that bastard today."

For just an instant I see my father lying in his own blood, and the certainty that Kayden had found his fiancée and his mentor in the same condition has me shivering. Kayden notices, too; of course he notices. He's somehow always aware of what I'm feeling, even when I'm not. He straightens and reaches for the blanket at the back of the couch that I know he intends for me. I take that moment of freedom and scoot to a sitting position, snatching up the tissues he'd given me and tossing them behind me, because already Kayden is wrapping the blanket around my shoulders. And while I am now covered, I am aware of every inch of his naked, muscular body. And when he holds onto the edges of the cloth, and those blue eyes, a shade paler now, capture mine, I can't breathe.

"Ella," he says, breathing out my name, compelling me to accept his proposal.

"Don't look at me like that."

"Like what?"

"Like you can't live without me."

"Stop making me feel that way and I will."

"What if I do? What if I stop making you feel that way?"

"Impossible," he assures me, "which is why you're marrying me. The end. We're going to find an insanely expensive ring, and we'll marry when and how you want. If you want your friend Sara there, we'll have her there. If you don't—"

"You can't just tell me I'm marrying you."

"Do you love me?"

"Yes."

"Do you want to share the rest of—"

"Yes," I say. "I do, Kayden. Very much, but—"

"Do you *want* to marry me?"

"That's not the issue. That's not even a question."

"Do you *want* to marry me?"

"*Yes,*" I whisper. "I love you. But Kayden—"

"No *but*. You want to marry me. I want to marry you. We're getting married."

"It's not that simple."

"It's as simple as we make it, sweetheart." His cell phone rings, his jaw clenching in response before he tightens his grip on the blanket and uses it to pull me closer, kissing me hard on the lips before he releases me.

He stands up and it's all I can do to not pull him back, reminding myself that this call could be news that we're waiting for about any number of things. Instead, I find myself once again staring at his gorgeous backside, a reminder that it could be mine to admire the rest of my life. And I want it to be. I want *him* to be.

But I don't just remember my father on that floor. I remember my mother collapsing at the funeral. I remember tears and torment, and the bastard of a drunken man she settled for, as if to punish herself for something I didn't understand and never will. I loved my father, but there was a reason he trained me. He knew that one day he could put us in danger. Yet he didn't stay away. He *should* have stayed away, even for his own sake. Maybe then he'd have been less distracted, and more ready for an attack—like Kayden will be without me.

I inhale on that hard-to-swallow reality, watching Kayden fish the phone out of his pants pocket and glance at the screen before answering the call. "Yes, Adriel," he says, and I know this is to let me know who is on the line. It's a respect I appreciate, one he gives me often. But he is still The Hawk, still dominant in every way, and when he's passionate about something, he's a stubborn force to be reckoned with. And he's clearly passionate about the topics of marriage and Paris.

"I'll be there in twenty minutes," he says, listening to whatever is being said to him and reaching for his pants again, while I catch the blanket before it slides away, the tape on my arm catching on the cloth.

I reach up, yanking what's left of it free, and in the process, my gaze catches on my new tattoo. I reach out and trace the pink wings of the hawk, and the truth is, I am already Kayden's wife to everyone who knows him as The Hawk. I know this. I also know that together, we made this choice and declared our bond. But Kayden felt pressured to protect me, while I . . . I love him. It really isn't a question for me, so why am I hesitating to marry him now?

Suddenly Kayden is sitting in front of me, his pants now on, his hand going to the back of my tattooed wrist and pulling it between us. "Wearing the bracelet to the party and getting this tattoo protects you, like I always will."

"I realize that, and I appreciate that you did this for me."

"I did this for *us*, Ella, and under different circumstances those things would have been choices, a commitment to me and us, to this life, but I realize that you really didn't have that option with Niccolo looking for you. Marrying me—*that* is a choice. It's you saying you want to spend the rest of your life with me."

And there it is. The reason I'm hesitating. I don't want to make the same mistakes my father made.

"Instead, you're doing what you said you don't do," he accuses softly.

"Which is what?"

"Running."

My defenses prickle. "I'm right here. I'm not running."

"Aren't you?"

"I'm the one who wants to go to Paris."

"That's suicide. That's what people do when they can't run anymore."

"I'm not running and I'm not trying to commit suicide," I say, but I hate that in the back of my mind I'm already questioning myself. "This isn't a choice either of us can afford for me to make right now. Not when we don't know who I am."

"We absolutely know who you are."

"We know things about me. We *don't* know who I really am—and most importantly, we don't know *what* I am. There's no way I'm working for that monster Neuville, but I could be working for Niccolo."

"Your memory snaps back when you're presented with pictures and people. You'd know at this point if that were true."

"What I know is that there is much more about me than we've pieced together."

"You're obviously leading me somewhere. What is your point?"

"I'm complicated."

"My life is a fucking foreign novel written in twenty languages, sweetheart. Complicated is what I do."

"You aren't hearing me again, Kayden. There is more to me than meets the eye."

"I'm more than aware of that fact."

"And I was aware of the French marriage laws when I eloped to Paris. I knew I couldn't marry him, so clearly I was using David. What does that say about who and what I may be?"

"Quid pro quo, sweetheart. You were smart enough to sense he was using you, even if you didn't know why."

"*Was* he using me? Or was that me setting him up? If I'm CIA—"

"I *am not* your enemy, if that's where we're going yet again."

"We don't know what I am, or what that makes us. And if you marry the wrong person and your men find out, it will damage you, Kayden."

He gently strokes just above my freshly tattooed skin. "To my men, this tattoo is a more powerful declaration than marriage. It's about trust and an invitation inside the secrecy of our organization, and at the highest level. It's done to them."

"You didn't have a choice, either."

"You're wrong on that, Ella. I could have sent you far, far away where you couldn't be found and cleared a path for you later. But I didn't—and by invoking Evil Eye, I made sure I never have to."

"And yet you fight me on Paris."

"I told you. Evil Eye or not, you don't taunt a monster

scorned, and you scorned Neuville. And this isn't about him right now."

"But it is. I'm a target. You're a target. I want to know that I can't hurt you. And you can't just dismiss my connection to the CIA, whatever that may be."

"Right. The CIA. Which I've explained does not put us at odds, but you don't seem to want to hear that. Maybe you think that if you're CIA, you won't approve of who and what I am. Maybe that's already happening. Maybe, for your sake, that's a good thing." He faces forward, grabs his boots, and starts putting them on.

I blanch. "What? No! It's *not* a good thing. It's not a thing at all. I know what you are. I know you. It's me we don't know." Wishing half my clothes weren't across the room, I wrap the blanket more fully around me and sit up next to him. "This is about me."

He finishes putting his boots on and grabs his shirt from the floor, pulling it over his head, and then settling his elbows on his knees. He doesn't speak, the dark edginess of his mood thickening the air, suffocating me, until I can take it no more.

"Kayden—"

"The truth is, Ella," he says, still not looking at me, "there are things about me you don't know, too. Things I've done. Things I'll do again if so needed. Maybe those things just won't work for you. And maybe I'm fucked in the head for suggesting this."

Those words punch me in the chest. "I know you walk lines," I say. "I *know* you beyond any of those things. I know—"

Finally, he turns his head toward me, his eyes sharp, cold,

when they'd been hot enough to scorch me only minutes before. "You choose who you are now and later, just like we choose what we are together. I was going to push you to choose me, like I choose you. That was wrong of me. Selfish, even. Why would you want this, why would I want this for you, when maybe, just maybe, you'll find yourself again, and you'll have a shot at a normal life complete with two kids and a dog and a big backyard?" He stands up.

"That is not where I was going with this," I say, popping to my feet and stepping in front of him before he can leave. "That is not what I want. My father—"

"Ella," he says, his hands coming down on my shoulders. "You were right and I was wrong. It's not the right time for us. Maybe it'll never be the right time. And right now, Adriel is expecting us in the store." He sets me aside and my heart all but jumps out of my chest.

"Kayden, please wait," I plead, whirling around to find him walking away, relieved when he stops, but discouraged when he doesn't turn. Instead he says, "You aren't going to Paris. Don't bring it up to Adriel." He is The Hawk with that command, and the instant it's issued, he starts walking, his stride long, sure, unstoppable.

My throat thickens and suddenly I feel as if I've been shoved into a dark, muddy pond that is slowly consuming me, and I've just pushed away the only man who can save me. I am cold inside and out, the nearby fire doing nothing to warm me up, and I know that it's adrenaline and emotions driving this sensation. How have we gone from marriage to this? But I know the answer instantly. Kayden is a fierce loner who let me inside the many layers of protection he's wrapped around himself, and in turn, I've hurt him. I hurt him badly, and that hurts me. Could I have screwed this up any worse?

I press my hand to my face. I was just trying to protect him. I don't want to leave him. I just don't want to destroy him by staying. I don't want to be selfish and hold onto someone I love to the point of destroying him, the way my father did my mother. My death or betrayal would impact Kayden fiercely, intensely, and hurt his entire operation. I don't know how to get around that if we stay together.

But what really worries me, what I can't live with, is the idea that he could end up dead. That he could become a target because of me, and end up the next one lying in a pool of blood. And that can't happen. It *won't* happen. That will be me, before him.

But right now, no matter how desperately I want to talk to Kayden and make things right, now is not the time. He's waiting for me and if there was ever a time to show him that I stand by him in all things, it's now, starting with the meeting with Adriel. I drop the sheet and waste no time putting on my clothes, mentally setting aside every emotion the past hour has stirred as I do. This meeting is with Adriel, and Adriel might be a friend to Kayden, but he is also a Hunter, and that makes him Underground business. This is not the time for personal matters to be aired.

I race for the door, having no intention of being late when Kayden questions him about when those pages in my journal disappeared, and it hits me and stops me dead in my tracks. I'm about to go tell Adriel his sister might be betraying him. I need to be sure I'm right. I need to look at the camera feed Kayden mentioned, which I should be able to access from the security room in our bedroom.

Decision made, I cut left and run up the double set of stone stairs, one straight and one cutting right, until I'm at the hallway above, the wide open archway leading to the living area in front of me, with our room to the left. Heading in that direction, the motion detector casts me in a dim, warm glow as I travel the walk down the long stone hallway, the ceiling towering above me. The eerie sensation of being watched that has become expected in this stretch of the walkway, which I've always played off as my resident ghosts, hits me. But tonight as I stop at our bedroom door, and turn the knob, I find myself pausing, struck by how similar this sensation is to the one in the entryway earlier.

My brow furrows, the possibility of an unknown camera crossing my mind, but I've seen every view Kayden has set up in our tower. Surely I haven't missed one in this location—and even if I have, that alone wouldn't make me feel watched when we're the only ones who can see that feed. Unless . . . could our cameras be hacked? The entire premise I've invented is crazy, but it still has me opening the door and entering the bedroom, not about to alert anyone watching that I might be aware of their existence.

Once over the threshold, I dial the lights up to the brightest level, shut myself inside, and lean against the heavy wooden door. Despite the urgent timeline I'm on, and the fact that the entrance to this tower requires a password that only Kayden, Marabella, and I know, I find myself uneasily scanning the spacious room. My attention lands first on the giant bed we didn't bother making this morning, my stomach knotting with the possibility that one day I might not be here to share it with him. Shaking off such thoughts, I force my attention to the fireplace on the wall opposite where I stand, then to the big-screen TV above the heavy dresser directly in front of the bed. Then, finally, to the bathroom door to the right that refuses to be dismissed.

Really, truly, I sense no danger, but that eerie sensation refuses to let me be anything but cautious, and I curse myself for leaving my gun downstairs. Nevertheless, I'm capable of protecting myself and I walk to the bathroom, the lights coming on as I touch one of the shiny white tiles, to find it empty. Completing my search, I dash down the white tiled path between the giant oval tub to the row of cabinets with double sinks to my right and flip on the light to the closet. No one is there but me, of course, but for just a few moments I pause in the doorway, my gaze catching on the rows of Kayden's clothes on the right side, and then the small row of clothes to the left, which are mine and a part of a new beginning. *You choose who you are now and later*, Kayden had said, *just like we choose what we are together.* Words I'd like to live by, but are they really true? Can I reject any reality the past tries to force upon me and us?

My gaze lands on the mirror in front of me, and my reflection blinks into view. What was I thinking? I don't have to wait and see who this woman is. I know her, and I don't want to be any other version of her but the one I am here and now with Kayden. I've even come to like my now dark brown hair, when

I've often craved my natural red shade. I need to tell him all of this, and I will. I'll scream it loud and clear if I have to, but right now I need to search the security feed. Fully intending to leave, I start to turn, but my gaze lands on the mirror again, and I am suddenly, abruptly even, transported to another time, to the point that I sway and lean on the closet door. Images race through my mind, my lashes lowering with the force with which they are thrust upon me.

∽∽∽

I stand in the closet, his closet, staring at myself in the full-length mirror, trying to see what he will see when I go downstairs. No. Trying to control what he will see. I'm dressed in an elegant cream pantsuit, my red hair draping my shoulders, the strap of a Chanel purse resting across my chest and at my hip. I see my familiar image, but not a woman I know or understand. Not the woman my father trained to be strong and fierce. Because that woman would not have allowed herself to be tied to a bed last night. And when she was released, she would have forcefully fled. My lashes lower and I inhale, sitting down on a bench in the corner against the wall, beside a row of fancy shoes Garner bought for me yesterday. I could leave, but where would I go? I still have no passport. I still have no money. And the more I've thought about this, the greater the odds of me randomly falling into the middle of whatever this is, it just doesn't make sense. I'm hiding with a monster, but that monster is necessary to my survival.

Inhaling again, I force myself to turn on my heel and march out of the closet, and never stop walking. I exit the bathroom into the bedroom and make the mistake of looking at the bed where I'd been tied up last night, swallowing the disgrace and anger I feel, the dread at knowing he's about to touch me again. I keep moving, and I exit into the hallway and start the walk down the windowless, red-carpeted stairwell. I'm just about to round a corner when I hear Neuville's voice speaking in French, followed by another familiar voice I know to be Bastile, his personal bodyguard. I freeze on the word collier, *or in English,* necklace, *icy cold reality hitting me. That monster I'm hiding with is the same one I'm hiding from.*

"I searched her hotel room again top to bottom," Bastile says, speaking in the French I pretend not to know. "There is no necklace. How do you want to proceed?"

"Search the property she brought with her when we're at lunch today."

"I've searched her property."

"Do it again," Neuville snaps.

"And if I don't find it?"

He won't find it, *I think.* I made sure of it.

"A man is dead and we got rid of the body for her. As far as she knows, we're hiding her from the murderer and the police. She'll give me the necklace."

Nothing he can do to me will make me give him that necklace. But somehow, some way, I have to figure out what makes it so sought after, and decide what to do with it.

"And if she doesn't? At what point do I torture her into talking and get rid of her?"

"You don't. I've decided to keep her."

∽∾∽

I jolt back to the present, sucking in air, disoriented by my equally sudden return to reality. I'm still here and I'm still alone, but Neuville's words are now living and breathing here as well: *I've decided to keep her.*

"Fuck you, Garner," I spit. "That didn't go so well, now did it?" I swallow bile in my throat, anger burning in my belly at the things he did to me, but I survived. And I will beat him.

Shoving off the door, I am more focused than ever on answers and an endgame, a motivation that has me hurrying into the bedroom and crossing to the security room in the corner next to the fireplace. Once I'm inside the tiny rectangular room, I sit at the small desk against the wall and key the computer to life. Clicking past the live feed now on the front of the castle, I struggle a bit but find the store security feed and the right date. With surprising ease, I'm watching myself chat with Marabella and Giada in the living area of the store in the Center Tower. I fast-forward and find the part where I left my journal in that room to inspect the delivery Kayden had sent to me that night. I watch Giada and Adriel interact in the living area, having some sort of heated words, but neither touches the journal.

I fast-forward again and find the moment Adriel's foot hits something and he bends down and grabs the journal from the floor by the couch, where it's obviously been knocked. He picks it up, but never opens it. He looks a little irritated, like I shouldn't be so careless, or maybe I'm just remembering his attitude when he handed it to me. He simply stands, leaves the TV room, and finds me in the main store, where he returns it to me.

He didn't take the pages out of the journal, but neither did Giada or Marabella. I sit back and stare at the computer screen without really seeing it. That day was the only time I've had my journal outside of this tower. And the only person who can get in here is Marabella. Sweet, loyal, wonderful Marabella. No. It's not her. I reject that idea. But . . . if it is, who is she working for? Niccolo, Alessandro, or the worst possibility of all: Garner Neuville?

six

The door to the bedroom opens and I barely have time to turn before Kayden appears in the archway to the security room. And oh God. He's so big and gorgeous and overwhelmingly male. He's also radiating a sharp, dark energy that cuts and bites with the certainty I created it. "We were waiting on you," he announces.

"I'm sorry," I say quickly. "I realized that before this meeting, I needed to know who took those journal pages."

"Because you still doubt my confidence in Adriel."

"Because you made me question when the pages went missing," I correct, "and the last thing I wanted to do was strain Adriel and Giada's already fragile relationship by throwing suspicion on her."

His expression doesn't change, but there's a shift in his energy that tells me he approves. "And what did you find?"

"Neither of them took it that day—and that was the only time I took it anywhere but here. And the only person who can get in here besides us—"

"It's not Marabella."

"Then who is it, and how did they get to my journal?"

"Maybe you tore pages out during one of your flashbacks."

I think of the moment in the closet when I'd returned to the present, disoriented, and I let out a breath. "It's possible. I'd really like to think that's it, but my fear is that it's not."

"We'll sit down tonight and go through the security feed. It'll take a long time, but we'll get it done. We'll find out."

"We?"

"Yes, Ella," he says, an emphasis on my name that is one part cold and one part hot. "*We.* But right now, Giada and Marabella are in the Center Tower. I had Adriel come here to talk to us to ensure our privacy. He's in the kitchen."

I stand up, the few steps between us feeling like a world, and he slowly backs up to let me exit but doesn't turn away. He holds his ground, almost willing me to hold mine, but I can't. I don't. I close several of the small spaces between us, stopping an extended arm's reach from touching him. "I don't want kids, who can get hurt. I don't want a dog, because even though I like them, I don't want to be licked all the time unless it's by you. But I like cats. Do you? Because I think that we, and this castle, really need a cat."

Still, there is no discernible reaction from him, his expression hard, his chiseled jaw harder, and it twists me in knots. It hurts, but what hurts more is knowing that his reaction is because I've made him feel what I feel right now. Rejected. Hollow. Empty. Unable to take the silence another minute, I start to walk away, but only manage a step before Kayden catches

my arm and turns me back to face him. I'm once again staring
into those unreadable eyes.

"He's not happy," he says, the warning about Adriel not exactly what I was hoping for.

"Does he know about my connection to the necklace?"

"I told him nothing more than what you did in the car,
which is part of the reason he's pissed, but I wanted you to decide what to share."

Kayden gives respect, and thus he receives it. It's only one
of the many reasons he's such a good leader. "Thank you, and
I'm not going to hold back. You were right. He should know
the truth."

His eyes narrow slightly, a hint of approval in their depths
before he gives me a barely perceivable nod, but when I expect
him to release me, when I think he intends to in fact, he does
not. Instead, he studies me, searching my face, probing, looking for something, I don't know what, but I hide nothing. I let
him see the emotions I feel. The regret, the fear, the love. But
too soon it seems, and without any palpable reaction, he releases me. "He's waiting."

My arm tingles where his touch was, a sensation I carry
with me as I give him a nod of my own. As I turn away from
him, moving across the room, I am hyperaware of him behind
me, close enough that when I would open the door his arm
stretches around me, his hand on the knob. His big body en-
cases mine, the scent of him, all masculine spice and dominance, teasing my nostrils.

He leans in and says, "He's going to attack."

"I can handle it."

"Of that, sweetheart, I am certain."

There is a hint of something in his words that I don't like, an implication that he's certain of this, but not of me or of himself, but I never get the chance to reply, not that this is the right time anyway. He opens the door and sidesteps to allow its movement, exiting into the hallway. Almost instantly the door shuts again behind us. We walk down the hallway, and I can almost feel The Hawk take over, the sense of focus on that part of him rising to the surface. In unison, we cut left under the archway and into the living area, where the fireplace is burning in the far corner, just beyond the leather couch and chairs, its warmth stealing the chill that extends beyond the nearly century-old stone walls to the kitchen to our right.

We cross the room and step under yet another archway to pause in the entryway of the kitchen, where Adriel stands behind the island, his dark, wavy hair a bit in disarray, his leather jacket gone. He's wearing a shoulder holster and not one but two firearms over his skull T-shirt, its deadly undertone rather appropriate considering how hard and cold his stare is right now.

"Who the fuck *are* you?" he demands, pressing his hands to the granite surface, that deep scar down his cheek giving his voice an even harder impact. "*What* the fuck are you, and what the hell were you doing with Garner Neuville?"

"Well, at least we don't have to worry about an awkward silence," Kayden says dryly.

I almost laugh, and probably would if there wasn't a throbbing vein at Adriel's temple I'm pretty sure would burst if I did. "CIA is a good guess," I say, giving him a direct answer, crossing to stand on the opposite side of the island.

He scowls. "A good guess? How do you make a 'good guess' you're in the fucking CIA?"

"I still have amnesia, Adriel. That isn't fake."

"Start at the beginning," Kayden says, appearing at the end of the island between us, "back in San Francisco. With David."

"The man you were traveling with that we can't locate," Adriel clarifies.

"Yes," I confirm, "but I'm not sure David is where this originated. The PI who visited us today revealed what I had already started to piece together. My father was a CIA agent and somehow, in some way, I believe that's relevant to all of this."

"Not just an agent," Kayden supplies. "A high-level, top-secret operative."

"How do you think he's involved?" Adriel asks.

"*Relevant*," I correct. "Not *involved*. He was assassinated when I was a teenager."

"*Assassinated* is a powerful word," Adriel states. "It implies a hit."

"It *was* a hit," I say, "complete with men in black and guns, though the agency never officially called it that or gave us an answer."

"It happened at Ella's family home while she was there," Kayden supplies. "Ella killed them before they escaped."

Adriel looks at him and then gives me a skeptical look.

"Didn't you just say you were a teenager then? And since we're talking CIA, I assume they were professional assassins?"

"I was already an expert marksman, which I doubt they expected from a teenager," I explain. "And it was my father's last wish."

"For you to kill them," Adriel says, sounding a little incredulous. "As a teenager."

"Yes. He lay there in his own blood and told me to kill them, and he knew I could. He'd been training me since I was old enough to hold a gun and fight."

Adriel's eyes narrow on me. "Was he grooming you to be an agent?"

"No," I say, ice sliding down my spine with the certainty that comes with my reply. "He was grooming me for the day they came for him or for us *because* of him." I fold my arms in front of me and look at Kayden, speaking to him. "I think I was looking into his murder. I don't know why I chose the present day, so many years after my father died, but whatever the case," I look between them, "I pissed off the agency, and the result was me taking this schoolteacher job and lying low. But I also don't know if that was my own choice or the agency trying to get me off the wrong radars."

"If you were lying low, how did you get into this?" Adriel asks. "It sounds more like you were undercover, to me."

"Maybe," I say, my brow furrowing. "But if I was CIA and pursuing the necklace—"

"The necklace?" Adriel asks, his tone sharpening again, his gaze shifting to Kayden. "She knows about the necklace and you didn't tell me."

"We're telling you now," Kayden states. "Only you, until we decide otherwise." And just that easily he ends the subject, glancing at me. "Tell him how you got the necklace."

"David gave it to me as an engagement gift—which makes the idea of me being undercover seem illogical. If I were after the necklace, I wouldn't have carried it to Europe and risked losing it. But it also seems completely illogical to think that I have a connection to the CIA and just fell into something this big."

"How did you go from eloping to knowing Neuville and Niccolo?" Adriel asks.

I give him the rundown, including my history with David, what happened at the hotel, and even Neuville showing up, covering pretty much everything. "I didn't know who Neuville was, beyond being a powerful French businessman."

"So you were intimately involved with Neuville," Adriel says, the statement hitting me in every wrong way possible.

My gaze jerks to his and I snap, "I fucked him or I died, so yes. I was intimately involved with him right up until the point that I held a gun on him in front of his people, and ensured he will *never* fucking stop coming for me."

"Easy, Ella," Adriel says, holding up his hands. "I was just trying to understand the dynamics."

"The dynamics?" I ask. "The dynamics are—"

"You don't need to do this, Ella," Kayden says softly, his voice somehow managing to deliver a cool caress I feel in every hot, angry burning nerve ending in my body, of which there are many.

"He's right," Adriel states, his hands pressing to the

counter. "I get it. Sasha's told me about his appetites. He needs to pay."

"He needs to do more than pay," I say. "He needs to die—but I'm fully aware of the concerns about whoever takes over being worse."

"Do you remember his second-in-command at all?" Kayden asks.

I shake my head. "No. I know his bodyguard, and I've remembered enough in the last few hours to know that he didn't accidentally meet me—not that we really thought that was a possibility. I also think he planned to kill me when he got the necklace, but changed his mind. He decided he wanted two possessions for the price of one."

"You hid the necklace from him?" Adriel asks.

"I hid it from everyone," I say. "I didn't know why it was important or what it was worth, but I knew at least one person had died because of it. I had to know why, before I knew what to do with it."

Adriel narrows his gaze one me. "And did you find out?"

"I don't know that answer yet," I say.

He studies me more intensely. "Did you offer it to Niccolo to get away from Neuville?"

"I want to say no," I admit. "I hope I can say no at some point, but Niccolo says that I did. And I was desperate to escape, and I did come to Italy. If I did make a deal with Niccolo, I have to believe I had a plan to protect the necklace."

"You know what I think about that?" he asks, his expression as indiscernible as his tone.

"That I suck."

"That you're honest," Adriel says, "even if it's painful, and I respect that. I've got your back. And I expect that our gun-wielding Lady Hawk has mine."

There is no question the "Lady Hawk" reference is about me being Kayden's woman, and considering all that is wrong between Kayden and me at the moment, it twists me into about twelve knots. "I do," I promise. "I have your back."

"We need to talk about Alessandro and Niccolo," Kayden says.

Adriel's gaze shoots to Kayden. "What about those two creates one sentence?"

Kayden gives him the rundown on the meeting and the ammunition Niccolo claims he has against Alessandro.

"I'm really fucking curious about what this file entails," Adriel says, glancing at his watch. "It's six o'clock now. So it's supposed to be here in the next two hours."

"And I want to be ready to act when it does, no matter what it turns out to be or not be," Kayden says. "I've contacted Nathan, Matteo, Sasha, and Carlo and told them to get here for a meeting at seven. I need you to try to get Sasha out of Gallo's bed in time to be here. I called her on a blocked line so that Gallo wouldn't recognize the number if he was with her, and she didn't answer."

"Sasha has our phone numbers coded with nicknames, so that's not a problem. I'll get a hold of her. Before I do, though, a word of warning. The last time I talked to her, she said that now that Gallo's suspended, he's got nothing to focus on but hating you and fucking her. A meeting, I see. But pulling her away from entertaining him beyond that is dangerous. Do we really want to move her out of the equation?"

"She told me," Kayden says. "And fucking Gallo from sunup to sundown is a poor waste of her talents. Just get her here for the meeting. She knows Neuville and Paris. I'll decide the next step with Gallo from there."

"Gallo will stalk me again if he gets the chance, but I can handle him," I say. "But it's Carlo who makes me very uncomfortable. Do we really need him involved?"

"He makes everyone uncomfortable," Adriel says. "And he enjoys it."

"Of that, I have no doubt," I say. "But is that good?"

"Considering he makes no one as uncomfortable as he does Alessandro," Kayden says, "it makes him a huge asset."

"Why does he make Alessandro nervous?" I ask, surprised by this news.

"Carlo was his Adriel at one point," Kayden explains. "They were as close as Adriel and I are, united in their rebellion against me, and Carlo got to know Alessandro's intimate thoughts and weaknesses in ways no other person has. But as they say, there's a fine line between hate and friendship, especially when a woman gets between them." His phone buzzes and he fishes it out of his pocket, glancing at his text messages. "Well, this is unexpected," he says, sticking it back in his pocket. "Marabella says that Giada wants to give me a gift of appreciation for all the time she's lived here. And per Marabella, and this is a quote, 'Come alone. She's nervous enough as it is.'"

"Giada?" Adriel says. "As is in my sister?"

"The one and only," Kayden says, glancing at me. "I'm beginning to think alien abduction stories are true, and she's been returned to us a different person."

"Not aliens," Adriel says, his gaze landing on me. "This is all you, Ella. You woke her up, and I appreciate that."

"Let's hope it sticks," I say, thinking of those missing pages of the journal, praying it wasn't her, despite really not knowing how she could have gotten it. "And for all we know, she's going to attack Kayden. He'll throttle her, and all will be normal in our world."

"I'll head on down," Kayden says, his gaze meeting mine, and the subject of Giada seems to already be set aside. "I want you in this meeting. It's in our War Room, but I'll meet you in the store when I finish with Giada and we'll go together."

Together. That word works for me, and when I look at him, I feel a punch in my chest with the connection. I sense that he feels it too, though he doesn't show it, but I'm not sure what that means to him at this point. "Okay. So I should go down there in about half an hour?"

"That works." He nods, giving Adriel a quick look. "Get me Sasha."

"I'll call her before I head downstairs," Adriel confirms.

Kayden nods and heads toward the living room, and already Adriel is dialing. I stand my ground, waiting for him to finish, making it clear I want to talk to him. His caller, Sasha I assume, answers quickly, and the conversation is over just as fast before he returns his cell to his pocket.

"Sasha's on her way," he says. "And clearly you have something else to say, so say it."

His directness doesn't surprise me. Adriel isn't exactly what one would call a warm and inviting personality. "I've been keeping a journal."

"I assumed as much, when I handed you a book labeled 'journal' in the store the other day."

"Right. I forgot that. Anyway. It's supposed to help me retrieve my memories," I say, "and it's helped. That's how I remembered the necklace. I started drawing it."

"Where are you going with this, Ella?"

"Two pages were torn out, and one of them was a drawing of the necklace."

Understanding registers in his eternally hard green eyes. "I didn't take it, if that's what you think. If I wanted to document something, I'd—"

"Take a photo," I say. "I know. I thought it was Giada, but I checked the security feed. No one touched my journal that day."

"So it was another day and place."

"I've only taken it out of this tower once—that day," I say. "And the only people who can get in *this* tower are me, Kayden, and Marabella."

"It's not Marabella," he says. "There's another explanation."

"That's what Kayden said. He thinks I removed it during a flashback."

"If you space out like you did today in the car, I can see that."

"Yes, but if it's Marabella—"

"It's *not* Marabella."

"It would destroy Kayden if she betrayed him."

"You're right, but this is one time that I can say I have zero, and I mean *zero*, doubt in someone."

"Those we trust—"

"Come up with another theory."

"Someone hacked our security system."

"Matteo has about four levels of hack notifications set up," he says. "He's truly one of the best in the world."

"*One* of the best means there could be another who's better."

"You're reaching, Ella. Someone is always here. If you're not in the tower, Marabella uses that time to clean and cook for you. And I'm usually in the store, as is Giada."

"You're right. Maybe I'm obsessing over the wrong thing."

"Caution is good. We'll stay vigilant and we'll talk to Matteo."

"That sounds good," I say.

"I'm going to head downstairs."

I nod, and he gives me another steady look. "You're safe here. Not that I think you're cowering in a corner, because that's not who you are, but you're safe. He can't get to you here."

"I'm not worried about me," I say. "I'm worried about what I bring to all of you."

"If they come for you we'll be waiting, and we'll enjoy every moment, because there are lines we can't cross other-wise. Okay?"

"Yes."

He studies me another beat and then rounds the island to leave. I stand there a moment that turns into ten before I whirl around and follow, heading through the living room on a path to the bedroom. Once there, I round the bed and walk to my nightstand, opening up the journal to start flipping through it, looking for any other missing pages, but there are only the two. I stare down at one of them that is, and will myself to remember ripping them out, but I don't. And right now, my memory is at 70 percent, the dark spots all seeming to revolve around the most traumatic events. I didn't tear this page out. I believe that, so if it wasn't me, where is it?

seven

Anxious to hear Matteo tell me there is no possible way we've been hacked, and to ensure the people surrounding Sara are good people, I hurry downstairs to our tower exit. The door lifts and as has become a habit I duck under it and find Adriel entering from the front door, a grim set to his jaw, the sound of a furious rain pounding outside. He motions to the porch, silently telling me Kayden is there. And though I have no explanation, I get the impression he thinks my joining Kayden is well timed. A knot of concern forms in my belly that something extending beyond Giada's frequent antics has gone wrong. Before I can ask for details, Adriel is across the foyer and headed toward the Center Tower's steps.

Steeling myself for whatever has happened, I walk to the door and open it, finding Kayden leaning on one of the two heavy pillars framing the porch. The chill of the night air mixed with the rain is nothing compared to the palpable edginess of his mood. His shoulder holster is back in place now, holding one firearm and not the two Adriel is wearing, but even now, with his back to me, there is an air of danger and power about Kayden that makes him lethal beyond any weapons or his willingness to use them.

I don't announce myself and he doesn't turn, though I have no doubt he's aware that I'm here. We feel each other that way. It's indescribable and special, the kind of feeling that makes you want to marry a man. I pull the door shut and walk to the opposite pillar, watching the ridiculously large droplets pound onto the driveway and the broad expanse of the gated yard. For several minutes, we just stand there, and it is not the unspoken words between us zigging and zagging but something else bothering Kayden, something I wait for him to share, and hope that he will.

"Rain," he says softly, "like tears, washes away the blood, but never the death."

I press my back to the pillar, and for just a few moments he remains in profile, tall and larger than life it seems at times, most assuredly now. It's the effortless power he radiates, I think, the calmness he projects, which still manages to be confidence and control. Things often mixed with just a hint of haunted torment, driven by tragedy that few see or choose to see, but I know it well. I see it in his eyes, taste it in his kisses. I hunger to ease the way it cuts him to his soul over and over and over again.

"Kayden, I—"

"Don't," he says, turning to face me. "Whatever you're going to say, don't say it. Not yet. Not now."

"Why not? Did something happen?"

"Because when we walk into this meeting, I'm The Hawk.

I make decisions that are cold, hard, and often brutal. I won't change that because you're present. But those things might change what you're about to say."

"They won't change anything." I don't offer him the reasons he doesn't want to hear right now. "What's happened?" I repeat.

He moves toward me, and by the time I straighten, he is standing toe-to-toe with me, close enough for me to smell that special blend of spice and masculinity that is the man I love. Close enough for me to feel the welcome warmth of his body without him touching me. "Giada gave me something of her father's," he surprises me by saying. "He was a good man, lost too soon, like others I've known, and will know in the future."

His comment about the rain makes sense now. Giada inadvertently stirred the demon named "death" to life, and with it, a reminder to Kayden that he's human, and so is everyone who counts on him, me included. And I won't give it legs or life by speaking its name. "What did Giada give you?"

He takes my hand and presses something small and round into my palm. "His lucky coin," he says, closing my fingers around it and his around mine, the warmth of his touch doing nothing to destroy the chill in the air and around him. "She thought he'd want me to have it, to protect me. Because her father admired me and felt I was making Europe a more stable region."

He is, but I don't say that either, not now, when I am certain it's not what he wants to hear, nor will it mean anything to him in this moment.

"But you see," he continues, "I don't believe in luck. It's

dangerous. It's the devil in disguise that tears down your guard and gets you killed."

"But you took the coin."

"That's *why* I took her coin."

Understanding hits me. "So she no longer thinks luck is on her side."

"That's right, and I told her that. I told her to believe in herself, and think for herself." He tightens his grip on my hand. "There is no such thing as luck, Ella," he repeats.

"I know that, Kayden. My father made sure I know that."

"There will be more blood and tears. There will be more death. I can't tell you there won't be."

"But there will be less because of you. Not just in Europe; Evil Eye established boundaries where there were none."

"And I convinced myself that by evoking Evil Eye I could protect you so I could really, truly make you mine. I'm not downplaying your abilities, which are many, but you need my protection in this world, and you seem to respect and under-stand how to navigate that and stay yourself. And I will protect you. The Underground will protect you—from physical harm. But the life I lead cuts deep beneath the surface."

My gut is twisted into all kinds of knots. "What are you saying, Kayden?"

"That I want to take you upstairs, strip you naked, and do everything in my power to convince you that I can heal every one of those cuts."

"You have, and you are, healing wounds. I would never survive without you."

"Only to create more." He releases my hand and steps

back, putting space I don't want between us. "And that would make me the same selfish bastard who proposed to you today."

"You are the least selfish person I've ever met, including my mother, who'd have baked cookies for a complete stranger."

"And yet I tried to make things simple, where they are complicated."

"But you like complicated. You just said that, and I like it, too."

"Do you?"

"*Your* kind of complicated." I hesitate only a moment. "Kayden, earlier, when you asked me to marry you—"

"*After* the meeting."

"The meeting will change nothing."

The door opens and I want to scream at the timing, but neither of us looks toward our visitor, who turns out to be Adriel. "Carlo is here," he announces. "And he's in a mood you might want to address before the meeting. Or, an option I'll throw on the table: as your newly reinstated second-in-command, I can knock the shit out of him and be done with it."

Kayden inhales and lets the breath out. "I need to make sure he sees the big picture, not just revenge against Alessandro."

The buzzer on the security panel goes off. "Nathan," Adriel says, holding up the security feed on his phone. "And Matteo is behind him." He's barely spoken the words when the wind gusts, splattering droplets of cold water all over us. Adriel curses, nearly in the line of fire even half inside the castle, while I yelp with shock, only to have Kayden reach out, shackle my arm, and pull me farther onto the porch, his touch fire and ice. I hate that combination. Just as I hate the wall I feel between us, holding us back, dividing us.

"I'm going to meet Nathan and Matteo," Adriel growls, disappearing into the castle without shutting the door.

"Let's go inside," Kayden says.

"Go ahead," I say. "I think I'm going to need a minute."

"I need to deal with Carlo."

"I'll be right in."

He looks like he wants to insist, but his grip on my arm slowly eases, his hand falling away, and I decide the warmth of his touch *did* do much to wipe away the cold, because now I am even colder. And then he is gone, walking inside the castle, the door shutting behind him. And I'm alone, hugging myself against the rain and storm that now suffocates me, wishing I could just grab him, kiss him, and explain my fears. But he's right. It's not that simple, no matter how much we both want it to be.

I turn and face the front lawn again, staring into the downpour he'd claimed washes away the blood. But in its depths I see my father's death, and I'm certain that my continual return to that image is my mind warning me. The past is connected to the present, but how? Perhaps it's not a direct link. Perhaps the connection is my mind reminding me of the choices my father made that I should not imitate.

The reality is that had my mother and I not hidden in the closet the day he was murdered, we might well be dead, too. Another reality is that my father trained me for a reason, not as a hobby. He knew that the day when he died could come.

He knew his life connecting to ours came with risks for us, not just him.

It's time to face what I've been suppressing—and while my mind resists, there is one part I can accept, if not embrace. If I'm to be honest with myself, no matter what happens with the necklace, and in spite of Kayden's confidence in Evil Eye, I know in my heart that Garner Neuville will come for me, like my father knew someone would come for him. And it will be the kind of mess you can't clean up. I can't let that happen.

But in the midst of that rain, I see something else. I see myself doing calisthenics in another downpour, my father yelling at me to keep going, to never give up. If I run from Neuville, if I hide, who am I kidding? If he knows that I'm with Kayden—and he will, if he doesn't already—he will use him and everyone around him to draw me out. I can't hide. That's where my instinct to go to Paris came from. I can't hide, so I have to be the aggressor. We have to be the aggressors and end this. And that starts with making sure Kayden understands that Evil Eye won't stop the insanity of Garner Neuville when he feels personally wounded. There are three ways I think he might approach this, all of which Kayden needs to hear before that meeting.

I open the door and step inside, shutting out the cold rain, but this part of the castle is always chilly—perhaps because this is where Enzo died. I shiver with that thought, crossing the foyer and starting the long climb to the Center Tower, my destination the dungeon-style arched wooden doorway directly in front of me and the entrance to the store where I'm to meet Kayden. Each of my steps is driven by my need to find him, tear down the walls between us, and make sure he knows the war he wants to prevent is already here.

I'm a dozen steps from my destination when the heavy door begins to lift, and I'm jumpier than I thought, because I reach for the weapon inside the purse that I don't have with me. Irritated that I haven't opted for a bra or ankle strap, I vow to remedy that right as Marabella appears at the top of the landing, her graying dark hair pinned at the nape, her robust figure highlighted by a dress with big red roses on it.

She grins at the sight of me, her cheeks even fuller with that smile, then covers her mouth as if she knows she shouldn't be happy in the midst of the Underground events obviously going on. Without shutting the door behind her, she rushes toward me, meeting me three steps from the top. "I know there is serious business happening now," she says the instant we've stopped in front of each other, "but did you hear about Giada?"

"I did," I say, and her joy is as palpable as was Kayden's dark mood, right along with her love for what has become her little family after losing her husband so many years ago. "I was very proud of her."

"So much pride," she beams, then echoes Adriel's claim. "You did this. We are lucky to have you here."

My heart squeezes with those words that pull me farther into this life, *this family*, which I want to be mine. Which I want to protect.

"Oh, and Adriel ordered her furniture for her new apartment," Marabella continues. "She's very excited about it." She sobers, lowering her voice. "I am glad she's out of the middle of the Underground business. It was never good for her, and the truth is, you either have to be in this or out of it."

"And you, Marabella?" I ask. "Are you in or out?"

"Do you have to ask? Kayden has offered me a lake retreat near Milan many times. But I don't plan to die at a beach re- treat near Milan. And who would take care of all of you if I'm gone?" She hugs me. "You are my new goddaughter." She leans back to look at me. "I know it's not official, but I say you are. So you are."

"I'm honored," I say, meaning it, certain in this moment that Kayden and Adriel are right. She didn't take the pages from my journal, not unless she was blackmailed or tricked— but I need to know for certain. "A random question for you, Marabella," I say, digging for my answers. "Do you remember seeing my journal by the bedside?"

Her brow furrows. "Journal?"

"A small notebook."

"Oh," she says. "The one you keep by your bed?"

"Yes. Did you happen to tear a page or two out?"

Her eyes go wide. "No. Of course not. I wouldn't do that. What would make you think—"

"It's nothing, Marabella. I'm sorry; I should have ex- plained. I've been having flashbacks, and I can't always re- member what I do when I have them. I'm pretty sure I tore the pages out and I'm just a little freaked out about that."

"Oh." Concern fills her face. "*Oh.* I don't like how that sounds. Have you talked to Nathan?"

"Talk to me about what?"

At the sound of Nathan's voice, Marabella and I turn to

see him standing at the top of the landing, looking every bit the Canadian preppy doctor that he is, in black dress pants and a light blue shirt rolled to his elbows, his brown hair neatly trimmed. Even his chin is stubble-free despite the late hour.

"Tell him what's going on," Marabella urges.

"What's going on, Ella?" Nathan asks, his brown eyes sharp.

Marabella gives my arm a quick squeeze. "I'll let you talk to him and I'll check on you tomorrow. Kayden ordered me to my tower before this meeting—and you know he likes to be obeyed."

I blanch at the statement that fits nothing I know of their relationship, almost thinking there's a sexual innuendo to those words, but this is Marabella and— *Wait*. She winks. There *is* a sexual innuendo.

"Of course, he's met his match in you," she says, her lips curving. She walks past me and I run my hands through my hair, blushing at whatever just happened. Maybe I don't know Marabella. Or maybe she's just more comfortable with me now.

"I didn't catch all of that," Nathan says as I close the space between us, "but a little color in your cheeks makes your doctor happy. What was Marabella worried about?"

"It's nothing," I say, certain I didn't take those pages myself, but if I did, life would be better right now. "Actually . . . when I'm having a flashback, I go very deep into the memory. Could I walk, talk, or write notes, and not realize it at the time?"

"Depending on the type of event, it's feasible to think you might," he confirms. "But are we talking the blackouts you were having before, or some different event?"

"The same blackouts," I confirm, and when he uses that word *blackout* again, as I have in the past myself, suddenly the idea that I pulled out the pages myself gets a little more possible. "Only now I tend to think of them as flashbacks. I guess that's a good sign."

"That depends on the reason. Are you accustomed to them now, so they are less traumatic, or have they improved and lessened in intensity?"

"Until today, they've been less frequent and easier to tolerate. But I'm not worried; I had some triggers, which is good. I'm really filling in the holes now."

"The private investigator," he says, "but that's another topic. Remembering is good, since we had no guarantees you would. But how do you *feel?* Did the increased flashbacks today trigger headaches of any kind?"

"No headaches," I say. "I just don't like that I lose time when they occur."

"Your brain is resetting, Ella," he says. "I think all in all, you've done very well. But I do want to do another full checkup soon."

Male voices sound behind us and I turn to see Adriel exiting the store. Matteo is by his side, his longish curly dark hair slicked back, his black tee imprinted with *I'm an Italian Stallion.* Which is kind of funny, since Carlo's the one who gives off that vibe, not Matteo.

As they cross toward us, Matteo is fully focused on me. "I

hear you're joining us in the War Room. Are you sure you're ready for that?"

There is a hint of something in his eyes and voice that I can't decide if I like, and can't quite name. "I'm with Kayden," I say. "That means I'm with The Underground, and I don't like to let Annie get rusty."

"Annie?" Matteo asks.

"My gun," I say, moving on. "Any update on Chris Merit or Blake Walker?"

"I'm still digging," Matteo says, "but so far nothing overly concerning."

"What does that mean?"

"Blake Walker has a reputation for being a wild card while in the ATF, but a good man," he says. "Chris Merit is a star in the art world who seems to keep his nose clean. He was raised in Paris, he moved in some of the same circles as Neuville, but I have no reason to believe that's intentional."

"I don't like the Paris connection," I say. "How are we checking that out?"

"Let's move this to the War Room," Adriel interrupts, flexing that second-in-command muscle with ease, a presence I am certain Kayden's been missing. "Ella will join us with Kayden," he adds, looking at me. "He's in the store."

I nod and as the three men start to walk away, I snag Matteo's arm. He stops walking and faces me while the other two men head down the hallway. "Just a quick question," I say. "Is there any way our security system could be hacked?"

"Here at the castle?"

"Yes. Here at the castle."

"You obviously don't know me well yet," he says, his tone irritated, when I've always known him to be far more easygoing. "I don't get hacked. I *do* the hacking. It cannot be breached."

"But anything you can create or hack, someone else, if good enough, *could* hack, right?"

"You do remember that I made you disappear, right?" he asks.

"I do," I say, "and I know that creating Rae Eleana Ward, and replacing my picture once Gallo saw it, took skill. I'm not questioning your skill."

"It took phenomenal fucking hacking to get into the international database and never be seen. No one gets into the castle that I don't want to get in here. And if they try, I have ten kinds of trouble set up for them. We're secure here."

"Matteo," Adriel calls.

He points at his shirt. "Trust in the Italian Stallion," he says, giving me my second wink of the day, and a glimpse of the man I know before he takes off down the hallway.

Still, I stare after him. His mood is odd, but I've never questioned his abilities before, and that could be what he's reacting to.

Either he failed to protect us or I'm blacking out in ways that are concerning, but at least it should be visible on our security film when I can finally watch it all. Shaking it off for now, I head toward the door of the store, about to enter when Carlo appears. And just as I remember, he has this edgy, dark, Italian Stallion kind of vibe that manages to make you think of leather and chains. His pants are, in fact, black leather. His twin guns are strapped over a black tee that's poured over his muscled upper body. That long dark hair of his is tied at the nape, while those green, cutting eyes are focused on me with the same all-consuming, too-attentive look I remember from the past.

"Carlo," I say, standing my ground, aware he enjoys the skill he has to unsettle people.

"Who are you exactly, Ella?"

"Aside from the girl who could draw your guns before you can?"

"You think you really can?"

"Try me," I challenge him before I can stop myself.

"As tempting an offer as that is, that would displease Kayden."

"And you want to please him?"

"Seems I do." He gives me an incline of his chin and starts to move before hesitating. "And you wouldn't need to draw my weapon if you had your own. You need to fix that."

With that rather too-observant assessment he steps around me, and my gaze lands on Kayden, who stands only a few feet away. And just like that the room is charged, the air thick, the distance reaching far longer than the few feet between us. But I won't let it win, not now or ever.

I cross the threshold and punch the button to shut the door behind me. "I really need to talk to you before this meeting."

"As I do you," he says. "We need to be upfront in this meeting about your past with Neuville and the CIA connection."

"I agree. I don't want them asking me who I really am, like

Carlo just did. Kayden. When I was standing on the porch, I realized why I hesitated when you proposed."

"Now is not the time for this."

"It's relevant to the meeting, or I wouldn't do this to you. I've been trying to be as convinced as you are that Evil Eye protects me and everyone here."

"It does."

"Not from a crazy, obsessed billionaire mobster with a personal vendetta. Garner Neuville *will* come for me and that necklace, and any thought I had that my leaving or hiding would save you and everyone here was a lie I told myself. He will just use the others and you to draw me out of hiding. Whatever decisions you make in that meeting have to take this into consideration. He's crazy, Kayden, and if he gets the necklace, terrifyingly powerful."

I take his hand and turn over his wrist, displaying his second tattoo, the box with a king chess piece inside, reading the English meaning of the Italian words trailing up his arm. "Once the game is over, the king and the pawn go back in the same box."

"In death we are equal," he says, stating the meaning. "Never underestimate your enemy. Garner Neuville and I will never be equal, nor have I underestimated him."

"You're counting on Evil Eye," I say. "But you don't want me to go to Paris."

"You aren't going to Paris, Ella."

"My point is your point. Evil Eye is revenge for the dead. I'd rather just make him dead before he kills you, Kayden. And he will kill you if you give him the chance."

"He would be a fool to cross Evil Eye. His punishment would far exceed death before death followed."

"I know that you believe that," I say. "I also know that you know Europe and The Underground and the mobs in both France and Italy. But I know this man. He's an insane monster. Please hear me, Kayden. I cannot lose you. And I can't bear the idea of someone here dying because of me. You told me not to go to Paris and you were right: I was just desperate to protect everyone here. But now, I'm asking you to hear me out."

His hands come down on my arms. "Easy, sweetheart. I hear you. I'm listening."

My hands go to his forearms. "You can't wait to maneuver his second-in-command out of the way before dealing with him. He will come for me, and if he gets the necklace, too—"

"He won't. I'll adjust my strategy going into this meeting, and I'll assume Evil Eye doesn't exist to him."

"And that means what?"

"It means when you walk into this meeting, Ella, you're going to understand how brutal I can be. And I'm not sure I want you to experience that right now."

"I'm ready for you to stop doubting yourself with me."

"I *proposed*, Ella."

"And I made you doubt that decision, but it was about this. It was about *him*, not you or us." His eyes are still guarded in a way I hope they'll never be with me again. "I hate that I did this to us."

His chest rises and falls, his face etched with shadows, his eyes shadowed as well. "Ella—"

There is a sudden pounding on the door. "Let me in!" It's Sasha.

"Hurry!" she calls out.

In another instant, Kayden has his weapon drawn and is at the door ready to open it, and I'm really missing Annie right now.

eight

Kayden yanks open the door and Sasha bursts inside, water pouring down her black trench coat, a hood covering her head. "No threat," she pants out. "No immediate threat."

"What the hell happened?" Kayden demands, locking the door before holstering his weapon.

She tugs down the hood, waves of chestnut hair falling in a beautiful mess around her shoulders. "My God. It's a nightmare out there. Hi, Ella."

"Sasha," Kayden bites out. "What the hell happened?"

"Gallo followed me when I left his apartment and I couldn't take a risk by going directly to the castle. I parked nearly on the damn moon and ran in this cold rain." She starts unbuttoning her coat. "I need out of this. I'm frozen to the core and it's soaked."

"Are you sure he didn't follow you?" Kayden asks.

"If I didn't lose him, he's an Olympian," she says, shrugging out of her coat, revealing black jeans and a black, low-cut sweater, before plopping the coat on the counter and rubbing her hands together. "You know me, Kayden—I'm good at what I do. I covered my tracks."

"What made him follow you?" I ask, trying not to think about her entertaining him in bed. "Do you know?"

"He's a paranoid, angry person," she says. "Even when we're fucking, he's angry, but at least he lets go of the paranoia then. The man needs to have a week of me naked in his bed to let go of some shit, I swear."

When she puts it that way her seducing him sounds a little better, because Gallo absolutely needs to let go of the past and his pain.

"He followed you, Sasha," Kayden says. "You're done. He's suspicious."

"He's paranoid," she repeats. "And believe me, that always leads to you. I don't know the man well, yet he talks about you. We need me in there, watching out for him and you."

Another point I hadn't thought of, and suddenly I'm on her side. "Maybe if he just steps back from things for a while, he'll check himself," I say. "Maybe she can help him."

Kayden's jaw sets in a stubborn line. "I'm not sparing one of my best Hunters during a critical time like this to fuck Gallo night and day. Gallo is being dealt with."

"If dealing with him includes Chief Donati transferring him," she says, "he'll turn in his badge."

"And do what?"

"This is the bombshell," she says, holding up her hands. "Wait for it . . ."

"Sasha," Kayden snaps.

She smirks and presses her hands to her hips. "He'll become a Jackal."

I gape and Kayden, ever in control, simply looks at her. "A Jackal," he says flatly.

"Yes," she confirms. "Which is why I think I should try and get him to run away with me, until you handle whatever it is this meeting is about."

"Has he been talking to Alessandro?" Kayden asks.

"I'm not sure on that one," she says. "It's really a miracle I know what I do. I've been in the man's bed a mere few days, but he runs his mouth after sex. It's like sex is a gateway drug, and his high is actual communication. I really think I need to stay close to him, Kayden."

"Yes," Kayden concedes. "You do. But right now, War Room, Sasha. We'll meet you there."

"'Get lost, Sasha,'" she says. "'I need to talk to Ella, Sasha.' Got it. War Room. Leaving." She turns on her heel and heads for the door.

Kayden and I watch her walk away, neither of us speaking or moving, the implications of Gallo and The Jackals spiking the air. "Don't slip in the puddle I left behind," she calls out over her shoulder, and then disappears into the hallway.

I face Kayden. "Alessandro and Gallo? That's bad, Kayden. He will influence Gallo in the worst way. What are you going to do?"

"Alessandro's connection to Niccolo is relevant."

"He said he'd handle Gallo," I say, following where this is leading. "You think this is part of his plan?"

"I think it's an odd coincidence if it's not," he concludes, "and since I don't trust Alessandro, you're right. It's a problem that could go badly for Gallo, us, or both. I'll call Niccolo and Chief Donati tonight, but right now I have a meeting to run and a big picture to navigate."

"And I have a meeting to attend. Before you try to warn me again about what I'll discover there, save your breath. I'm going, Kayden. Not to prove a point, but because I'm in this fight with you now."

He doesn't immediately respond, nor does he reach for me or even offer words of support or otherwise. He doesn't even give me a look or expression to read. There is just silence, and the thickness of the air, before he says, "I meant what I said. I won't hold back in this meeting to protect you."

"That wouldn't be protecting me or us, Kayden. Any of us. If you did that, you wouldn't be the man I know you to be. And if I asked or needed you to do that, I wouldn't be the woman who's supposed to be by your side."

He gives me the slightest incline of his chin. "Then let's go."

⸎

Side by side we exit the store, and Kayden seals it shut behind us. We then cut left down a path I have never traveled, a part of the castle I've never explored, the stone beneath our feet. But this long, high hallway is not so unlike the one leading to our bedroom, and identical to the one leading in the opposite direction. So much so that as we pass one wooden arched door after another, I think of the one I'd approached not long ago, to find Enzo lying in a bed while Nathan tried to save him. And failed. Enzo died as I watched the desperate attempt to revive him. It is also in this tower that Kayden's fiancée and mentor were murdered, and at times I envision what Kayden must have been like on that day. What he would be like if he found me the same way. I think . . . I am strength to him in many ways, a needed partner to fight by his side, but I am a weakness as well, and I don't know how to reconcile that fact.

"Death lives here," I say softly as we round a corner, a chill running down my spine as huge, open double wooden doors come into view. "I feel it."

"As do I," he agrees. "Every damn second I'm in this tower."

"Somehow that makes the War Room being located here feel like perfection," I say.

"Exactly my thought," he says, his voice a tight band of tension that seems to rip and pull around us as we step in unison, his energy shifting and changing with each second that passes, the walk seeming to last forever.

The sound of our booted feet on the stone floor is hypnotic. Unbidden, it delivers me back in time into a new memory.

I'm inside some sort of gym, a training facility I believe, and a group of students in the same blue sweats and T-shirts are standing around a mat to watch a fight. I blink and discover that I'm in that fight and my opponent isn't a woman. It's a man who I've managed to flatten on his back, land my foot in his chest, and twist his arm.

"You fight like a girl," he mocks.

"Says the girl on the ground," I retort, laughter erupting around us.

"Finish him." I look up to see our instructor, a big, intimidating black man standing on the other side of my opponent.

"He's down," I say.

"And mocking you. Make him hurt."

"He's another student. This isn't like—"

He leans in closer. *"He's mocking you. And guess what, little one? Your fellow agents can turn bad. Targets will grow on you, and many will feel like friends, but you still have to take them out when they turn on you. Grow some balls or get out of my facility."*

"I've proven I can take him out."

"Halfway out," he corrects. *"We win here, no matter what that takes. And if you think compassion erases your past, it doesn't. If you think anyone in the agency will work with you, trust you, or like you because you have compassion, think again. You will be the girl who won't kill the enemy trying to kill her."* He looks up and around at the students. *"The ones who end up on the ground are out. You're gone. You die this death on the mat, and I save you from another death."*

The man on the ground makes a move, twisting toward me, and instinct kicks in. I'm small; he's large. If I go down, I won't get back up. I stomp on his chest and twist his arm as he tries to sweep my leg out from under me, and the result is bone crunching, his shoulder snapping. He screams in pain and my stomach knots.

My instructor leans in close. *"That's the daughter of Charlie Ferguson I was looking for. Win at all costs, or die forgotten."*

∞

I blink again and we're a foot from our destination, a million thoughts in my mind that I don't have time to dissect. We are at the wooden doors, and I am about to become part of Kayden's world in a whole new way.

He knows it, too, I know he does, and that's why he stops and turns to look at me. "Ella—"

"Win at all costs or die forgotten," I say. "Something someone said to me once. It's true."

"Who said that to you?"

"It doesn't matter who," I say. "It's what it means to you and me. Whatever it takes, Kayden, and whatever that means, win. And I plan to win with you."

His eyes narrow, some emotion in their depths I cannot name before he gives me a small nod and faces the door. Together we seem to breathe in, as if bracing ourselves for something life changing or relationship changing before we step forward into the room. All voices go silent at the sight of us, despite the expectation I would be here for this meeting. Maybe it's seeing Kayden and me together like this. Maybe it's sudden distrust. I do not know. But there is an obvious, drawn-out pause in the room in which all eyes are on me.

I catalog the room, taking in what is before me, remotely aware of a wall of monitors on one side of the space and a wall of maps on the other, while my key focus is on the giant round stone table in the center of the room. Eleven black leather chairs surround it, and one brown, that one etched with a hawk. Of those twelve total seats, five are filled with the Hunters Kayden has chosen for this challenge. But it's the table that really draws my attention, particularly the etched design in the center that matches Kayden's tattoo on his arm. A box, with chess pieces and the Italian words translated to "Once the game is over, the king and the pawn go back in the same box." In death we are all equal. *Win at all costs or die forgotten*. It's the same message. How is it the same message?

Kayden motions me to the right, and I shake off that thought better explored later, quickly rounding the table toward my seat next to the brown one, and beside Sasha, while Matteo is on her opposite side. Since the last thing I need is to look like the supporting cast that needs support, I quickly reach for my chair, praying Kayden doesn't attempt to be the gentleman he is and help me with it. Thankfully, he's in tune with me on this and does no such thing, settling into his spot beside me at almost the same moment I do mine. Fortunately, Kayden is angled at just the right position for me to see his face and gauge his reactions to whatever takes place. Unfortunately, Carlo, of all people, is now sitting directly in front of me, center to Nathan, who is to my right, and Adriel, to my left.

"Everyone here has been briefed on the necklace," Kayden states, getting right to the point, "and those of you chosen to attend this meeting were chosen for something unique you bring to the table. You all know what that reason is as it relates to you. But hear me on this: in turn, you're being trusted at a level that reaches well beyond that of your fellow Hunters. Should you betray me on this, you will see a side of me that you have never seen. Are we all clear?"

Each of them raises a hand, as if this is standard, and I follow suit, only to have Carlo home in on me, silently questioning my presence in a way he soon will not.

"If that necklace falls into the hands of the wrong person,"

Kayden continues, "it will give their illicit organization the kind of power we never want them to have. This isn't a treasure. Anything worth this kind of money, with an active buyer who wants it, is a weapon we have to protect."

"Who is the buyer?" I ask.

"Two billionaires who are willing to bid against each other," Kayden says. "The ceiling seems to be three hundred million, the actual evaluation of the necklace is closer to two hundred million. And why are they willing to pay this kind of money for a necklace? It seems to be a game to them. It's all about the power."

Carlo chimes in on that one. "Two rich men with mobs, cartels, and governments chasing their tails. It's insanity."

"It *is* insanity," Sasha agrees. "These men have no regard for the damage this could do to entire countries. I don't even want to think about the impact of Niccolo or Neuville adding three hundred million dollars to their treasure chest."

"At least Niccolo and Neuville operate with a mob code, no matter how fucked up it might be," Carlo replies. "Alessandro has no code but greed, and that's a dangerous way to operate."

"Indeed," Nathan agrees. "I've seen too much blood, thanks to the Hunters he turned into lawless pirates." He eyes Kayden, shifting the topic. "I take it we have a lead on its location," Nathan surmises, "or we wouldn't be here." It's a statement rather than a question.

"We have a lead," Kayden confirms, and then offering little more by clear intent, adds, "but not a definitive location."

"What's the lead and the source?" Carlo presses.

"More importantly," Matteo asks, "is there anything I can do on my end to make that lead a little more solid?"

"More importantly," Sasha says, "*if* this lead does pan out, if we find the necklace, what's next? What do we do with it to ensure it doesn't end up in the wrong hands?"

"We deliver it to the British government's museum vault," Kayden replies. "They have now officially contracted our services, with the understanding that we remain anonymous to avoid any backlash."

"I want to go on record as saying I have reservations about handing over the necklace to the very people who lost it in the first place," Carlo states.

"They own it," Adriel reminds him.

"Finders, keepers," Carlo says. "That's the Jackals' motto."

"And ours," Kayden says, "is to do our jobs right and get paid. That said, I'm no fool and I don't expect you to be. Our job is to find the necklace and set up security that ensures it doesn't disappear again; in return, I've negotiated a generous fee. After all, we are handing over three hundred million dollars."

"How much?" Carlo asks. "Because in my experience, governments are cheap-ass—"

"Five million apiece," Kayden says.

Palpable shock radiates through the room with this stunning news, and Matteo lets out a whistle. "That's a big prize. I'm counting seven of us in this room, if Ella is included in the split."

"I'm not in that number," I say.

"She is in that number," Kayden counters, his eyes meeting mine. "You hunt. You get paid."

"I don't—"

"You do," he assures me, his attention landing on Carlo. "You're getting paid. That's the point here."

"Hear that?" Sasha asks, holding a hand to her ear. "That's the sound of silence while Carlo eats his tongue."

Kayden continues. "Moving on to the players competing in this game, I count four."

"Four?" Nathan asks. "I count Niccolo, Neuville, and Alessandro. Who else is there?"

"I've loosely added Raul Martinez," Kayden explains. "After the Enzo debacle he made his interest clear, but we'll come back to him. I want to start with Niccolo, as our local major player."

"Who was, interestingly enough, hunting Ella," Carlo comments.

"And who wants the necklace," Kayden says, not taking the bait, and making it clear that he'll talk about what he wants, when he wants. "He also wants us to work for him while Alessandro works for him as well."

"Which we declined, correct?" Sasha asks.

"Many times," Kayden replies, "but we're allowing him to believe we could be swayed, because (A) he says he's made a deal with Raul to get him to walk away from the necklace and we have a finger on that activity, (B) he's blackmailing Alessandro and promised me the documents being used against him, (C) this gives us insight into three of the four players, and finally, (D) we believe Niccolo has cancer and we need a bird's-eye view of how that affects his operation."

"Wait," Sasha says, flattening her hands on the desk. "Of

all the things you just said that blew my mind, Niccolo having cancer is the only one I can process. That's almost too bittersweet to digest. It's karma. Pure, unadulterated karma."

"Before you celebrate," Nathan says, "keep in mind that people who are dying have nothing to lose. That makes them unpredictable, and Niccolo was dangerous before that word came into play." He glances between Kayden and me. "How do we know this? Do we have medical proof?"

"I've been working on proof," Matteo chimes in, "and yes, he has cancer. He's got an aggressive form of leukemia; it was caught in the late stages. He's recently undergone an experimental treatment, though with good results."

I glance at Kayden. "That's what his coded references to beating karma were in the car."

"Agreed," he says, and then to the entire table, "and as much as I want to kill that bastard, or even better, see him suffer a slow, horrible death, we've determined that the longer he's in play, and we're in play with him, the longer we'll have that three-for-one navigational hit."

"Considering our concerns about his successor," Nathan interjects, "I need to caution here that no matter what his current prognosis is, cancer is an unpredictable beast. We could see him turn for the worse at any moment and be left with a replacement that lends havoc to the entire country."

"Which is exactly where I was going next," Kayden says with no hesitation, his eyes meeting mine for the briefest of moments before he scans all eyes looking at him. "We choose to be mere Hunters or far more, and I have, and always will, see us as equalizers. Regardless of where the necklace may be, but most certainly with it in play, we will take the responsibility of ensuring stability in Europe. In other words, we take out Niccolo's second."

Kill him, he means, and I wait for that to punch me in the chest, to turn my stomach, but it doesn't. There is a bigger picture here indeed, and I can almost hear voices in my past telling me that fearlessly taking the action no one else will is often necessary.

"Our man is close to Niccolo's second," Adriel says. "And we need to keep him there, which means this needs to look like an accident."

Kayden turns his attention to Nathan. "What do you have for us?"

"Heart attack in a vial," he says with no hesitation. He's my compassionate doctor, a man who cares about lives the way I see Kayden caring about lives, but he's cold, and focused, in this reality that is a silent war.

"I need it tonight," Adriel replies. "I can reach out to our man under the shelter of rain and get this done in the next seventy-two hours."

"I can make that happen," Nathan confirms.

"Then I'll consider this handled," Kayden replies, shifting topics. "Circling back to Raul. If Niccolo takes a turn for the worse, any deal between the two can be assumed void. Matteo, I need you to create some kind of disaster in his U.S. operation that will guarantee Raul's return to the States."

Matteo rubs his hands together. "I love this kind of project. A huge dose of chaos coming up. Consider it done."

"What about Alessandro?" Carlo asks, going back to his sweet spot.

"He's a problem for reasons I haven't even begun to discuss," Kayden says. "But I've given Niccolo an ultimatum. If he wants our help, we get the goods on Alessandro, which he claims will be delivered here by sundown."

Carlo lifts his arm and glances at his watch. "That would be now. Are we sure he's going to come through?"

I tune out Kayden's reply as my gaze lands on the Cartier watch on Carlo's wrist, so like the one Kayden threw away because it resembled the watch Garner Neuville wears. I have a flash of images in my head, familiar hated images that Kayden has done much to wash away but they are here now, demanding I put together another piece of my puzzle. A hand touching me, that watch below a white cuffed shirt. But those images are of Garner Neuville. Why do Carlo, Kayden, and Neuville all have that same watch? That's too much of a coincidence for me to believe is possible.

Carlo leans forward, resting his arms on the table and lacing his fingers together. "Why are you staring at me, Ella?"

"You're a hard person to figure out."

"No," he says, the air suddenly crackling around us. "That's not why you're staring at me. If you have something to say, say it."

I now have to decide if I'm going to confront him or take this to Kayden privately. I want to look at Kayden, but to be the woman by his side, I have to stand tall, like he does. I'm cornered and if I don't punch my way out, I'll have no respect in this room and beyond. But accusing one of them of betrayal might not be smart, either. I'm about to let it go when a horrible thought occurs to me.

As if he senses it, Kayden reaches down and squeezes my leg, urging me to look at him, but another sudden, horrible thought crosses my mind, and all calculation goes out the window. "Where did you get that watch, Carlo?"

I feel Kayden's attention riveted to Carlo's wrist; feel the moment he realizes what that watch looks like, even before he says, "Yes, Carlo," his hands in front of him, lacing his fingers as if forcing control. "Where did you get that watch?"

"Gifted by a client last week," Carlo says with no hesitation, and my bad feeling about this gets worse.

"That's a twenty-thousand-dollar watch," Kayden says. "A generous gift for a job I wasn't briefed on. What client and what job?"

"It was on the books, Kayden," Carlo says. "Matteo sent me the assignment, like he does all the jobs I take now."

"Matteo assigns jobs?" I ask. I need to learn the internal workings of The Underground now, not later.

"I keep the database and check out the clients," Matteo replies. "If they aren't standard fare, they go to Kayden for approval. This one was standard fare."

"Name," Kayden bites out.

"Alicio Petit," Carlo supplies.

"I checked him out," Matteo says. "Married guy looking for a file with pictures of him and his girlfriend that his ex–business partner was using to blackmail him. Carlo and I found it and returned it to him." He grimaces. "I, however, didn't get a twenty-thousand-dollar watch."

"Find a connection between that man and Garner Neuville," Kayden commands. "Somewhere, it exists. Open your computer and find it now."

Carlo looks between us. "What is this about?"

"Yes," Nathan echoes, "what is this about?"

Ice runs down my spine and settles in my veins, my gaze finding Kayden's. "It's a message. He knows I'm here."

nine

Kayden's eyes hold mine, and everything we talked about on the porch tonight is in the air between us before his attention shifts back to the table. "Everyone," he says, drawing their attention and placing his finger to his lips, silencing everyone before motioning for Carlo to take off the watch. "We need to know if it's bugged and how much damage control we have to do," he tells me softly.

"That doesn't sound good," Sasha murmurs, obviously close enough to hear him.

"It's not," I reply, the words rasping from my dry throat.

"Here," Nathan instructs, pulling a small leather case from his pocket and unzipping it.

Carlo passes the offending watch to Nathan, who opens the case to display a mini tool set, yet another example of there being more to the doctor than meets the eye.

While he works, Kayden angles toward me, and me to him. "I'm not going to tell you this is a scare tactic," he says for my ears only. "Though it may well be."

"It's a promise," I say. "It's him being bold enough to say he's coming, and then do it."

"We won't leave this room without an aggressive plan to deal with him, which was already my intent."

"You mean kill him? Because that's the only way to stop him."

"Yes," he promises. "I mean kill him."

"No bug," Nathan announces.

The room seems to sigh in unison, only to have Matteo throw us all another punch. "But we have another problem," he warns, looking up from his MacBook Air as all eyes fall on him.

"The client no longer exists," Kayden supplies. "He's been wiped away as easily as Ella was."

"That's exactly right," Matteo confirms.

"Can you find an internet signature of who, where, and when?" Kayden asks.

"I'm trying, but unsuccessfully. Whoever did this was good. Really damn good."

"This from a man who claims to be one of the best hackers on the planet," I say, not secure with his claim that our security system can't be broken into anymore.

"I *am* one of the best hackers on the planet," Matteo snaps back sharply. "But you don't go head-to-head with someone like me, unless you're someone who can keep up."

"What the hell is going on?" Carlo demands. "And how was I used to make it happen?"

Kayden's response is to look at me in a silent question. Do I want to tell my story or let him? "Me," I reply, as if he's spoken. "I'll tell them." I inhale and glance around the table, then get right to the point. "Some of you know pieces of this. Matteo for sure, because he's been helping look into my past. Adriel, because we just told him."

"What the fuck is going on?" Carlo demands. "And how many times do I have to ask that question?"

"You really are charming, Carlo," Sasha says. "A prince, in fact."

"I'm your lead to finding the necklace," I say. "That's why Niccolo was looking for me. I wasn't just some random person who was at the wrong place at the wrong time, as we initially thought."

"Your identity being wiped out completely was a pretty good sign that something didn't add up," Matteo says.

"Obviously Niccolo believes you don't remember where it is," Sasha says, "or you'd be under lock and key."

"She's protected under Evil Eye," Carlo reminds her.

"He's fully aware that I have amnesia," I say, "and, unfortunately, he's using me to try to get Kayden to work for him."

Kayden is quick to weigh in on that. "He lost that leverage when Alessandro led the private eye hired by Ella's friend right to her."

"But the PI did help jolt some of my memories," I say, "which I hope will help me remember where the necklace is."

Sasha asks, "Are you saying you actually had it, or just a lead on it?"

"I had it," I say. "I'll start at the beginning and tell the entire story, which is somewhat convoluted with chunks of my memory still missing." I begin with David, the engagement gift, everything I told Adriel, and finally David dying in the alleyway and me calling Garner Neuville.

"You were staying with Garner Neuville?" Sasha asks.

"Yes. It didn't take long for me to figure out that he wasn't what he seemed, and that I'd been set up. I was his possession in his eyes, set up for the murder of my fiancée if I went to the police, my complete identity erased. I figured out he was after the necklace, but to my knowledge I never knew why or what it was worth. I just know that I hid it."

"And that no one has found it," Kayden adds. "They're all still looking for it."

Carlo narrows his gaze on me. "How did you get here, and why was Niccolo looking for you?"

"He claims I promised him the necklace in exchange for protection from Neuville," I say. "There's no way I'd have promised him that necklace. I'd have had a plan to avoid giving it to him."

"In other words," Carlo says, "he believes you have the necklace."

"He's aware of my amnesia," I say. "But yes, he believes I'm the key to finding it and he's right. I had it the night I called Neuville for help, and I remember the night I overheard Neuville talking to his bodyguard about me having it. My thought was—it's hidden; you'll never find it. But I didn't remember that until two days ago."

"The good news here is that she hid it well enough that no one has found it," Nathan offers. "It's bought us time to remove some of the players." He glances at me. "What's the story behind the watch?"

"It's Garner Neuville's watch," I explain. "It was him telling me that he's coming for me, and that he can get to any of you to do it. He wanted to own me and the necklace. He doesn't have either, and when I left, per Niccolo, I held a gun on him in front of a crowd. He's obsessed with me."

"You humiliated him," Sasha says. "Which the bastard deserved, but he won't let that go."

Carlo looks at Kayden. "And now we know why you invoked Evil Eye."

I feel those words like a slap.

"I invoked Evil Eye because I want Ella by my side," Kayden corrects. "I needed a solution that sent an off-limits message to Neuville and Niccolo, long term. Otherwise, I would have hidden her away until this was over."

"Evil Eye won't keep him away," Sasha says softly, her hands flattening on the table as if she's bracing herself for a fight.

My gaze goes to Kayden's, a silent push to remind him that this is exactly what I've said, as well. He gives me a small nod, while Adriel offers Sasha the same response Kayden gave me earlier tonight. "He'd be crazy to risk Evil Eye," Adriel says. "Not even Alessandro is that foolish."

Her gaze snaps to her sometimes lover. "You don't understand who and what that man is," she says, and I realize that she's set her hands on the table because she's trembling.

I'm reminded then of the night of the party, and her mentioning that she'd fled Paris after crossing Neuville. I can easily imagine the many ways he might have created the anger—and *the fear*—radiating off her now.

"Let's step outside, Sasha," Adriel says softly, a tenderness in his voice that tells me their relationship might contain a real connection that neither has allowed the other to explore.

"No," she says, twisting to direct an appeal to Kayden. "Please listen to me."

"Carlo's right, Sasha," Nathan argues. "Evil Eye—"

"Won't matter," she bites out, keeping her attention on Kayden. "I experienced that man's capabilities, and he just saw me as a fling. He sees Ella as a possession that you took from him, Kayden. He will come for her." She looks at me. "He will come for you." She gestures around the table. "He will come for us. He will kill us all, if we let him. Do you all hear me? *He will kill us.* And then what damn good is Evil Eye? Tell me!"

The room goes silent, everyone staring at this strong, bold woman who is no longer able to hide her trembling. I want to grab her and hug her and tell her I understand, but I know that isn't the answer. Not here and now.

"We're going to kill him, Sasha," Kayden promises, his voice soft, strong, and absolute. "We're going to make him pay for his many sins."

"When, Kayden?" she demands. "When is someone finally going to kill that man?"

"We are going to end him now. But you need to go take a breather with Adriel. We'll detail a plan when you get back."

"Respectfully, no," she says. "I'm here. I'm fighting." She shoves fingers through her brown hair, still a mess from the rain. "And I'm perfectly composed. I just needed to get a point across."

"At the risk of sounding like the sane one here," Nathan says, "I'm going to be the voice of reason. If we kill Neuville, his entire operation will come after us. And both his second and third are problems."

"Which is why it can't look like we did it," Kayden states. "And they have to die with him."

"If we didn't do it," Nathan asks, "who did?"

"Raul would make a damn good fall guy," Adriel suggests. "Pit him against Neuville. He's brutal and he's hungry to expand his power here."

A buzzer goes off, and Kayden picks up a remote control to bring one of the dozen monitors on the wall to life, revealing a person in a raincoat at the street door of the store. "That should be our delivery."

"I'll get it," Adriel says, already on his feet and moving toward the door.

Kayden eyes Matteo. "Go with him for backup."

As Matteo follows Adriel, Kayden's phone rings. He pulls it from his pocket, glances at the number, and heads for the door, leaving only Sasha, Nathan, Carlo, and me at the table.

"Any drugs you can give her to jolt her memory, Doc?" Carlo asks, talking to Nathan but looking at me.

"No," Nathan says. "But I have a few to shut you up."

Carlo ignores him, fingers thrumming on the table. "So, let me get this straight. We're supposed to believe you were a schoolteacher who eloped with this doctor, but you can fight and handle a weapon as well as any of us?"

I tell him about Blake Walker. I tell him about my father. "He was covert CIA. He trained me from a young age."

"My experience is that the CIA is a shady operation," he comments. "Most of the agents, especially the highly covert ones, feel they have no rules or boundaries to follow. In my experience, the dirty agents outnumber the good ones."

"You're such an ass, Carlo," Sasha says. "This is her father, who was murdered on the job."

"Why was he murdered?" he asks. "And by who?"

That's the question. Why? By who? And the word *dirty* is grinding through my mind with dogged insistence. Was my father dirty? Is that why he was killed? Was I an agent? And was I, am I, dirty?

"What about you, Ella?" Carlo asks, as if reading my mind. "Good agent or bad agent?"

"Schoolteacher," I say. "No one has found any proof I'm an agent."

"Let it go, Carlo," Nathan warns.

"Yes, Carlo," Sasha says. "You really are a piece of bad work. Tell me why you're here again?"

"To take down The Jackals," he says, never missing a beat. "Who have been known to have a few CIA contacts of their own. As does Niccolo."

The obvious accusation hits a nerve. Anger comes at me hard and fast, and I don't even know what root it's sprouting from. "This from the Jackal himself?"

"I'm no longer a Jackal," he snaps.

"No?" I challenge. "Because once a bottom feeder, always a bottom feeder."

"Don't push me, Ella," Carlo warns.

"What are *you* doing to *me*?"

"Trying to get you to get your fucking memory back," he snaps.

"By being an asshole?" I demand. "That's been tried. It fails. All it does is piss me off. So let me tell you what I know, Carlo. I'm loyal to Kayden, which means I'm loyal to The Underground. I will fight for it. I will kill for it, and it would not be the first time I've killed. I will protect your back and your life, but if you come at mine with bad intentions, you won't like the outcome. Because I am my father's daughter, and he taught me to win—and that means other people die, not me. And not the people who I'm protecting or standing beside."

I inhale, realizing then that I've leaned forward in an aggressive stance, and I force myself to ease back into my seat. Adriel and Matteo have returned, standing behind their seats, while Kayden stands in the open doorway, his presence sucking all of the air out of the room, a force to be acknowledged. Our eyes lock, the connection stealing my breath. We stare at each other for several long beats, and I see amusement curving his lips.

"I see you found out Ella's no pushover, Carlo," he says, moving forward to stand between the seats Adriel and Matteo reclaim.

"I guess you could say I did," Carlo confirms, his gaze meeting mine. "It's my way to test people. And believe it or not, it makes me a damn good Hunter."

Thinking of the nerve he hit, I say, "Actually, I do believe it."

"Truce it is, then," Kayden declares, drawing our attention and holding up a folder. "Alessandro stole three million dollars from Neuville."

"He's officially insane," Sasha says, echoing the words in my head.

"He's a dead man walking if Neuville finds out," Carlo replies. "I fucking love it."

"He's going to find out," Kayden says. "Because you're going to make sure he finds out." He slides the envelope across the table to Carlo, who catches it easily. "Get that to the Jackal you know will sell out Alessandro and go to Neuville, preferably in Paris, but don't let yourself be the source. When Alessandro falls we're breaking up The Jackals. The existing members will have these options: follow my rules, leave the country, retire, or suffer great consequences. They'll report to me through you."

"Understood," Carlo says, all of his cockiness remarkably, if only momentarily, washed away. "I won't let you down."

"Then hear me, and hear me well, Carlo. Alessandro does not die until Neuville and his second and third are dead, and it's assumed to be retaliation. Do not get trigger happy and blow that. You communicate with me. We'll design the timing. When he leaves for Paris, you and I will, too."

It's what I expected him to say. He wants to end this. I knew he would. Adriel, however, isn't pleased. "You can't get anywhere near this."

"I'm ending this," Kayden says. "One way or the other."

"Aside from incriminating yourself," Adriel argues, "this is dangerous as fuck. You're too important to the stability of Europe to take that risk."

Adriel convinces me he's right and I open my mouth to agree, but somehow, some way, I remind myself that for now, at least, Kayden needs me to argue with him behind closed doors.

But Nathan doesn't stay silent. "You can't risk being connected to this."

"I can back up Carlo," Sasha says. "I know it leaves Gallo exposed, but Alessandro will now have other things to worry about. And I know Paris, and Neuville's people. And I'd be happy to kill any or all of them that survive Alessandro."

"You can back us both up," Kayden says, his gaze warning me not to debate my role in this in this room.

A concern outside of Kayden's safety hits me, and I speak up. "Niccolo will know that you released the information he sent you."

"Here's the piece of the puzzle you need to put it together," Kayden replies, to me and everyone else. "Niccolo didn't give me this file to satisfy me, or to offer you protection. He's not that honorable. He knows what Neuville did to Ella. He knows I want Neuville dead. He led Alessandro into crossing my path and endangering Ella. He *wanted* me to use this to get rid of a stepbrother he wants dead."

"Without starting a mob war," I supply.

"Exactly," Kayden says. "But we aren't doing his dirty work, leaving ourselves that exposed. We'll clear the path for him or someone he trusts to do the job. And that's what I'm going to tell him in person tonight." Kayden considers a moment. "In fact . . ."

He glances at Adriel. "Contact our man inside Neuville's operation. This is starting to read like a setup by Niccolo. I'm betting Neuville's still wearing his watch, and the gift to Carlo was a plant, meant to hit a trigger with Ella and make me go after him." He looks at me. "Niccolo knows you were running from his stepbrother."

"We can't assume it was Niccolo," I warn. "It could have been Neuville."

"It fits Neuville's style of manipulation," Sasha says, quick to support my worries.

"I'll tell Niccolo I'm going to kill Neuville, which is what he wants," Kayden says. "If he did send the watch he has no reason to deny it, and will likely gloat about how brilliant his plan was."

"I'll look for a connection between the customer who gave it to Carlo and Niccolo, just in case he tries to play coy," Matteo says.

"Do that," Kayden says. "And I need a final word on Blake Walker and Chris Merit tonight."

"You'll have it," Matteo assures him.

Kayden looks at Sasha. "Deal with Gallo until we're ready for you." His attention shifts to Nathan and Adriel. "You know what you have to do." He then scans the room. "Any questions or input?" After several beats of silence, he says, "We're done, then."

Everyone stands, including me. Only, as they disappear out of the War Room, I close the space between myself and

Kayden, him watching my every step, his expression unreadable, those pale blue eyes hooded. Ridiculously, in those final few steps as he turns to face me, butterflies attack my stomach, ridiculous when this man is my soul mate. My shelter in every storm I will ever face, and in all the ones I now relive.

He doesn't reach for me, standing there, all power and masculinity, his gaze sharp, unreadable. "I'm going to be a few hours. Maybe longer."

I want to ask where he's going, aside from seeing Niccolo. I want to tell him to be careful. But this is one of those moments where I must ensure that one of the fears I voiced doesn't become reality. That I don't become a distraction, one that changes how he makes decisions, and places him and the others in danger.

"I'll be here when you get back," I say.

He doesn't immediately respond, and the wall I placed between us is still there, still dividing us. "What you said to Carlo—"

"I meant every word."

Again he is silent, studying me. "There are many things I want to say to you right now." There is a low, rough quality to his voice. "But I can't right now, before I—"

"I know, Hawk," I say. "Go. Lead. Take care of business."

"I'm leaving Matteo and Sasha here with you, and I have men on the exterior keeping watch. You know you're safe here, right?"

I think of the hacker that out-hacked Matteo and wonder how true that really is, but that's not what he needs to hear now. I have guns. I have suspicions. I have guards. So I say, "Yes, I do. I'll be here when you get back."

He hesitates a few beats, then turns and is gone. I stare after him, already wishing he were back.

Every answered question in my life seems to lead to another, but the ones I hate the most are the ones I created in Kayden and me and us. But I'm going to make them go away. Tonight.

ten

I have no idea how long I stand in the War Room replaying Kayden's proposal, but it must be a while, because Sasha appears in the doorway, a concerned look on her face. "You okay?"

"I am," I say, standing, having at some point sat back down at the table. "Just deep in thought. How are you?"

"You mean because of that little incident in the meeting?" She waves it off. "That was nothing. I won't let it be anything, because Garner Neuville doesn't get that kind of power. Besides, he'll be dead soon."

"He will be," I agree, waiting for some guilt or distress to form, but all I feel is regret that I won't be the one to kill him. "But every person who touches our lives leaves a mark. He's left a mark on both of us. Even when he's dead, that stays. You know that, right?"

"Not if I don't let it."

"You can deny it, Sasha, but eventually it demands notice."

"Are you talking to me or you?"

"Both of us," I say, accepting now that my mind is blocking everything that leads to Garner Neuville. "Obviously my mind thinks I can't handle the truth, and it's frustrating."

She leans on the door frame, studying me for several long moments. "At least if he's dead, the fear of knowing he's on this earth is gone."

"That's true," I say. "That's some closure, and I admit I'm hungry to find that. I wanted to go to Paris and finish it myself. Kayden wasn't happy with that idea."

"If he was, I'd personally have to kick his ass, Hawk or no Hawk. You know what Neuville is like."

"I thought returning to Paris might jog my memory and help me find the necklace."

"It also could get you killed. But"—she pushes off the frame, her hands settling on her hips—"I do have an idea. I know Paris well. We could print out pictures of Neuville's neighborhood, and any other area you remember. Maybe they will help."

"That's a great idea."

"We can use Adriel's office," she says. "He has a printer."

"Technically my office now," I say, joining her and walking down the hallway. "I'm taking over the store now that he's returning to hunting."

"That's a misuse of your talents, as it was his," she says.

"Kayden isn't exactly ready for me to dive into hunting, even after Neuville is gone."

"Yes, well, he's always believed Niccolo was behind Elizabeth's and Kevin's murders."

"He's all but admitted it."

"That doesn't surprise me. Neuville is a crazy person, but make no mistake, Niccolo is an evil bastard. Kevin must have crossed him in some big way, though we'll probably never know the details."

"And now there's Evil Eye."

"Yes. And it really does work. One thing you'll learn once you meet all our field Hunters, here and around the world, is that The Underground has the power to destroy empires. And Neuville is just a crazy person. Literally."

"You know, maybe I could take over dispatching from Matteo," I suggest. "That's a safe way to get involved and ease Kayden into the idea of me working with him."

"That's also a misuse of your skills. I've seen you in action, and heard from others about how you handle yourself in a fight."

"It would allow me to get to know the Hunters, the types of jobs, and the ins and outs of things. And it seems a misuse of talent to have 'one of the best hackers on the planet' being a dispatcher." I laugh. "His words, not mine."

She laughs as well. "How could I not know that?"

I make an Italian Stallion joke in French, and she gives me a surprised look. "You speak French."

"I do," I say. "I have no idea how I learned it or why, but I remember the language."

"You think you're CIA?"

"I really don't know," I say, but in my gut, I am certain my connection to the CIA is far greater than just my father. "I think most likely my father taught me the trade, like he did so many other things."

"Maybe he worked in Paris," she says. "That would mean he most certainly knew Garner's parents, and maybe even him."

"That's an interesting thought," I say, "but he's been dead a long time. It's not impossible, but I'm doubtful he has any real connection to any of this." But she's now got me thinking about my father and his murder. *Could* that be connected to the French mob? Could I have wanted to go to Paris to follow a lead, and that's why I jumped on the elopement? Something about this feels more right to me than any other explanation.

"As for you doing the dispatching," she says, thankfully changing the topic, "think about how that would consume Kayden. He needs to be thinking of the big picture. You'd pull him into the small pictures."

"Hmmm," I say, as the door opens. "That's a good point." We enter the store to find the lights have remained on, and I punch the button to lower the doors, which is mandatory for security. With the doors down, anyone who gets into the store can't get to the rest of the castle.

"Now that the meeting is over," she says, as we walk toward the front of the store, passing glass cases filled with collectibles, "Marabella is out of exile. You think she might be convinced to bring us food? That woman makes the best everything. Her cooking is a guilty pleasure. Well, that and Adriel. It's a two-for-one when I'm here."

"I'll call her, on one condition," I say. "You have to tell me the real scoop on you and Adriel."

She laughs. "There's nothing to tell," she says, making it clear she's not going there.

We round the counter to find Matteo sitting behind the small wooden desk, full bookshelves surrounding him, and I feel a little like I'm in a crowded elevator with the three of us in the small space. "We need the printer," Sasha announces. "You have to find another spot to work."

He shoves fingers through his wavy dark hair and says something to her in Italian, which she answers in English. "We're trying to jolt her memory and find the necklace. Are you convinced to get up now?"

"That does the trick," he says, shutting his MacBook and standing. "I'll be in the TV room. I'm calling Marabella to bring food."

"That's what I'm talking about," Sasha says as he exits. "Ask her if she has any of those chocolate croissants she makes," she calls after him, but he ignores her. "Maybe we should call ourselves."

"She'll take care of us," I assure her, claiming the visitor's seat while she sits down behind the desk and powers up the desktop.

"I'm sure you're right," she says, and then moves on. "Okay. I know you were at Garner's place, so I'll start by printing out things around his building." She grabs a pad and pencil and hands them to me. "Write down other locations you want me to focus on. And really, *anything* you remember. I'll try to turn that into a destination and photo."

"Chocolate shops," I say. "I went to one the night I called Neuville for help, and I'm hoping that finding the one I visited could flip a memory switch."

"I'll go out on a limb here and estimate that there are

about a hundred chocolate shops in Paris," she says. "Can you narrow it down at all? Was it near his home?"

I write down the address I found inside the necklace and hand it to her. "Near this location. And I need pictures of anything and everything around this address."

She types in the address. "Five chocolate shops within only three blocks. I'll start printing them out."

"What about within eight blocks? I went that far after the murder."

"Trying to disappear," she says. "Smart." She keys into the computer. "Another four." The printer begins to hum and I start writing down the places I do remember.

A few minutes later, I'm looking at a printed image of the store and street fronts for all nine shops, and I see one that I'm certain is the location I've been looking for. I stuff it at the back of the stack, not wanting to black out in a flashback right now.

"Anything?" Sasha asks.

"Not yet, but when Blake Walker shared things with me, I didn't immediately feel the trigger. It came later in the day."

"Well then, let's just print out everything and get you armed."

I hear the exterior door opening and I push to my feet, exiting the office as Marabella calls out, "Chocolate croissants have arrived."

I round the counter and rush to meet her, finding her lugging two picnic baskets, and I have this sense of belonging, of rightness here in the castle. Death might live here, but so do new beginnings, healing, and perseverance. I belong here, no matter what my past might try to say otherwise. It's at that moment that a peal of thunder rattles the store windows, as if I'm being told the calm before the storm is over.

∽∽∾∾

An hour and a half later, my stomach is stuffed, my stack of papers is substantial, and there is no word from Kayden, which has me feeling pretty antsy. "I think that's about everything," Sasha says, finishing off a croissant before handing me one last page. "I even printed everything I could find here in Rome that's near the alleyway where you were found. But there's one other place in Paris I wanted to mention. Did you ever go to the club?"

Ice slides down my spine and I quickly shove away the memory of being tied up, the whip biting into my skin. "He took you there?"

"Fool that I am," she says, "I went by choice. Naively— who'd ever think to call me that—I didn't see that we're his targets. He likes powerful women he can break. If they submit easily, he doesn't want them. But I guess that's good. I mean, think about how he affects us. Can you imagine what he would do to someone with a different nature?"

"I don't even want to consider that."

"But maybe that's the point," she continues. "He wants to be able to push and push and push some more."

"Why were you involved with him?"

"We had a contract with a French diplomat who wanted to take him down once and for all. The paycheck was huge and I'd get to take down the brutal head of the French mob. I was so inspired that I stayed even when it got bad. Did he ever make you call him Master? That was where the trouble started for me. I have this 'never surrender' mentality that he saw as a challenge."

My mind starts swimming with images, and I begin to tremble. I drop my head forward, fighting the flashback I can't have here. Not in front of Sasha, and with Matteo nearby, perhaps walking in at any moment. I fight hard, but it's no use. Suddenly I am in the past, though not at the club. I am in his bedroom. Garner Neuville's bedroom.

※※※

I am naked. He is not. He's dressed in slacks and a button-down shirt. I'm on my knees and he's holding the flogger I hate so damn much. I stare at the floor, willing myself to just get through this.

"Look at me," he orders, and I ignore my warning to myself and his command. "Look at me."

I can't do it. I just . . . can't.

His fingers tangle in my hair and he yanks my head back, the tug against my scalp biting. "I see that defiance in your eyes, my love. You dare to look at me this way? The man who saved you? The man who owns this city, as I own you? The man who deleted the security footage that showed you leaning over a dying man?"

And there it is. A promise to destroy me should I not submit, delivered by the mob boss. A laundry list of the many ways he can, and will, hurt me if I leave him. And a reminder to me that I can't kill him yet. Not when I've seen enough of his operation to know he will be avenged. Not until I know I'm ready to disappear and take the necklace with me.

"Say thank you," he orders.

"Thank you," I force out.

"You don't sound like you mean it." He leans in and brushes his lips over mine. "I can taste your disobedience. Ah, love. The moment I break you will be the most erotic of my life." He nips my lips, a painful punishment that draws blood, his voice roughening. "I am your Master. You will say it before this night is over."

He tightens the grip on my hair and reaches down and smacks my nipple with the flogger. But I don't give him what he wants. I do not cry out; I do not so much as whimper. "Master," he repeats.

I want to kill him.

I want to hurt him first.

I want this night to be the night I get to do those things.

"Say it," he commands. "Master."

I don't say it, but he doesn't even wait to realize that. He releases my hair and thankfully drops the flogger, only to produce a rope from his pocket. "Put your hands in front of you."

The moment I let him tie me up, the real torture will start and I'll be unable to kill him.

"Hands," he demands.

Kill him!

No.

Not yet.

Survive. You have to survive, or you won't enjoy his death.

He grabs my arms and pulls me to my feet, turning me to face the bed before shoving me down, half my naked body on the mattress, my backside in the air. And then he has my arms, and I know that this is it. I have only moments to decide how this ends. In thirty seconds I could snap his neck. But then what? I can't get to the money I stashed tonight. I can't get to the necklace tonight. He binds my hands, thinking he's forced me, having no clue that I let him. And then his hand is on my lower back, and he shifts. I steel myself for what I know is coming, fearing it and him, not because I couldn't kill him. Because I can't yet, which means I am this man's property.

And then it happens, the expected, and yet it's still a shock. The flogger smacks my backside with vicious force. He lets that first hard smack sting, lets the promise of another linger in the air, and then he's punishing me. Hitting me again. Once, twice, twenty brutal times, and then it's his hand on my flesh instead of the flogger. Over and over and over again. In some part of my mind, I know that pain is his way of telling me that to survive, I must surrender. And I hate that it's true. But he's going to really hate the moment he finds out that my surrender is my *control—not his.*

⚬≈≫⚬

"Ella. Ella."

Sasha's voice permeates the flashback, bringing me back to the present, and I become aware of my elbows on the desk, my chin to my chest and my hair draped around my face. I inhale, willing myself to regain my composure, and suddenly my mind goes to earlier today with Kayden. To us naked on the couch, with my hands taped and him promising to spank me.

"Why aren't you afraid, Ella?" he'd asked.

"Because you're not him," I'd said.

I have never appreciated Kayden as much as I do in this moment, and how easily he could have made me feel like a prisoner but never did.

"Ella," Sasha repeats softly.

"Yes," I say, shoving my fingers through my hair. For the briefest of moments, I realize I was a redhead in my flashback and yet now, with brown hair, I am so much more myself than I ever was with Garner Neuville. "I'm sorry," I add. "The flashbacks come fast and hard, and if I don't let them happen, I lose the memory. Unfortunately, it wasn't useful."

"Sweetie," she says softly. "I know who you were with in that flashback. I saw how you trembled. But that's between us."

I swallow against my suddenly dry throat. "Thank you, Sasha."

"I hate that you have to relive Neuville to find that necklace."

"I'm not sorry," I say. "I have to do this. My surrender is my control."

She arches a brow. "What?"

"He can't have my fear. I'm angry that my mind keeps sheltering me—but not for long. I'm going to remember it all. I'm close. Very close."

"Any luck?"

At the sound of Matteo's voice, I twist around to find him in the doorway. "I'm armed with potential triggers," I say, holding up the papers we've printed. "But the memories come as they please, not as I will. It's no miracle fix. What about you?"

"Chris Merit and Blake Walker check out," he says. "I can find absolutely nothing to suggest otherwise."

"What about Chris running in the same circles as Neuville?"

"There's nothing there that looks like a problem to me,"

he says. "And I dug deeply. I've sent a detailed file you can review to Kayden's email."

The buzzer at the front door goes off and we all frown. Matteo pulls his phone from his pocket and eyes the screen. "It's a man with a trench coat and a hood on." He walks around the desk. "I need to see the larger view." He reaches over Sasha and types, then clicks.

"What the—" Sasha starts. "That's Gallo. He couldn't have followed me. That's not possible." She grimaces. "I should have put a man on him."

Matteo hits the volume, and we hear Gallo shouting through the rain in Italian, but I catch the word *Kayden* several times. "He's obviously not here for Sasha," Matteo says. "But we need to know what's wrong. I'll go talk to him." He eyes Sasha. "Get someone on him now."

"Let me go talk to him," I say, standing up. "I'm still an outsider like him, someone he wants to save. I have the best chance of finding out what's wrong with him."

"I'm not letting you open that door," Matteo says. "Kayden trusts me to protect you. We do this together or not at all."

"He trusts us to be a team," Sasha says. "And I know Gallo. He's not dangerous."

"And yet he's going to join The Jackals?" Matteo counters.

"Which will end with him dead—not someone else," Sasha says.

"The poor man is getting drenched," I remind them. "You're both right here in the office."

Sasha punches buttons on the computer. "There is no one

else dumb enough to be outside, Matteo. It's a ghost town. We're right here with her; she'll be safe."

He grimaces. "I'm going to be squatting behind the counter. Sasha will be in the office with the lights out."

That's all I need to hear. Matteo takes his position behind the counter. Sasha flips the light out behind me, and I head toward the door. Flipping the locks, I open the door and step back, bringing a drenched Gallo into view. He scowls at the sight of me, or maybe he was already scowling. Whatever the case, he charges through the door, water pouring off of him, and shuts it behind him.

"Where's Kayden?" he demands, tugging down the hood on his tan trench coat, his hair a rumpled mess, but then it always is, his gray eyes etched with anger. His impatience wins over and he repeats himself a bit more gruffly. "Where the fuck is Kayden?"

"He's not in," I say. "What's got you so riled up?"

"Kayden fucking happened," he proclaims, the puddle at his feet becoming wider. "If he's not here, why are you in the store?"

"Is there some rule in Italy that I don't know about women and stores? Since when do I need Kayden to be in here? And while it's none of your business, I'm taking over the store. It's mine now, and I'm working late to put my personal touches on it."

"You're staying with him, then, Eleana—is that it?"

"Yes, Detective Gallo, I'm staying with him. And call me Ella. I know you've heard people call me that. Hell, *you've* done it a few times before. I prefer it."

He reaches in his pocket and holds up a picture of a young

woman with an *X* over her face and some Italian words written across it. "Do you know about this? Is this the kind of action you condone?"

"What is that?" I ask, already knowing I'm not going to like the answer.

"A photo of my sister who lives in Milan, with a threat against her life. This is the kind of man you're with. Is this the kind of person you are?"

"Kayden didn't do this," I say quickly, certain this is Niccolo and Alessandro's handiwork. "He would never do such a thing, and I just talked to him about you—"

"I don't want to hear your ridiculous efforts to defend him." He shoves the photo into his pocket. "You know what is sad? You're going to wake up to a brutal reconciling of the real man and whoever he's pretending to be for you. You don't know him." He shakes his head. "Tell Kayden his methods backfired. This is war." He turns and walks toward the exit, and he's wrong about Kayden. Without question, I know him, but I also know how Gallo is right now, and that's angry and desperate, two dangerous things. He yanks open the door, pulls up his hood, and disappears into the rain, slamming the door behind him.

"I need to go after him," Sasha says, stepping out of the office, and Matteo stands up behind the counter. "Before he ends up in Alessandro's web," she adds.

"He could be baiting you, and waiting for you to leave," I warn. "You need to exit the castle in a car, and without visibility."

"She's right," Matteo says. "Did you get someone to follow him?"

"I sent a message to our neighborhood lead," Sasha says. "He's on it and he'll text us both with updates." She looks at me. "And you're right about the possible trap. I'm going to call Carlo and see if he can find out anything from inside The Jackals." She heads back into the office, leaving me with Matteo.

"I'm calling Kayden in case Gallo does something crazy and ends up standing in front of him," I say, punching in the auto-dial and walking toward the TV room for privacy.

He answers in two rings, his voice deep, concerned. "What's wrong?"

"I'm safe," I say, "but I need to give you a heads-up to make sure *you* stay that way. Gallo showed up here in a fury. He had a picture of his sister with a huge *X* over her face, and some writing in Italian that basically equates to a threat. He thinks you did it. I told him it's not you, but he's out of his mind right now."

"Where is he now?" he asks, receiving the information as calmly as he does everything.

"We've had him followed, but he just left. He was standing in the pouring rain, pounding insanely on the store door. My worry is that he'll connect with Alessandro and alert him to where you are. Or he'll wait and try to confront you when you return to the castle."

"You did right by calling me," he says. "I just left Niccolo. Obviously I need to get back and have another conversation with him about Alessandro and Gallo."

I want to ask what happened in their meeting, but this isn't the time. "Sasha wants to go to him, to try to get him under control, but—"

"No. Gallo followed her earlier. This could be a setup."

"That was my thought as well," I say. "Right now, we're waiting to see where he goes and what he does."

"Text me if there are new developments. Call me if you feel it's urgent."

"I will." I bite back another "be safe" that I know isn't what The Hawk needs to hear. "While you're talking to Niccolo, just remember that he's afraid of dying. And fear—"

"Is punishment," he supplies. "That idea is going to make me sleep better tonight. Make sure someone calls Adriel and updates him."

"I will."

He's silent for a moment, then two, and I almost think he's hung up before I hear, "Ella."

"Yes?"

He says something in Italian, his voice low, gruff, intimate, and then he hangs up—leaving me wondering what he said, and why he wouldn't say it in English.

eleven

I end the call with Kayden and head toward the store again, Sasha meeting me under the archway dividing the TV room from the store.

"I just called Adriel and filled him in," she says. "He's already successfully handed off the cocktail to our man inside Niccolo's operation, and he's pulling into our driveway now. Did you reach Kayden?"

"I did," I confirm, "and he was worried about Gallo setting you up before I even mentioned it myself."

"I really don't think that's what that was. Not based on how upset he was, and per our man following him, Gallo parked at the front of the castle and is making his way to his car in the pouring rain. If he set me up he'd be waiting around and would surely have a better plan than pounding on the door in the rain."

"You have to remember that Alessandro is involved with him now, and by reputation, he's devious."

"Alessandro already knows I work for Kayden. Oh, crap! I

don't think Gallo knows my story yet, but Alessandro could tell him at any time."

"He might have hinted at it, or told him and Gallo didn't want to believe it, so he followed you."

"Maybe. Either way, now that I've had time to process Alessandro's involvement, I can't reconnect with Gallo. He's too volatile. I could ignite new anger that might send him into the deep end."

"Yeah," I agree. "And I hate that, because Gallo really is a mess. He needs someone to ground him. I'm hoping he just goes home tonight and drinks or sleeps this off."

"His sister is in danger," she says. "He's not going to just let this go."

"What are you thinking?"

"That he'll go to Milan," she says, and we both look at each other as the light bulb goes off. "And," she adds, "that's exactly what the goal was."

"He leaves the city," I supply, "and he's no longer able to cause trouble."

"It's a temporary fix, but a fix," she says. "Unfortunately, I don't think that means his sister is safe. Not with the people we're dealing with."

The sound of the door between us and the castle lifting sends both of us in that direction, and we arrive in front of it at the same moment Adriel appears. "Where's Gallo now?" he asks, his dark hair slightly damp, the scowl on his face seeming to deepen the scar down his cheek.

"He's headed toward the airport," Matteo announces, joining us. "I hacked the database and he leaves for Milan on the last flight out tonight. I've already contacted our people in Milan and arranged coverage at the airport when he arrives and at his sister's place immediately."

Sasha and I glance at each other. "We were right," she says.

"*You* were right," I say, glancing at Sasha. "They got him out of town."

"They did," Adriel says dryly, his hands settling on his hips. "It was, in fact, brilliant, except for the part where they threatened his damn sister, which makes an angry man angrier."

"Not to mention making him think it was Kayden," I comment.

"Obviously intentional," Adriel supplies, "and my guess is that it's Alessandro's way of convincing Niccolo that he did what was requested, while still ensuring Kayden has a problem to manage."

"He probably didn't expect Gallo to show up here and show his hand," I say. "Kayden's taking it up with Niccolo now."

Adriel's jaw tightens with his voice. "Fuck, I hate when he goes to see him alone."

"If anyone's going to die, it'll be Niccolo."

"Exactly," Adriel replies. "You can only sit across from the man who murdered your family so many times before you put a bullet in his head. And the hell that will follow, if that isn't planned, and planned well, is not the bitch you want in your bed, believe me."

"He won't kill him now," I say. "He's too capable of seeing the big picture, which includes making Niccolo suffer."

"Niccolo suffering sounds like the promise of sweet dreams," he says, "and a good thought to say good night on." He eyes Matteo. "Go home and get some rest. We'll sneak Sasha out in the morning."

Matteo scrubs a hand through his hair. "I'm not going to argue that, but I'll be in touch if there's an update on Gallo." He starts walking and calls over his shoulder, "Someone needs to watch the gate when I leave, and make sure no one sneaks in."

"Call me before you pull out." Adriel's gaze then lands on me. "Kayden's going to be a while. I'd feel better if you were secure in your tower."

Secure. That word hits a nerve that refuses to be ignored. "Speaking of feeling secure," I say, immediately reminded of the watch and the torn pages in my journal. "If Matteo was out-hacked with the watch situation, couldn't he have been out-hacked here at the castle?"

His eyes narrow and then he shouts, "Matteo!"

Matteo groans and then backs up, rejoining us. "What went wrong in thirty seconds?"

"Talking through recent events," Adriel says, "Ella and I have concerns that the castle security might have been breached."

"It wasn't breached," he says, giving me an irritated look that says he knows this is from me. "That didn't happen."

"Is it impossible?" he asks. "Or improbable?"

"Your form of dry smart-ass doesn't work for you or anyone," Matteo says. "Some fucker with a watch who knows how to create a fake identity does not an expert hacker make. But

I'll hack for hacks, if that's what we think is the best use of my time."

"Hey, man," Adriel says, holding his hands up. "We're just trying to keep everyone safe. We're dealing with Alessandro and two mob bosses, one of whom killed Kayden's family, while the other one is obsessed with Ella."

Matteo's expression tightens, right along with his voice. "You're right. You're right." He looks at me. "I get a little defensive about hacking. It's my thing." He points to his shirt. "Italian Stallion and all, you know?"

"I know you are," I say. "I'm just worried about someone getting hurt because of me. I couldn't live with that."

"No one is going to get hurt, Ella," Adriel says firmly. "We won't let that happen."

"We *can't* let that happen." The numerous ways Garner Neuville might strike are too many to fathom.

"I'll double- and triple-check every possible breach when I get home," Matteo promises. "I'll text you both."

"Thank you, Matteo," I say. "I really do appreciate it."

"He was just being an asshole with an ego," Sasha calls out, which Matteo replies to in Italian that is distinctly snarky, and then he's turned and disappeared into the hallway.

"You think there was a breach in the castle?" Sasha asks, concerned. "How and when?"

"I'll fill you in on her concerns myself, Sasha," Adriel says, his brown eyes falling on her.

"She's standing right here," she says. "Why can't she tell me?"

"Because you and I have a lot to talk about, on many topics. Conversations better had in private, in my tower."

Translation: in his bed.

For just a moment they stare at each other, the sizzle between them making me feel like I'm invading their privacy. I
delicately clear my throat. "I should go to my tower."

"Are you sure?" Sasha asks, immediately turning her attention to me. "If you don't want to be alone, I can join
you."

"I appreciate it, but I'm actually eager to get back to
Kayden's and my private space and focus on the data we
printed out. I'm going to grab it and get out of here."

"What data?" Adriel asks.

"I'll tell you in your tower," Sasha teases, and I turn away, a
smile on my lips. There is something about these two together
that works, but I have a feeling that's also the problem. There
is a lot of something between them, but both of them have
plenty of reasons to fear trust and love.

I make my way to the front of the store, pausing before I
round the counter, and I eye Gallo's puddle of water that I
should clean up but decide to ignore. Puddles of water are
fine. Puddles of blood are not. Entering the office, I reach for
my stack of papers, noting that they are face up now, not face
down. Either Matteo or Sasha looked through my papers.
Maybe Sasha just wanted to recap and see if she could think of
anything more. Or maybe she added images from near the
club. Or Matteo might have been curious. Thinking back to
the meeting, he was pretty excited about the five-million-
dollar payday, maybe more so than the others. My brow furrows. Why am I even spending time on this?

I snatch up the papers and leave the office, ready to go to

my private space with Kayden. Even more eager for him to return.

⚬⚬⚬

Once I'm alone and inside the foyer of our tower, I grab my purse from the coat rack where I'd hung it earlier, settling the strap on my shoulder. I fully intend to head up the stairs, but my gaze catches on the office that is now officially where Kayden proposed to me. Drawn in that direction, I cross the foyer and enter the room, where my gaze lands on the couch, random memories from earlier today assailing me. Namely, the spanking that wasn't a beating or really even a spanking. It was this sexy, erotic, consuming rush. Intimate and right in ways that I don't think it could be with anyone but Kayden. And I swear I can almost feel him next to me again. And damn it, I can almost feel the way I hurt him, too. I inhale the scent of him lingering in the air, and promise myself I'm going to make up for that every day for the rest of our lives.

My attention moves to the desk, with the roll of tape still sitting on it, and I cross to pick it up, more memories flitting through my mind.

"What are you doing?" I'd demanded, when he'd started tearing the tape.

"Proving a point," he'd said.

And boy, had he.

I trust him completely. Considering how badly I handled this afternoon, I need to tell him this again. Actually, I need to tell him so *many* things. And I'd love one of them to be the location of the necklace, so we can start putting all of this mess behind us. Motivated by that idea, I open the top desk drawer and scavenge for the supplies I need to create a memory wall. I leave with scissors, thumbtacks, and my trusty roll of tape. Once I'm upstairs, I stand at the edge of the stairs and wait for some sense of unease, but I don't find it. I head down the hallway and reach our door, and stop dead in my tracks with a realization. Where's that creepy "I'm being watched" feeling I've come to know as normal? I turn and face the hallway, waiting for it to wash over me, but it doesn't. Have I finally killed the paranoia by talking about it to everyone? And my imaginary ghost with it?

Not sure what to make of this new development, I enter the bedroom and flip on the light as well as the fireplace. The bed is now made, which of course is Marabella's doing. She is always on top of everything. Shutting the door, I toss my things on top of the blanket and cross to the security booth, where I check the entire tower just to be sure I'm alone, and then do a scan of the store and random other locations. Once I feel good about there being no safety concerns, I return to the bedroom and stare down at my supplies. I play with the idea of setting up a wall of memories in my dance studio, where memories of my past, and my mother, already live, but I really want it to be here in this room for some reason. I could use the security room, but it's so small. So . . . where?

An idea hits me and I snatch my journal from the nightstand, scoop up my supplies, and head into the bathroom, making a beeline for the closet. Once I'm in there, I set everything on the bench in the center and then glance around the room, finding a section of Kayden's clothes with a little extra space. With my wardrobe small at this point, I quickly move my things to his section, pausing momentarily to savor the sight of our things hanging together. I've never shared a life with anyone. Of this I am certain. I want to share this life with Kayden. That was never in question, but now it is for him. And no wonder, really. Everything in his life is danger, questions, problems. Closing the door to my questions, remembering everything, is something that isn't just for me. It's for him.

Turning to face the area where my clothes no longer hang, I note the concrete wall and decide tape is a good idea. I go to work and start creating a map. The hotel. A restaurant I remember passing. Various places that strike the familiar, if not true, memories. But I have no immediate flashbacks, and a good hour later, when everything is where I want it, even the re-creation of the alleyway still provokes nothing more than feelings and random glimpses of non-useful images in my mind. I sit down and set my phone next to me, picking up my journal and a pen, thinking I might jot down thoughts. Instead, I stare at the place where one of the pages was torn, willing myself to remember tearing it out, but I just can't.

Grabbing my phone again, and thankful that at some point Kayden keyed in a list of important contacts that includes Matteo, Marabella, Nathan, and Adriel for me, I pull up Matteo's number but hesitate. He's just so darn sensitive about any suggestion anyone could get past his safeguards. I start to dial Adriel when I spot and laugh at the name "Sasha the Great" that she must have inserted herself sometime tonight. But I hesitate again. Something tells me she and Adriel are a little busy right now.

Matteo it is, I decide, but I bypass the call and settle on the less offensive text message question: *Any word on the security concerns I had?*

He replies almost instantly: *Aside from a ghost or two I can't get rid of, you're safe.*

I blink and laugh at his joke. Ghosts? Well, I have always thought the castle was haunted. I set my phone down and pick it back up, fighting an urge to type: *Are you 100% sure?* But that would really agitate him and he's good at what he does. I know this.

I set the phone down firmly. There isn't a security problem, anyway. There's a me problem, and a little thing called blackouts. Why is my mind still protecting me, after that flashback in the club and then today? *Just give me back everything and let me get it over with!*

I study the wall before me, the images in full color and with street views, and I decide to start with the hotel in Paris. And just like that I'm in the hotel room, and things come to me as memories, not a flashback. This makes me smile. I see the room. The bed. The chair. The fight with David and the moment after he leaves the room, when I yank off the necklace in anger.

"Ah, damn it," I murmur as it falls to the floor. *"Sometimes I get way too into character."*

I blink. "Way too into character? What does that mean?"

It has to mean I'm CIA, but I still find no memory that solidifies that for me. My hand flattens on the hotel photo. I remember leaving, with a hat and glasses on, then discreetly searching for an address that has nothing to do with David. I inhale and let it out. I used David, who was good-looking and full of himself and clearly using me as well, to get to Paris so that the CIA wouldn't suspect I was following a lead about my father's death.

"I'm remembering," I whisper. Hoping this means I can remember what I did with the necklace, I move on to the image of the chocolate shop. I see myself go inside. I feel like that moment is important. I need to go to the security room and get online.

I turn around and Kayden steps into the doorway, his entrance having evaded my knowledge for the consumption of my memories. He pauses there, his holster gone, dark stubble on his square jaw that tells of the incredibly long day we've had. His hair is mussed up, as if he's been running his fingers through it, which would imply he was fretting. A hint of being out of control that he never allows himself.

"Hi," I say. "I made a memory wall and—"

I never finish the sentence. In a blink he's in front of me, his hands on my waist, walking me against that wall of locations that may or may not have played a role in bringing us here to this moment in time.

"I ordered the murder of five people in that meeting today, Ella."

"I know. I was there."

"The assassination."

"Why are you telling me this?"

"Because this is my life. This is who I am—"

"When forced."

"I don't hesitate to do what is necessary."

"To save lives."

"I ordered the murder of five people," he repeats. "Why are you okay with this, Ella?"

"Because some people are built for this kind of life—like you are. Because I'm my father's daughter, and you're your father's son."

"Your father could not have wanted this life for you."

"My father wanted me to be fearless."

"I told you on the porch that proposing to you was selfish. I wanted you with me. That's all that was on my mind."

"Wanted? As in past tense? I didn't decline."

"This is where I should tell you that proposal is void, past tense." His fingers flex at my waist. "This is where I told myself that loving you means getting you the hell out of here. This is where I promised myself I wouldn't be selfish."

"Kayden—"

"But I'm still the same selfish bastard who proposed this afternoon, Ella. I don't want to let you go. I want you. I need you. I didn't want to, and I still don't, because it would destroy me to lose you. I want to convince you that you belong here."

"I was convinced the moment I met you, Kayden. We were strangers, yet you were familiar and right."

He repeats what he'd said to me on the phone in Italian.

"What does that mean?" I ask.

"You belong with me, and I'm not going to let go of you."

There's something odd about the way he says that. "Why would you have to let go of me?"

"You're CIA. Covert—even more than your father was. As in, part of an elite group most of the agency doesn't even know exists. My contact wouldn't tell me the name of the group, if he even knew it. They recruited you right out of high school and paid for your college. Apparently your father had used every CIA exam in existence to train you, and they located those when he died."

I inhale, memories of my father timing me while I took quizzes filling my mind. "How do you know this?"

"I have a contact here in Italy. A guy named Trigger. He's hard to reach, which he says is because he's retired, though I'm doubtful that's true. He didn't know your father, but he knew of him. And he knew how to get information on you that no one else could."

I search his face, and suddenly, his intensity, his edgy dark mood, has me worried. "I know you, Kayden, and there's more to this. Tell me. Just say it and get it over with."

twelve

What I know," he says, tangling his fingers in my hair, "is that your instant worry over being CIA is why I wanted it confirmed. And it is now, but the last damn thing I want to talk about is the CIA. What I want is to be clear: this changes nothing. We are not divided or in danger. We're okay."

"Tell me you know that as certainly as you know that I'm CIA."

"Yes, sweetheart," he says. "We are absolutely okay. In fact, we're perfect."

"I want to embrace those words," I say, "but the CIA reminds me of my father, and my father reminds me of blood and death—and those things are far from perfect."

"But *we are perfect*, Ella," he repeats. "And I won't let you forget that." His mouth slants over mine, his lips warm, his tongue warmer, his body hot against mine: passionate, deep, a demand and a caress in every stroke. "You're mine," he declares, his voice soft yet fierce. "You're marrying me, and yes,

I'm *telling you* that. This time, fear and worry don't win. They don't get to wake up with you every day. I do."

Emotion charges though me with that declaration, jolting me with the realization that I was reverting back to this afternoon, and for someone who doesn't let fear win, I was then. I am now. But before I can say this, he's kissing me again, and the taste of him is all dark torment and a deep, ravishing hunger for some unnamed thing I still manage to know and understand so very well. It's about pain, loss, the need for control those things create in him, and perhaps in me. But there's more. There is need. There is decisiveness. There is a certainty that I'm right for him, and him for me, things that I made him doubt today and never want him to doubt again. But he doesn't. With each swipe of his tongue, he tells me that he rejects a life without me and wants the same from me.

Desperate to give him that, I shove against him, tearing my mouth from his. "I'm not going there again, Kayden. And really, truly, I was never mentally or emotionally anywhere but here with you. I choose you and I choose us. I will *always* choose us."

His eyes darken, then heat. "Then you'll marry me?"

"I thought you had already decided for me?"

"*Will* you marry me, Ella?" he asks with a gravelly quality to his voice.

"Yes," I whisper, so many emotions welling inside me that I'm trembling. "A million times over, yes."

His lashes lower, relief showing in the way his shoulders ease, the way his expression softens, telling me that this amazing, powerful man was that on edge over me, confirming what I'd suspected. I hurt him today. "Kayden—"

I never finish the sentence. His fingers tunnel into my hair and his mouth slants over mine again, tongue licking, caressing, tasting, his hands now at my waist, moving, touching, and suddenly it's just not the time for words. I need what he does, what I feel and sense he craves. Body against body. Passion meeting passion. And I stop holding back. I meet his kiss with a demand of my own, with hunger. I savor and use his touch, his taste, to try to drive away the fear that lives inside me, the fear that I can't deny. Not when it's what drove my hesitation earlier today, not when it haunts my every waking moment. Fear of losing him. Fear of this being our last kiss, our last touch, our last taste. It has me tugging his shirt up, urging him to remove it. It has me pressing my hands to his warm skin. He feels the same; it's on his lips. It's in the way he tears away my clothes while I tear away his. And when our clothes lie on the floor, he gazes at me for several intense, emotionally charged moments that I swear steal my breath, and then as I've become accustomed to, he scoops me up and starts walking.

I curl into him, my hand settling on his chest, his heart thundering beneath my palm. Because of me. This man, who I called beautiful, who I thought was too perfect to be real, is affected by me in every way that I am by him. All the emotions, all the desire I feel, I don't even question him sharing. Nor do I discount what a gift it is for two people to share that same intense reaction to one another. Or what it is like to feel safer with him than alone. I never thought I'd ever feel that—and with that realization, splintered pieces of the past, the damaged parts of my life that formed that opinion, promise to reveal themselves.

He settles me on the mattress, the sweet weight of his body on mine, his hips spreading my legs, the thick pulse of his erection between my thighs. His elbows frame my face, his lips close, his breath a warm trickle on my mouth and cheek. And then it happens, the way it happened that very first night together. We linger there, breathing together, being together, feeling every inch of each other where we touch, and where we soon will touch. Slowly, he pulls back, those blue eyes of his hot with desire, with love. They meet mine and I am naked, inside and out, in every way with this man.

He rolls with me, settling us on our sides facing each other, his hand cupping my backside, his shaft settling between my thighs. "No spankings," he says. "Nothing to prove, Ella. No point to make. Just us." His lips brush mine, a seduction and a tease that still manages to be a promise. No, many promises that manage to be both erotic and romantic. Sexy and sweet. And then he is kissing me again, a slow, sensual slide of his tongue against mine, which I feel in every part of me as his fingers lightly caress my nipple, then the side of my breast.

I moan with the sensations rolling through me, with the way he feels so much a part of me, the way I know he wants to please me, to love me. Things no other man has ever made me feel. Even before I knew my past, I knew Kayden was different, a part of me in ways I didn't understand. His hand slides down to my hip, his lips trailing my jaw, finding their way to my lips. "Where do you want me to touch you?"

"Everywhere, please," I whisper. "But right now I just want you inside me." I can feel him grow harder between my thighs, and I grow wetter. "I need to be that way with you right now."

"You won't get any resistance from me, sweetheart," he promises, lifting my leg to his hip, his teeth giving my lip a gentle tug, his tongue licking a soothing, seductive line over my bottom lip before he presses inside me.

My breath lodges in my throat, my fingers flexing into his shoulders with the feel of him stretching me and slowly inching deeper and deeper, until we are fully connected, bodies melded together.

"Is this what you needed?" he asks, with that low, gravelly sexiness in his voice.

"Yes," I say, barely finding my voice. "Oh, yes."

"Like I need you, Ella." He cups my backside, pulling me more snugly against him. "You understand that, right? I *need you.*"

"I need you, too, Kayden," I whisper, and he swallows my words, his mouth coming down on mine, hot with a demand that says "you are mine, you belong with me." And he belongs with me. It is a powerful taste and feeling and I press against him, trying to get closer, to get more of everything and anything that is this man.

Then comes the welcome squeeze of my backside, followed by a deep, intense thrust of his body into mine. I gasp and then pant into his mouth where our lips have parted, my fingers stroking the rough stubble on his jaw. And what follows is this sultry dance of bodies, moving, touching, melding together. It is perfect, and yet Kayden proves that not even perfection is enough with him. There will never be enough of anything with this man.

It is slow, sexy, romantic, and erotic. And yet we aren't wild and frenzied, although I love wild and frenzied. That would end too soon. There's just this savoring of each moment between us that creates this burn and ache in every part of me. But it is too good not to take me to that sweet spot that's the edge of release, where I'm about to tumble over that edge. "Kayden," I warn, "I'm—"

"No," he orders, no longer moving, no longer giving me those seductive strokes of his cock. "Not yet."

I swallow hard and bury my face in his shoulder, breathing deeply, calming my body. He must know the moment I've succeeded, because only then does he kiss my neck and whisper in my ear, "I get to own your orgasm for the rest of my life."

Kayden Wilkens announcing he owns my orgasm isn't exactly the way to prevent me from having one. "Careful," I murmur, tilting my head back to look at him. "Or you'll own it right now."

He laughs, a low, sexy sound that strokes along my nerve endings, the sound a promise that I'm about to be right back on the edge any moment now. Kayden must know it too, because he doesn't start moving again. He kisses my neck, teases my nipples, and scrapes his teeth on my shoulder. And then finally, finally, the slow, seductive sway of our bodies begins again.

Twice we repeat this process, starting and stopping, but there's a point where we both cave to the inevitable, and he promises, "We have all night for repeats," before he thrusts us both into oblivion, a place where pleasure and forever live, but nothing else can survive. A place we linger even after the storm of pleasure has become the calm sea of its aftermath, holding each other. Breathing with each other.

"I'd better get you a towel," he finally murmurs, dragging my head back and kissing me before he pulls out of me and disappears.

I inhale and somehow, of all the things I could remember in this blissful moment, the words *You're CIA* are the ones that come to me. But I shove away the million questions I still have about his meeting and this Trigger person. Kayden matters right now. What happened this afternoon matters right now. Remembering that moment when he'd walked out of the office, leaving behind jagged, broken emotions, and fixing it. That's what comes first.

Kayden reappears, now wearing his jeans low on his hips, sans underwear, offering me the towel.

I accept it and as he takes my arm, helping me sit up, the chill of the stone walls has me shivering. "For you," Kayden says, indicating his shirt in his hand. "Because it's cold in here and I like you in my shirt."

Those words and the look in his eyes warm me even before he sits down and slips the shirt over my head. I settle it over my body, the material soft, while I'm quite aware of it having been next to his hard body. Like I just was. Like I want to be again. "Thank you," I murmur.

"Thank me by going to bed in my shirt every night for the rest of our lives."

And just like that, we're in the place I wanted us to be,

staring at each other, the air pulsing with unspoken words I'm ready to voice. "You do know that there was never a moment when I doubted wanting to marry you, right? And that nothing in today's meeting was ever going to change that. If you really believed that, why did you ask me to marry you?"

"When you hesitated over my proposal, it made me take a step back and ask myself if I was wrong about what you felt and what I thought—"

"Don't say that," I say. "You were not wrong."

"No," he says confidently, "I wasn't. But regardless of understanding your reason for the hesitation, when a man asks a woman to marry him, he wants a yes."

"I'm sorry, Kayden. I handled today horribly wrong." I inhale and let it out. "And the truth is, if I'm honest with myself and you right now, as ironic and wrong as it is, when you started to doubt us, it hurt."

"There was never any doubt, sweetheart. I explained where my head was. And like I said, I'm a selfish bastard when it comes to you. I'm owning up to that. I want you here, despite all the risks that are part of The Underground."

"Don't say you're selfish. Because how am I not selfish, if I bring danger to you with Neuville hunting me? Or if I'm CIA—"

"You are CIA," he corrects.

"Then what about the danger I might bring from that? The point is that if you keep saying you're selfish for marrying me, then I see where that leads. If something happens to me, you'll say it was because you were selfish—and you can't. Because if I die, Kayden, I promise you I will have fought hard, taken someone with me, and enjoyed every moment I had with you. You have to promise me you'll remember that. You have to, or you know what? I won't marry you. Because I won't—"

He cups the back of my head and kisses me. "You're marrying me."

"I know," I say. "But promise me that you won't say you're selfish, or even think it."

He doesn't promise. He holds me there for several beats and then releases me and stands, leaning toward me and pressing his fists into the mattress and meeting my stare. "I'm going to be protective."

"That's understandable, since one mob boss killed your family and another one is after me. But eventually promise me that we can work together and get there."

"We're going to fight," he warns.

"That's okay, because I'll win."

His sexy, oh so talented lips curve. "You have a lot to learn," he teases, "but I'll teach you." I laugh and shake my head while he straightens and offers me his hand. "Let's go to the kitchen. I'm starving, and we have a lot to talk about." I give him a tentative look and slide my hand into his, and he notices. "We're just catching up on everything for the day. That's what husbands and wives do."

"Husband," I say softly.

"Wife," he says softly.

I haven't missed the fact that he hasn't let go of his self-proclaimed title of "selfish," and I fear for how he'd deal with my death. But we have plenty of time to work on a remedy for that, since I don't plan on dying.

"Come on," he says, helping me off the bed.

My gaze catches on his new Rolex, and I hate that it's pulled me from our sexy, romantic mood.

My hand comes down on it and he turns to face me. "You want to know about the watch given to Carlo."

"Yes. Was it Niccolo?"

"I didn't ask him."

"What? Why?"

"Because as I was standing in front of him, he made a comment that reminded me that he is a desperate, dying man. If he didn't send it, it will make him feel his brother is moving faster than he is. He'll push you for the necklace, and who knows what that will mean."

I give a slow nod. "Yes. I believe he would. Thank God you thought of that."

"But on that same note," Kayden says, "I think that is exactly why it could be he who did this. He needs you to feel the urgency that he does to find the necklace. Scaring you and worrying me could be a strategy."

"That works for Neuville as well," I point out. "Would Niccolo really think of the watch being a trigger for me?"

"Would Neuville?"

My mind goes to a memory of me tied up, of him looking at that watch and setting a deadline. *One hour. Then I'll come for you.* "Yes. He would. I want to believe it's not him, but he's the one who would know what my reaction would be to Carlo's watch."

"They both have spies inside each other's operations. They know each other well. If Neuville favors that watch—"

"He does. He makes notice of it often."

"Then remember that Niccolo is highly intelligent and manipulative. And Matteo found a link between the customer who gave Carlo the watch and Alessandro."

"Who could be working for both brothers."

"Yes," he confirms, "and even as we speak, Matteo is trying to find a path that connects Alessandro, the watch, and one of the two brothers. In the meantime, we assume it's the more dangerous of the two."

"Which means we assume I was right: Garner Neuville is coming for me."

"No," Kayden says, his hands settling at my waist. "That would make us victims, sweetheart, and we are not victims. This is war, and we will win. He's not coming for us. We're going for him." He brushes a lock of hair behind my ear. "Let's go eat and plan our enemies' demise. Or our wedding. Whatever you want."

What I want is to turn back time, hold that gun to Neuville's head again, and shoot him. Because I fear that lost moment will be my greatest regret and loss.

∞

Ten minutes after Kayden and I use the words *wife* and *husband* for the first time, I've pulled on black leggings under his shirt. He's now wearing a plain white shirt that hugs his muscles to perfection, the way I plan to again before we sleep. Both of us wear warm UGG slippers and we've made our way to the kitchen, where he's doing a scavenger hunt in the fridge and I'm making coffee. For reasons I don't analyze, despite my earlier urgency I'm not eager to dive into the topic of Trigger and the CIA, but there's plenty else to talk about anyway.

"Any word on Gallo?" I ask, flipping on the pot and getting the brew started so it will be ready when we've finished eating.

"He boarded that plane to Milan," Kayden says. "He also booked a flight back here in two days, so this plan to get him out of town for a while didn't work."

"What did Niccolo say about the threat to Gallo's sister?"

"I changed my mind about discussing that particular topic," he says, removing a plate of sandwiches from the fridge, shutting the door, and motioning to the table where we've already set up plates, bottled water, and a fruit salad.

"I don't understand," I say, claiming a seat. "Why?"

"Niccolo doesn't like to be crossed," he says, sitting next to me. "He'll kill Alessandro if we aren't careful, and we need him as our fall guy for the death of Neuville and his men."

"I see." I watch as he sets a croissant sandwich on each of our plates. "That makes sense, but what do we do about Gallo?"

He opens a bottle of water and takes a deep drink. "For starters," he says, setting it down, "Chief Donati is going to give Gallo reason to believe the threat came from a criminal Gallo took down last year, who later escaped and disappeared." He takes a bite of his sandwich and motions for me to eat.

"Well, since Niccolo claims to have Donati under control, that seems like a smart move. So why does 'for starters' suggest there's more to this plan?"

"In premise it *is* a smart move," he agrees, setting down his sandwich, "but Alessandro is obviously looking for a way to use Gallo against me. He'll go after Gallo the minute he's back here—and considering the dangerous direction this has now taken, I'm sure Sasha has figured out that her involvement is just too risky."

"She has," I confirm, "but what about having her go to Milan and try to keep him there until things settle down a bit?"

"Considering Gallo's in volatile state, I'd just as soon cut the jugular and kill any power Alessandro has to corrupt him."

"That sounds like a plan already formed."

"Ultimately, Gallo's a good cop. A bitter pain in the ass, but still a good cop. We'll just tell him some version of the truth."

"He hates you too much to see the truth, Kayden."

"I'll have Adriel and Sasha talk to him."

"That would be weird," I say. "Sasha's been sleeping with Gallo, and she and Adriel have more than the casual fling they pretend exists. Gallo might get that vibe, and it could turn him in the wrong direction on this."

He arches a brow. "Do they, now? That's news to me."

I nod. "They haven't told me that, but it's in the way they look at each other and interact."

"I'll trust you on that, so we'll cut both of them out of this. I'll prep Nathan to talk to Gallo when he returns." He studies me a moment, lacing his fingers together on the table. "Trigger told me nothing more than what I've told you. I promise."

"I didn't ask."

"You didn't have to. Did that wall of memories you created in the closet help you remember anything?"

"I just put it up, so no. Not yet, but I do feel like I'm starting to form real memories about things that aren't requiring flashbacks."

"Anything you feel is important?"

"Well, it's not the location of the necklace, or any time or place that places me as a CIA agent." My brow furrows. "Actually, maybe that's not completely true." I shove my plate aside and rest my arms on the table. "Aside from the combat training memory I had, there's one of David back in Paris. As I told you, we had a fight and he left. I slammed the door and leaned against it. I ripped off the necklace, and then scolded myself for playing my character too deeply."

Kayden's eyes sharpen. "Are you saying he was an assignment?"

"No," I say, certainty in my reply, "yet I see why that memory makes you assume that." Frustrated that I can't remember more, I push to my feet and walk to the coffeepot, removing two cups from above the sink. And right when I reach for the cups, I remember more about that night with David. I've just ripped the necklace off, and I'm staring at how truly stunning the stones are. It's beautiful, and I ripped it off, and for what? This is a character I'm playing. I suck in air with that thought and then shut my eyes, and silently plead with my mind to give me more.

❧❧

I squat beside the necklace and reach for it, noticing the piece of paper hanging out of it. Snatching it up, I note the address written on it. "Damn it," I murmur. I'd already decided he was a dud assignment, a man mixed up with someone else, and I'd be pulled off it any day now, yet clearly I was wrong. He's using me, just like I'm using him. I stare at the piece of paper, obligated to investigate, but I'm not doing it right now. I'm here not for him or for my job. I'm here to follow up on a name and address I found in my father's copy of Carrie *by* Stephen King.

❦

My eyes pop open. "I was wrong. He *was* an assignment."

"You sound more certain than ever," Kayden says, stepping beside me.

I face him, both of us resting our elbows on the granite surface, while I quickly recap my memory. "I thought of him as an assignment, Kayden, and that explains why I'd jump all over the crazy drunk proposal. That's how that happened: he was drunk and he proposed. I was like—great, Paris. I need to go to Paris, and the CIA won't be suspicious. They assigned me this guy."

His jaw sets and he turns my back against the counter, his hands coming down on either side of me. "Answer every question I'm about to ask you with the first thing that pops into your head. If David was an assignment, why not call the CIA for help when he died?"

"I was looking into my father's death, and I wasn't sure I wasn't being set up."

"Why?"

"It was a gut instinct."

"But you were desperate to escape Neuville. You never called them at all?"

"Once, from an untraceable line. But the number I was to call in to wasn't working. That's when I surmised that someone at the CIA was working with Neuville, hence why no one had come to save me or kill me."

"Where'd you hide the necklace?"

"I don't know yet, but I keep thinking about this one chocolate shop in Paris. I went there that night. It has to be there or close to there, and I don't know why I just can't remember this."

"There's something your mind still thinks you can't handle."

This is not an idea I welcome. I've relived my father's murder and I keep reliving what Neuville did to me. What could possibly be worse?

thirteen

sara

I t's raining.

The bed is warm.

Chris's hard body wrapped around mine is even warmer.

I can hear the storm pelting the windows of our master bedroom, see the dark sky beyond the panes peeking through the small part in the curtains. I've come to know that rain in Europe is not like rain in the United States. Here in Paris, when they say it's going to rain, they mean a steady, all-day-and-all-night drenching that you cannot escape. I've also come to know that when Chris holds me this way, with his leg tangled around mine, he can't escape the tragedies of his past or the demons they've created. Demons that once would have driven him to a dangerous need to use physical pain to drive away the emotional pain.

Often that need delivered him to that damn club that supposedly caters to the elite of Paris with darker hungers. Where the owner, that monster of a woman, Isabella, happily helped feed Chris's need to escape reality with whatever punishment he ordered her to deliver. Though in most cases, Isabella doesn't need to be ordered to do such horrid things, but Chris never gives away control. In whatever role she plays, though, Isabella thrives on delivering pain, and ironically, gut-wrenchingly, considering my worries for Ella, that club—and therefore Isabella herself—is the one thing that Chris and Garner Neuville share in common. But Chris is ultimately all about control, and that means he wants to please and protect me, sometimes to the extreme. Chris would do anything for me, as I would for him.

But Neuville is no bad-boy version of Chris. He's the mob, and the stories that have trickled to us say that he's brutal to the point of evil, in both the bedroom and boardroom. Stories that have kept me up at night, worrying about Ella.

Right now, though, what keeps me awake is discovering that we've inadvertently involved this organization called The Jackals in Ella's life. What if Kayden is Ella's safe haven, as Chris is to me, and me to Chris, and in my desire to protect her, I've stolen that away?

∞ *ella* ∞

It's raining.

The fireplace is glowing amber.

Those are the first two things I think when I blink awake in the dark bedroom, Kayden's hard, warm body wrapped around me from behind, the fireplace glowing in front of me. Safe. Warm. *Loved.* I am no longer alone, and neither is he.

And we both were alone, even when we were with other people. He nuzzles my neck and pulls me tighter against his body. The dark room, the thrumming of the storm on the window, and him make for a seductive combination. I love the rain in Europe. It's eternal, and it soothes all the hot spots in my mind. I shut my eyes and savor the perfection of the moment. I'm safe in a way that's indescribable with Kayden, in a way that has nothing to do with the physical. I can't lose this or him. Garner Neuville will not take this from me.

If he tries . . .

The next time I open my eyes, the darkness has become more of a dull, light haze cast by the storm, and Kayden is no longer in bed with me. Certain he hasn't gone far, I roll over and find no note, which means I'm right. He's probably in the kitchen fielding calls for Underground business and drinking coffee. I glance at the clock. Nine o'clock. Oh, yes. He is most certainly in the kitchen. Stretching, I smile with the realization that I'm still wearing his shirt, drawing in a deep, yummy whiff of his spicy scent before climbing out of the bed and pushing my feet into my slippers.

Fully intending to join Kayden for a caffeine fix, I hurry into the bathroom and take care of things like brushing my teeth and my brown hair, which I dare to imagine red again. Maybe, just maybe, I'm close to being me again. Just one mobster to kill, and a few other problems to solve, and I'll be a redhead again. No matter how I try to convince myself brown is beautiful—and it is—it's just not me.

Stepping into the closet, I grab my leggings from last night, pull them on under Kayden's shirt, and turn my attention to my new memory wall. A few seconds turn into a minute, but apparently memories require coffee, because I get nothing this morning. Except . . . my gaze lands on that chocolate shop, Hermés Le Chocolat, and I press two fingers on it. "Is this where you are, little butterfly?"

I tear the page off the wall to show it to Kayden and start to turn, only to have my gaze land on my ballet slippers. In my mind, I see my father in my bedroom, holding one of them, talking to me about my lessons. It's not a good or a bad memory. It's just a memory.

I feel Kayden before I see him. "Morning," he says in that low, gravelly, sexy tone he sometimes has, and I always love.

I pick up one of the ballet slippers and turn to find him in pajama bottoms, a snug white T-shirt, and slippers, his rumpled hair and shadowed jaw deliciously masculine.

"'Well, honey,'" I say, imitating my father's low voice, "'I guess if you have to do this dance thing, at least they'll never expect a ballerina to kick their ass.'"

His lips curve. "I take it that's a quote from your father."

"Yes," I say, setting the slipper back on the shelf. "That was right before he handed me a quiz on types of ammunition."

He laughs. "What else would a father quiz his daughter on?" He folds his arms in front of that broad, impressive chest and leans on the door frame. "Speaking of ammunition: Blake Walker. I want to know what he knows. And I want to be sure our men guarding Sara don't conflict with his. I arranged to bring him here."

"Here? Can't he be tied to Sara that way? Should we allow him to be seen here?"

"Exactly why I don't want us in public with him. Adriel is doing a covert pickup. And he'll enter the castle in the car, out of sight."

"Of course," I say. "Why would I even question you having thought of this?"

"Better to bring it up than not," he says, proving yet again why I feel he's a great leader. He makes decisions. He makes demands. But he is confident in himself and in his role to listen to others and welcome input. "I do miss things."

"Doubtful," I say, "but you know I'm still going to give my two cents."

His eyes warm, and while yes, there is a hint of that sin and sex he does so well, there is a different kind of warmth I decide is even better. It's trust and friendship. When he glances at the piece of paper in my hand, he asks, "What's that?"

"This is the chocolate shop I keep remembering," I say, offering him the paper.

He reaches for it and looks at the page, then at me. "I know where it's located." He folds the printout and sticks it in the pocket of his pajama bottoms. "You think the necklace is there?"

"I can't imagine there would be a place to hide it there, but I went there with it in my possession. Going there, when it's possible, might be the final trigger to unlock my memory."

"I can at least go there and search the place when I'm in Paris."

"When you're in Paris," I repeat, my gut twisting with that idea. "I hate you going without me."

"You know—"

"I know what you're going to say. Sasha said it, too. But consider this: I could be used as a good distraction. I—"

He reaches for me and pulls me to him. "No. Not this. You can help plan everything, and be involved in every way except putting yourself in his reach."

"Can we at least—"

He cups my head and kisses me. "No. If that means we fight, we fight."

My hand flattens on his chest. "I'm really not feeling like fighting with you, Hawk, but I reserve the right to change that at any minute."

A low rumble of sexy masculine laughter escapes his lips. "Duly noted, future wife of The Hawk. We need to get you a ring."

"You choose it. That will make it special."

"I have something in mind."

"Then that's what I want."

He gives me the tender, warm look that defies the dark, hard parts of him, and makes him even sexier and more alluring. "Blake won't be here until this afternoon," he says. "We have plenty of time for you to grab those slippers and use your studio upstairs. You can show me your moves."

The suggestion is unexpected, as is the jolt it delivers. "No," I say, that jolt turning to a squeeze in my heart. "It reminds me of my mother, and right now, I need to just deal with my father. I'll revisit that other part of me later—but I wouldn't mind hitting the gym."

"I want to see you dance," he says, his voice a gentle, stubborn prod.

"You think I'm hiding from something."

"You haven't resisted the idea of dancing before now, sweetheart. Something else is going on. I think you're afraid that giving yourself permission to do something you love, just because you love it, makes you weak. It doesn't."

He's hit a nerve I didn't know existed, and it's far closer to the truth than the answer I'd given us both a few moments before.

"When was the last time you danced?" he asks. "*Really* danced?"

Okay, maybe there is truth to both answers. Because my chest tightens and I look to the ceiling, fighting an unexpected wave of emotion. "A little here, when I was alone one night."

"Before that?"

"The day my mother died," I grudgingly admit, refocusing on him. "And I haven't relived losing her yet. I guess there are more things my mind is hiding from me than I realized."

He gives me a three-second intense look. "Would she approve of you turning your back on ballet?"

"She'd roll over in her grave."

"And how long has it been since your mother died?"

"Years," I say, a firmer answer coming to me. "Right after my college graduation."

Those blue eyes of his fill with challenge and mischief. "In other words, you don't remember how to dance."

He's goading me and I don't want it to work, but I grab the slippers anyway. "I promise you, I can handle these slippers as well as I handle a gun any day."

"How would I know that? You won't show me."

"Fine," I say. "Let's go."

He smiles, and when this man really smiles, it's devastatingly sexy. And before I know his intentions, I'm over his shoulder, his hand on my ass, and we're moving.

I inhale his spicy, almost woodsy scent that's so addictive. "It's a good thing you smell so great, because that's the only thing making me forgive you for making the blood rush to my head."

Rather than putting me down, he simply says, "I'll walk faster."

And that proves true. In a blink we are in the hallway and making our way up the narrow wooden stairs that lead to a small passage and an office halfway to the left. Continuing onward and upward, we enter the gym. "I'm seeing spots, Kayden," I murmur, and moments later he sets me down in the middle of my newly finished dance studio.

I sway and he catches me at the waist, his big hands strong and welcome. "We really have to talk about this habit of you carrying me everywhere," I tell him.

"I don't do it often enough?"

I laugh. "That's it," I tease. "You need to carry me everywhere."

"Careful what you ask for," he teases back, and I feel his mischievous, light mood becoming contagious. "Put your slippers on and let's see you dance," he orders, because he can't help but give commands, but he doesn't let me go. He glances around the rectangular room with the new hardwood floor that he, Carlo, and Adriel installed over the old flooring for me just last week. "You need a bench to sit on and mirrors in here. We're still a work in progress." He refocuses on me. "I'll hold onto you so you can change into your ballet slippers."

I grab his arm for balance and make the change, staring down at my pink-covered feet, memories exploding in my mind. Dancing. More dancing. "I auditioned for Juilliard."

"What?"

"I auditioned." The memory is sharper now and I wait for some emotion to hit me, but it just feels like a fact.

"And?"

One of the questions we'd wanted answered is my answer. "The CIA showed up."

"Did you make it into Juilliard?"

"I don't know. The CIA withdrew my application the minute I said yes to them."

"Why'd you say yes?"

That sharpness becomes focused, and I know why I'm recalling this again now. "I was never a dancer after I killed my first two men."

"Your father's murderers."

"Yes."

"How do you feel about that?"

"Oddly unemotional. Joining the CIA appealed to me because they were an extension of my father. I think I wanted a family unit. Little did I know that's not how the CIA operates, but I made it work."

He doesn't comment, but I know he gets it. No family. No one to worry about. Until there was us. "Do you remember anything else?" he asks.

"No, but I will." There is confidence in my tone. "That's becoming evident."

"It is. For now, though"—he kisses my forehead—"be a dancer."

A bubble of excitement fills me. "I'm eager to try out my new slippers."

"Good. I'm eager to see if you really *can* handle them like Annie."

"Game on," I say, accepting the challenge. "But I need music."

"I have about every song released in the States in the past five years, as well as the biggest hits by decades. They're programmed into the panel in the corner." He walks that way. "Any idea what you want?"

Feeling determined to steal any power Neuville still has, my answer is quick. "'Take Me to Church,'" I say, choosing a song that we both know reminds me of that monster.

Kayden returns to me instantly, his hands settling at my waist. "No. You will not dance to a song that reminds you of Neuville raping you. This place is about you having something special for you. Should you invite me here on occasion, I would love to join you. But this is your place, our new life, and he doesn't get to be a part of it. Understand?"

In this moment, Kayden slides a little deeper into my soul. This man who can be hard and cold should he need to be, yet so very tender and gentle. "The many shades of dark and light that you are, Kayden, is so damn sexy and perfect."

His eyes soften, and those sensual, sometimes punishing

lips curve. "I could say the same of you, sweetheart. Now. What music do you want?"

I shove his chest. "You go stand somewhere. I'll pick it." He hesitates. "*Not* that song."

He smiles, obviously pleased with my eagerness, and so am I. I haven't felt this light-spirited in a very long time and I want to enjoy every moment. I walk to the electronic panel and find it's pretty close to having the entire iTunes library installed. I scan my choices and smile when I see Jason Aldean's "Just Gettin' Started," deciding to connect with the Texas boy Kayden is at his core.

I turn it on and move back to the center of the room, finding him leaning on the wall, hearing the song begin: "*I knew the minute that I picked you up, it was gonna be a wild ride.*" "That doesn't sound like ballerina music," he says.

"The ballerina gets to decide what ballerina music is," I say, feeling pretty darn playful.

I lift my arms and try out the first position, my eyes meeting Kayden's, a smile mixed with heat in the depth of his. I go to my toes, and oh, how I love this. Toes. Arms. First position. Second position. Plie. I am back. I start dancing, falling into my old steps far more easily than expected, and throwing in some new moves. Giving a sexy shake of my hips here and there, and throwing Kayden an equally sexy look over my shoulders.

"That doesn't look like ballet," he accuses.

"The best dancers have a creative side," I say, moving around the floor, and as my confidence grows, so do my sexy little moves, and before long we're having a great time, both of us singing and laughing. I really love that he's singing too, that he lets down his guard with me. That he can let himself be my man, not The Hawk, right now. It's just us having fun, and there's not a flashback or inhibition in sight. I love that, too.

I go all out and present him with my backside, pull up his shirt, and dare complete silliness. I twerk. I have no idea how I know how to twerk. Probably the kids at school, but I seem to be good at it.

"You can't do that to Jason Aldean," he objects. "It's just wrong, though it looks very right when you do it."

I face him, both of us laughing, and knowing the lyrics coming up, I close the space between us to stand in front of him just as the words I'm waiting for fill the air: *"Ain't even had a taste of your love."* "I haven't had a proper taste," I dare.

"What is proper?" he asks, dark hunger in his blue eyes, and I suspect my green eyes are dancing with the same.

My hands settle on his hips, then find their way under his shirt to shove it upward. He rewards me by pulling it over his head, his delicious muscles flexing as he tosses it aside, while my palms have already pressed to warm skin and hard, ripped abs. The instant he looks at me again, I slowly lower myself to my knees.

He gives me this heavy-lidded stare that is all sex and hunger and that does all kinds of crazy things to my body, warming it all over, driving my motivation, my desire for him. My lips find the line right above his pajama bottoms and I trail my tongue back and forth, while my hand lightly strokes over his already thick shaft through the thin cotton material. Just the idea of pleasing him this way, of him completely letting go for me, as I have for him, has my nipples aching and my sex clenching.

But before I can lead him down that road his hands come down on my shoulders and he lifts me to my feet, turning me and pressing me against the wall. "We're equals," he says, snagging the hem of my shirt, his shirt. "Which means you have on too many clothes." He caresses the cotton slowly up my body, his hands now warm on my skin, branding me in a way only he can, his touch radiating through me. My breasts are heavy, nipples tight, and my thighs slick.

Finally, he pulls the shirt over my head, tossing it aside, and while my unbound breasts had not been ideal for dancing, the hot swipe of his stare, followed by his hands, prove them quite ideal. He strokes my nipples, tugs and then thumbs them until I am panting, aching. Then, he repeats exactly what I had done moments before. His eyes find mine, and he lowers himself to one knee, anticipation burning through me.

"I wanted to do things to you," I say, wondering how I lost the chance to please him for once.

He gives me a steamy look. "You can. You will. I just can't stop thinking about how you taste." As if those words weren't enough to melt me, his lips find my belly, as mine had his, but there is no me pulling him to his feet. His tongue flickers, licks, teases. He takes his time. He builds anticipation that is killing me.

"Kayden," I plead, and demand.

This must be what he was waiting for, because he drags my leggings down my hips, and doesn't stop there. They are at my ankles and then over my ballet slippers in a few blinks. He tosses them away and then looks up at me, his hands wrapped over the pink ribbons at my ankles. "The slippers stay," he says, and when he looks at me, there's a message in his eyes that he wants me to read.

I think . . . he's telling me that the person I am when I dance stays with us. I'm not just an agent. And I have officially never been so willingly naked for any man, ever.

He begins trailing his palms up my calves, goose bumps rising in their wake, every inch seducing me, like he seduces me. But the moment he's at my thighs, about to touch me where I need him to touch me the most, the music changes. While it's changed several times before, this song, Tim McGraw's "Live Like You Were Dying" has a meaning that renders us immobile.

At any moment, we can die. Any moment, we can lose each other. We both freeze, our eyes locking and holding, the words speaking to us about past losses and fears of more to come: "I hope you get the chance to live like you're dying." That line, which is all about living right now in case you die tomorrow, jolts me. It must jolt Kayden, too, because he stands up, his hands tangling in my hair, his stare meeting mine, a million words in his eyes that all land in one silent place: I can't lose you.

A moment later he is kissing me and I am kissing him, and we are wild, hot, desperate. In stark contrast to last night's slow, seductive lovemaking we are all over each other, touching, licking, biting. And it isn't long until his pants are gone and he's lifting me, the thick, hard length of him pressing inside me, all the way inside me. He holds me. I hold him. All my weight is on him, our bodies melded close, my face in his neck, my nostrils inhaling that delicious scent of him I never want to stop smelling.

I lose everything but him, and this, and I don't even know where we start and end.

When it's over, he turns and leans me against the wall, and despite the fact that his legs have to be exhausted, he doesn't put me down. "No one is taking this from us, or taking you from me. You have my word."

"Don't do that to yourself," I warn again. "Don't put that pressure on yourself or us. Let's just spend every day like this. Let's live—"

"Like we're dying," he says, his forehead finding mine.

"Yes," I whisper, my fingers curling around his jaw. "Live like we're dying."

fourteen

After Kayden and I have showered, we both coinciden-tally dress in black jeans, boots, and T-shirts. I'm not sure what that says about his mood, considering our amazing morning, but I'm shifting gears, moving from pink slippers to Warrior Princess, should I need to be her. And, I just want to be sure Blake Walker takes me seriously. He needs to hear what I say to him. He needs to protect Sara.

By noon we've joined Marabella in the kitchen and she is all about stuffing our faces with pancakes, and filling our cups with delicious frothy coffee.

"I need to hit the gym. I can't keep eating like this." I look at Kayden. "Maybe we should come up with a routine. We go in the morning before we do anything else?"

He sips his coffee, his gaze warm, a wayward strand of light hair brushing his brow. "A routine would be good."

"A routine for Kayden," Marabella says, hands on her ro-bust hips, and ironically, her dress a pale ballerina slipper pink.

"We could continue exactly as we did this morning," he offers, mischief in his voice.

"Did you work out this morning?" Marabella asks innocently, making my cheeks heat.

"We did," Kayden replies, winking at me. "A perfect way to start the day." His phone rings next to his plate and he grabs it, pushing his seat back. "Carlo."

I nod and he walks out of the room, which hits me as interesting. He never talks business in front of Marabella, so what are the lines he's drawn with her? What does she know and not know?

"Anything else before I leave?" Marabella asks. "I can swing by and clean up later."

"I'll do it," I say, eager to regain some privacy. "You've done enough."

"Are you sure?"

"Of course. Thank you for breakfast."

"Okay. If you don't get time, I'll be here tomorrow." She tilts her head. "You feel good?"

"Yes, good as new now. Well, except for a few holes in my memory."

"Did you talk to Nathan about that thing with the journal?"

"I did. He says these things are normal with amnesia. I'm improving, and that's what's important."

"That's good." She starts to turn away. "One thing. Giada really wants both of us to go shopping with her for her new place."

"When?"

"Friday."

Two days from now. I'm not sure I feel good about anyone going shopping this week, and Kayden and I need to talk about protecting Giada and Marabella. "I should know tomorrow if I can make it happen."

"It will make Giada so very happy. I won't tell her until we're certain, though."

"Sounds good," I say, watching her disappear, fairly certain we have to get her and Giada on lockdown for now.

I stand and carry the plates to the sink, taking care of the mess by the time Kayden returns.

"Carlo seems to have a solid handle on dealing with the aftermath of Alessandro's demise," he says, joining me on my side of the island and leaning against it. "We're going to sit down in the next few days and hammer it all out."

"What about Niccolo's second-in-command?" I ask, leaning against the counter directly across from him.

"The drug goes in his drink tonight, and he shouldn't wake up tomorrow."

I hug myself. "That's good," I say, though the word *good* chokes in my throat.

"Ella—"

"I don't need coddling, Kayden. I don't like calling death good, but sometimes it is. Sometimes monsters have to die."

"Monsters always have to die, sweetheart. Because if they're really monsters, they can't be saved."

"I know," I say. "Believe me, I know. And changing the subject: what can I say and not say in front of Marabella?"

"Anything that extends beyond basic hunting, keep to yourself."

"Enzo wasn't basic hunting."

"Enzo made a mistake while hunting," he reminds me.

"Should we get her and Giada under lock and key until this is over?"

"The last thing we want is Niccolo seeing us act suspiciously when his second dies. I have men watching both of them. Now, I'm changing the subject. Adriel tells me you pressed for Matteo to check the security system."

"I did. I still don't think I tore those pages from my journal."

"We'll spend tonight going through the security feed together."

"I'm glad you aren't discounting my concerns."

"There is nothing about anything you do, say, or think that invites me to discount any concern you can't shake." His cell phone buzzes with a text and he glances at the screen, then me. "Blake and Adriel just pulled into the garage."

He motions for me to follow and we head out of the kitchen.

"Isn't this earlier than expected?"

"Apparently, Blake called Adriel for help and needed an early pickup. He was being followed, and he didn't know the city well enough to ensure he broke free without support."

"We didn't even get time to talk about what to discuss with him," I say as we head down the stairs. "Is his wife with him?"

"She distracted the person following Blake, and stayed behind."

"Where are we meeting him?"

"Right here in the office," he says as we reach the foyer. "I don't want him getting the run of the castle." He looks at me. "Leave the necklace out of things, and the part where we dispose of our enemies. But to protect Sara, he needs to know that there's dirty CIA and the mob involved."

"Dirty CIA?"

"Yes. Someone set you and your father up." He punches the button on the wall and the door begins to lift.

A minute later, Adriel and Blake are standing in the archway. Today must be "black" day, because they're both wearing the uniform as well. Blake and Kayden lock stares, and I don't know what passes between them, but what concludes seems to be some sort of mutual respect, even if it's temporary. Adriel gives Kayden a nod, and then disappears. Kayden motions Blake into the tower and seals us inside.

"This is an absolutely fucking amazing place," Blake says as we move into the office.

Kayden simply motions him to the seating area, where Kayden and I sit on the couch.

Blake sits to my left, angling toward us and leaning forward, elbows on his knees. His intense brown eyes look at me. "Are you safe?"

"As safe as I ever am."

"What does that mean?"

"It means I'm not what I seem."

"Are you happy?"

"Yes."

"Do you need help?"

"Yes," I say. "I need to make sure Sara is safe."

"You have my attention, and my resources. My men are

the best of the best. Those with me on this trip are ex-FBI and ex-SEAL."

We tell him the story, including my fake life that brought me together with Sara. Blake asks a lot of good, thoughtful questions that do much to give me confidence in his ability to protect her. "All right, then," he says. "And I take it you aren't going to tell me what this is ultimately about, or how you plan to resolve it?"

"Not a chance in hell," Kayden says.

"Right to the fucking point," Blake says. "I respect that. Now. How long are Chris and Sara in danger?"

"We don't know that they are in danger," Kayden says. "But we want to keep it that way."

"I could get them on a plane out of Paris tonight," Blake says, "but that's going to get press, since Chris is headlining a huge charity event at the Louvre Saturday night."

"That's three days from now, counting Saturday," I say. "That's too long. I want them out of there."

"No," Kayden says. "If they skip that show, it tells Neuville that Sara is important to you. We don't want her getting on his radar, because once that happens she won't get off."

"Kayden, I don't like this," I say.

"Trust me, sweetheart. This is no different from not going on lockdown here. We need to act like all things are as usual."

"Sara's been on Neuville's radar in the past," Blake says. "He had her followed at one point, thinking she would lead him to Ella, and there was even a confrontation between Sara, Chris, and Neuville."

"When?" Kayden asks.

"Four months ago," Blake replies.

"Then we damn sure don't want to give him a reason to look at her again," Kayden says. "But if he's looked into her in the past, he could be doing it now, and he might well try to grab her. But he could do that in the States, when everyone's guard is down, too. At least here, you have your men and I've got a half dozen to help you."

"Are you suggesting we keep them in Paris until you resolve this?" Blake asks.

"No," Kayden says. "Get them on a plane Sunday morning. We'll ensure Neuville is distracted then. If all goes well, I'll contact you before you land and tell you this is over. But right now, you need to get back to Paris discreetly. I'll get you on a private jet that won't be traced. Don't connect Sara to Ella, and being here now could do that. Protect your client."

"I have men in Paris to protect Sara and Chris," he says. "My client wants me to protect Ella."

"I'm CIA, Blake," I say. "I can handle myself."

"Then I'm just a little extra backup," he offers.

I reach toward him, yank open his jacket, and take his gun.

"Fuck," he growls.

"I can protect myself," I say.

"I let you do that," he counters.

I offer him his gun. "You did not let me. Protect Sara."

He takes his gun and holsters it. "My client—"

"I'll pay you double what they're paying," Kayden states. "But you protect *them*—not Ella."

"Chris Merit's a billionaire, man," he says. "You don't want to pay me double."

"Double," Kayden repeats.

"I don't want your money," he says. "I know you operate on paydays, but I'm about what's right."

"What's right," I say, "is protecting them. Don't let Sara get hurt because of me."

He studies me for several beats. "All right. I'll go take care of her. But I do not look forward to the moment I tell Chris Merit what's going on. He's intense about protecting Sara."

"Good," I say. "If he wasn't, I'd be concerned."

"She's in good hands with Chris," he says, narrowing his stare on me. "She was never going to give up on you. She loves you."

"She probably won't after she finds out that everything about me is a lie."

"Your friendship is not a lie. I see that clearly. She will, too." He looks at Kayden. "What about The Jackals? How worried do I need to be about them?"

"If they show up, I wouldn't hold my gunfire," he says.

Blake gives him a long, hard stare. "Holy fuck. I hired them." He scrubs his jaw. "How do I get that ride to Paris?"

Kayden pulls his phone from his pocket and makes a couple of calls. Five minutes later we walk Blake to the garage, where Adriel waits by his Mercedes. Blake walks to the passenger door, but before he gets inside, he turns to me. "My father always told me, kill or be killed. Don't get killed, Ella." He disappears into the car, and Kayden and I watch them depart.

"What distraction is planned for Sunday?" I ask, facing Kayden.

"Saturday night, we'll make sure Alessandro gets a lead on

the necklace being in Paris," he says. "He'll get on a plane and go there. Sunday morning, we'll make sure Neuville not only finds out Alessandro stole from him, but that he's in Paris and he has the necklace. I'll also be in Paris."

"So Sunday is the day this all ends?"

"Yes. The minute I know Sara and Chris are gone, I'm ending this. Sunday is the day."

"I want to go with you."

"No. End of subject."

"Kayden, damn it—"

His hands come down on my shoulders and he pulls me to him. "I'm ending this, Ella. And then we're getting married." And any objection I might voice is lost as he kisses me soundly.

fifteen

ours after Blake's departure, Kayden and I are both in sweatpants and tees, sitting on the bed with several MacBooks in front of us as we take on the tedious process of looking for a security breach. Regardless of the work under way, Kayden and I are together, in our room, in our private space, and it's cozy, warm, and right. There are brushes of our hands and legs, kisses and laughter as we watch Marabella fret over the messes we've made. And neither of us says it, but there is a heaviness in the air, a fear that this weekend will not end well.

Finally, after several hours, all but done with our review with nothing to show for it, our laughter turns into his hand on my face and a shared, lingering kiss that does me in. I capture his hand. "Let me go with you. No one will have your back like I will. I'm trained. I'm lethal. Test me—"

"Ella," he breathes out, a gravelly quality to his voice.

"Kayden, please."

He turns us so that we're facing each other and holds my

hand. "I know how skilled you are. Blake Walker is a skilled ATF agent and far from a rookie, yet you made him look like one."

"Then take me with you."

"If you go with me, all I'll be thinking about is your safety."

"But you just said you know I have skills," I argue.

"This is a man who raped you, Ella. As it is, I'm personally involved. I want to make him suffer. I want to bring someone to his house and watch him get raped. But I won't. This isn't about me shutting you out of any operation that ever requires a fight. This is about this fight. I need to know you're safe. And while I told you I'm going to need some time to get over being protective, this particular case doesn't even count in the mix of things. It's a whole different beast. So I'm asking you to please listen to me on this, and not see it as me suffocating you, or having no faith in you, or—"

I press my lips to his, lingering there a moment as so many emotions expand between us. "I understand," I whisper, easing back to look at him. "It's going to be torture to wait for you, but I'll do it." My lashes lower and my throat thickens before I look at him again. "I'll do it."

"I'll come back to you," he promises. "But he never will. He *never* will."

"I believe you," I say, remembering my advice to myself: I have to make him stronger, not give him doubts. "You will win. I know that."

His phone rings and he grimaces. "Bad timing."

"No, it's business. It's about ending this. Take the call."

My response pleases him. I see this in the admiration in his eyes, which in turn pleases me. It also earns me a fast, hard kiss before he grabs his phone where it rests on the bed, answering it. In the meantime, I refocus on the computer screen and tab through more footage, laughing yet again as Marabella grimaces at one of our messes. Over and over today, she's entertained us without even knowing she's doing so. She ignores my journal every time she sees it, passing it by to worry over some dusty or dirty spot, more interested in cleaning and cooking than my inner thoughts.

"Everything is on target on Carlo's end," Kayden says after his call. "He's stirred buzz among the Paris Jackals that Alessandro stole from them and from Neuville, and our plan to have proof landing in the right hands at the right time still looks right on schedule."

"But can he do it without making it seem like a setup?"

"I didn't make him a Hunter for no reason, sweetheart," he says. "The magnificence that is Carlo is in his ability to manipulate people and situations." He glances at his shiny new Rolex, and I try not to think about that watch delivery. "It's four o'clock. I don't know about you, but those pancakes wore off a good hour ago."

"I'm starving, for sure," I say.

"We could raid the kitchen, but we're pretty comfortable here. Why don't I just bring us whatever I can find?"

"I'd like that," I agree, just as eager as he is to keep our private little escape alive and well.

He kisses my forehead, a tender act I've come to expect and cherish from him, before he heads toward the door, effortlessly graceful and powerful. I inhale and watch him disappear into the hallway, still bothered by how I've felt watched there, and now I just . . . don't. My lips thin and I turn back to the computer, but this seems almost useless. We've found nothing, not even an oddity in the film that might indicate a splicing. And the bathroom and closet have no cameras, so I might have torn the pages out there.

Still, this nagging feeling that something isn't right won't go away, and I start scanning footage again, finishing the last few screen shots we have to review, then starting all over again.

"I have something for you," Kayden says, drawing my attention back to the door, where I find him approaching with a book in his hand.

"That doesn't look edible."

"Not edible," he says, "but I do think you'll like it." He stops beside the bed and hands me what turns out to be a copy of the book *Carrie*, the same book my father had owned. "I thought it might help you remember more about your father and your past."

"I can't believe you have this. Thank you."

"Kevin was a die-hard King fan, and he was a big reader. He always said that a good Hunter was an educated Hunter, and that meant reading often and broadly, fiction and nonfiction." He motions toward the door. "I'll leave you to it and grab that food."

"Okay," I say, amazed at how he hits every right mark for me.

He walks away and I call out, "Kayden."

He stops at the doorway and turns to me, arching a brow. "Really," I say, holding up the book. "Thank you for this. It feels like a little piece of him right here in Italy."

"I'm glad," he says softly, giving me a tiny nod and then disappearing.

I turn my attention to the book and start flipping through pages, and in my mind, I see so very much. I grab a piece of paper and start writing. Events play in my mind and I can't wait to tell Kayden. I keep hold of the piece of paper, and I run down the hallway and into the kitchen.

"What is it?" Kayden asks, setting a plate down on the island, clearly reading my urgency.

I meet him on the opposite side of the island. "I just remembered things. Lots of things. This is what I found on the paper inside my father's copy of the book, and it wasn't his handwriting. It was someone else's." I rotate the pad to show him what I've printed:

Urgent: Tell DOD, Candycand5 to RumbleRed11, bury deep.
That problem is a problem.

"What's this address you've written underneath it?" Kayden asks.

"I found it in another part of his copy of the book," I say. "Both were torn off in tiny strips that were barely noticeable. I'd been cleaning out the house to sell it and I wanted to feel close to my dad, so I took it to bed with me to read."

"Sounds like the book was a way someone delivered him information."

"That's what I thought at the time, too," I say, "and I wanted to know who DOD was, so I started digging for anything I could find with that name. One of his old Rolodexes had a David Densen in it, but I found nothing. So I started going through every one of my father's hundreds of books, starting with the common denominator of Stephen King novels."

"And you found something."

"An email address."

"And?"

"Every option had flaws, but I finally settled on going to a public computer and emailing as my father. The message was: *Tell DOD I'm alive. Must talk. Candycand5 to RumbleRed11. Meet in person.*"

"And then what happened?"

"Somehow the CIA knew it was me. They showed up at the house. Told me DOD was now dead, thanks to me, and that I was to never speak of such things again. They questioned me and asked where I found the information. I lied and said in a desk drawer. I wanted to go through the rest of the books. The next morning, I was sent on an assignment in Washington, D.C. that lasted a month."

"What assignment?"

"A double agent I was supposed to expose and deliver, which I did. Upon returning home, I was handed a check for my family home that had burned down, which they said was related to the DOD murder and the reason they got me out of town. And why I was being assigned to San Francisco as a schoolteacher."

"Where were you living?"

"North Carolina, right across the border from the Virginia training facility for the CIA."

"Just far enough to not make it obvious your father was CIA," Kayden assumes. "You used a public server to email that message?"

"Yes. A local copy shop. And I cleared my history, but that can be retrieved."

"They'd been watching you, thinking you'd lead them to something connected to your father."

"They had to be, which must mean whatever it was is big. I mean, I was a long shot, but . . . it can't be the necklace, right?"

He taps the address I've written down. "Paris and the CIA are common denominators. I don't think we can rule that out. I'll go to this address myself while I'm there."

"Why would the necklace show up now, not a year ago when I sent that email and the CIA came to my house? That makes no sense."

"Unless DOD wasn't dead, but hiding, and he knew where RumbleRed11 was."

"And RumbleRed11 was the necklace," I supply. "Maybe."

"What do you remember about the CIA now?"

"I was—am—in a program called Black Forest. We don't exist to the rest of the CIA."

"Who did you report to?"

"A man named Drew Nelson, though I have no idea if that's his real name. I met him once. He said he knew my father, and that's why he recruited me."

"If you only met him once, how did you get your assignments?"

"Phone calls that told me to go to a lockbox. I also had an emergency extraction phone number that, as I mentioned, wasn't working when I called for help in Paris."

"Whether this is connected to your father or not, it's obvious that someone is dirty in the CIA and used you to transport that necklace, because you're a woman and you have skills. Which could be as simple as Drew Nelson knowing you and targeting you."

"But that feels too simple, doesn't it?"

"It does, and I'd say I'd try and find out who Drew Nelson is. But right now, anything we do could alert Neuville to a setup. This will come after Sunday."

I inhale and let the breath out, taking back the piece of paper and staring at what I've written. Then I turn back to Kayden. "Why can I remember this, but not where the necklace is?"

"We've talked about this. You're blocking something to avoid a trauma."

"There can't be anything left to protect me from." My lips tighten. "The chocolate shop has to be the answer." I consider this for a moment, images fluttering in my mind, as do facts. "I hid it there. In a planter by the downstairs bathroom. I was sure I'd be followed, so I went to several other places, and walked a good mile before I called Neuville for help."

"But?"

"But that still doesn't feel right, even though I'm saying it and I even remember doing it. I had to have moved it."

He presses his hands on the counter and leans closer. "You'll remember."

He's right; I know I will. But if my mind is blocking me, what else is coming? What nightmare has yet to be exposed?

∞∞∞

We go to bed with the confirmation that Blake is now with Chris and Sara, as are Kayden's men. Apparently Chris Merit is not happy, which is good news to me. He cares; he loves her. He is not another Neuville. And with Kayden wrapped around me, I sleep remarkably soundly, but I dream. Of dancing. Of my mother's laughter and the smell of her chocolate chip cookies, but even better, my father is there, and this time, he doesn't die. There is more laughter. There is love. There is a tomorrow.

I wake when Kayden shifts beside me, realizing that his phone is ringing. He rolls over and grabs it from the nightstand, pushing himself up to rest against the massive wooden headboard.

I roll to my stomach, watching his unreadable face, trying to make out the conversation despite it being in Italian, to no avail, but it's short and sweet anyway. "It's done," he announces, ending the call. "Niccolo's second is dead."

No tomorrow for him, I think, the news creating a pinch in my chest I know as respect for life lost, but not guilt. I've understood killing for necessity ever since the afternoon when chocolate chip cookies ended with me shooting my father's murderers. "Now what?"

"I'll take you to one of my favorite restaurants. It makes us look like we have nothing to hide, and I want you to try it anyway. Dress warmly. The outdoor seating is the best."

An hour later, we've driven one of Kayden's four Jags, the silver F-TYPE, to a spot near the Spanish Steps. The restaurant is on top of the building, and our little checked-tablecloth-covered table is on a balcony, where we sit side by side. "The view is amazing," I say, scanning the multicolored stucco rooftops, thankful for the heat lamp near our table. "But I'm glad I wore a turtleneck. It's chilly." I eye his thin, long-sleeved black T-shirt. "Aren't you cold?"

"Hot blooded," he teases. "It's your fault."

I laugh, and his phone rings for about the tenth time. "Sorry, sweetheart," he says. "We'll come back when it can be a real enjoyment." He answers his phone, and the waitress sets cups of coffee in front of us. I give her my best Italian *grazie* and sip the outrageously strong beverage. "Gallo decided to stay in Milan for a few extra days," he tells me.

"Why do I get the idea that you aren't pleased? Isn't that good? He can't get into the middle of everything we have going on, right?"

"Something about it doesn't feel right."

"No. Something doesn't feel right," Niccolo says.

I have all of two seconds to stiffen at the sound of his voice behind us before he sits down in front of us, and for once he has color in his face and sharpness in his eyes.

"So nice of you to join us for lunch, Niccolo," Kayden says, eyeing his heavy coat. "Take off your coat and stay a while."

Niccolo taps the table and stares at Kayden before cutting his gaze to me. "My second is dead," he announces, obviously looking for a reaction, not knowing what a damn good actor I am.

"Oh God," I say, my hand going to my neck. "I'm so sorry. I didn't even know you were married."

"What?" Niccolo asks, grimacing. "I'm not married. Where did that come from?"

I give him an equally baffled look. "I thought . . . I . . . isn't a *second* the translation for *spouse*?"

Irritation flashes in his eyes and he looks at Kayden. "What do you know about this?"

"I've never heard that translation, and I had no idea you were married," Kayden says, and it's all I can do not to laugh.

Niccolo is not amused. "Do not test me, Hawk."

"You're wasting my time," Kayden says. "I have no interest in your second. Maybe your third got word that you're dying and decided to make a path for himself."

His eyes dilate to almost black. "No one knows about my"—he seems to reach for a word—"situation but you. And if they find out, I'm coming back to you."

"Well then, I guess I should delete you from the cancer treatment center's database," Kayden replies. "That way you won't go blaming me when someone else finds your record."

"Those records are—"

"Easy to get to," Kayden says. "We're The Underground. There's a reason why Evil Eye is so damn evil." He leans forward, damn near in Niccolo's face. "If you were to cross the wrong Hawk, that Hawk might just displace you from that program and give someone else your spot. And you won't be alive to get a second chance." He leans back in his chair. "Good thing that you represent the stability this region needs."

I hold my breath, certain Niccolo is about to threaten him, but there's the slightest hint of fear in Niccolo's eyes and I get the feeling it's unfamiliar to him.

"Our local kingpin, Raul Martinez, had troubles in the States. He left. Would you know anything about that?" Niccolo asks.

"I know something about everything," Kayden says. "That's what makes me such an ally, isn't it?"

"Do not mistake what an enemy or ally I can be, Hawk," Niccolo warns. "I will not leave this earth without rewarding and punishing those who deserve it." He turns to me. "I'm growing impatient with your amnesia. You have one week."

He stands up and leaves.

Kayden and I watch him depart, the seconds ticking by before Kayden says, "How was the coffee?"

I give him an incredulous look. "That's all you're going to say?"

"That was predictable."

"He's a problem."

"He's necessary for stability, just like I said. Besides, the fear I just saw in his eyes was the sweetest damn revenge I could ask for."

"What about the necklace?"

"As far as we know, someone stole it from you that night in the alleyway and it ended up back with the British govern-

ment. He should have protected you better. Niccolo is a problem checked off. Gallo is not."

"What are you thinking?"

"I don't want him to end up dead, and Niccolo might just
do it to lash out at me at this point. And, what I couldn't do
with Gallo in the past, I might be able to now, with his sister
involved: pay him off. I'm going to send Nathan to him and
offer him money and protection for him and his sister, to get
them far, far away. Let's hope like hell that checks him off the
list, as well."

My phone buzzes with a text in my purse. I remove it and
glance at the screen with a groan. "Marabella and Giada are
determined to get me to go shopping with them, on Saturday
of all days." My gut twists a little, and the twist of weird emotions that follow is unsettling. "What do you think?"

"It sounds like hell, but it helps drive home the idea that
we're not planning anything and we're not involved with
what's about to happen in Paris. In fact, plan it late enough in
the day that I can meet you for dinner right before I leave."

"You aren't worried about safety?"

His gaze narrows on me and he rests his elbow on the
table, leaning in close. "The watch is messing with your head."
It's not a question.

"No. Yes. Damn it, I hate that I let Garner Neuville make
me blink. The first time they brought this shopping trip up to
me, my first thought was hell, no. I wanted to lock them away
and hide them until this is over. And I really like that I can say
that to you. But maybe I shouldn't. My father said: Don't give
fear a voice. Don't give it that power."

Kayden reaches up and strokes my cheek. "Saying it to me is the same as thinking it to yourself and working through it. We all work through those things in our heads, Ella."

"Even you?"

"You know I do. I know you know I do. Especially when it comes to other's people's safety. I'm protective of you and responsible for everyone who sees me as Hawk. This isn't Paris the eve before an operation directly related to you, or even Paris on a normal day, where we always tread lighter. This is Rome, our operational center. Niccolo may own the city, sweetheart, but we own the core neighborhoods, where the real heart and soul rests. *We own* the heart and soul. And those people, those eyes and ears, are layers of protection and loyal followers, Hunters and otherwise. No one makes us afraid here, and that's a message we send loud and clear in every action we take. We have people everywhere, and when I get back next week, I'm going to make sure you start meeting more than a small core group of Hunters."

"I'd like that," I say. "Actually, I wouldn't mind sitting in while Matteo dispatches for a few days, to see how it all works."

"I think that's a great idea," he says. "We'll have him come over the next few days. You'll get a feel for how deep our resources are before Saturday. And just as Evil Eye exists, there is 'The Code,' which is universal for all Underground operations. It's meant to ensure Hunters are never Jackals. They're a breed made of uncompromised morals and loyalty."

"And that code is what?"

"There's actually a book, but the bottom line for this conversation right now is: Loyalty and life above all else. You steal, you're out. You betray us and that results in putting someone in danger, Hunter or civilian, you die. It's brutal, but it's the only way we keep order in a business this rogue and driven by money."

I like that he's included civilians in that code, but even more, I admire his passion as he speaks of life and loyalty. "Have you ever had to kill a Hunter?"

"Once. A massive payday was in play and the Hunter killed his partnering Hunter, a good man with two kids. I found our betrayer, ended him, and I have no regrets. And the money from that treasure went to that man's family."

"You kept none of it."

"You know I don't need the money, nor would I sleep at night had I kept it. More so, my people need to know they come first, to follow me. But the real moral of this story is that after that, there's no one who questions my willingness to back that code up—and you, my Lady Hawk, are an extension of me. If you face anyone who dares threaten you or one of our own, or even a civilian, you deliver the message that code requires, and you do it with my support. Don't hesitate because it's someone you've sat across from and thought you trusted."

My mind goes to my father's bloody, lifeless body and my certainty that someone close to him stabbed him in the back before the bullets landed in his chest. "No hesitation," I assure him.

"Then go shopping. Show the world that Lady Hawk is in the city and she owns it. The message to anyone Garner Neuville might have watching is that you're so unconcerned about them, you're shopping for lingerie for me. Feel free to actually do that, by the way."

My lips curve. "Lingerie."

"Yes. Think of the entire shopping experience as a final 'fuck you' to Garner Neuville before I put a bullet in his head."

sixteen

On Thursday, Nathan heads to Milan to deal with Gallo, and Kayden spends much of the day in the War Room with Carlo, coordinating the aftermath of Alessandro's rule, and then deciding to take Carlo to Paris with him. I sit on the opposite side of the War Room with Matteo, learning the ins and outs of dispatching, truly impressed with all the resources at our fingertips. Matteo manages the process well, but it turns out Sasha was wrong about me pulling Kayden into the day-to-day operations. He's already involved in them. Every action Matteo takes is fed directly to a console Kayden keeps live on his phone and iPad, and as I watch, he actually intervenes and declines a job Matteo intends to take.

Matteo's reaction is similar to when I questioned him about security. He doesn't like it, but of course Kayden can't see this re-action, with the technology wall between them. And he thinks he hides it from me, but my father used to turn people into puzzles I had to solve. And while I understand having pride in your work, it rubs me wrong, and I make a note to talk to Kayden about it.

However, when finally Kayden and I retreat to our private tower and sit down to a light dinner Marabella has left for us, his focus is wholly on the life-threatening mission ahead of him, and talking through plans and backup plans, rendering Matteo's pride a less-than-important issue. My mental note made about Matteo, I am more than eager to help Kayden prepare for Neuville.

We've just finished eating when he finally gets a call from Nathan, who's in Milan with Gallo. When the brief call ends he tells me, "Gallo accepted five million dollars to just go away."

"You don't seem pleased."

"He took it too easily."

My brow furrows. "It's five million dollars, Kayden."

"It's a gut feeling, sweetheart."

"Well, I hope it turns out to be nothing."

"It won't," he says. "I feel it." He reaches for his fork. "Let's eat before I lose my appetite."

We both dig in and it's not long until we're pushing aside the plates and he's fixed me with a long stare. "What?" I ask.

He grabs the tube sitting next to him and pulls out a blueprint. "I'm going to ask you to do something uncomfortable."

"What?"

"I have a blueprint of Neuville's house, but I need to know what might be different. I need to know details that other people might not tell me or know."

I scowl at him. "Stop acting like he makes me a delicate flower." I grab the blueprint and we get to work, but the interesting part in going over the details with Kayden is the absence of even one flashback. It's just . . . odd.

I'm still thinking this when we fall into bed, my back to Kayden's front, his body wrapped tightly around mine. If there's still some big emotional explosion waiting to erupt in my mind, keeping me from finding the necklace, why did talking about Neuville's house, where most of my hell happened, not trigger a single image of those things?

$$\infty\infty\infty$$

On Friday we're back in the War Room. Kayden is wrapping up details with Carlo, while I am back with Matteo, who is back to his normal, funny self, and I surmise that perhaps Kayden keeps him behind the computer for that very reason. By early afternoon Matteo and Carlo depart, and Sasha and Adriel join us in their place. The four of us take up residency at the table, our seats close, and begin reviewing the Paris plans, with Adriel and me playing devil's advocate on each of three possible plans. Considering plans A and B require Sasha to make contact with Neuville, and use herself and the necklace she'll claim to have as bait, I'm pleased to find Sasha her normal sassy, confident self.

Finally we move to Plan C, the only one that requires entering Neuville's home, and Sasha and I compare notes, talk through security, and generally work through any problems that could be encountered. And again, she's driven, focused, and ready for this fight, and I'm pleased she is the one by Kayden's side. And oddly again, I have no flashbacks during this recap of Neuville's private space. Maybe the chocolate shop is the final answer. Maybe I'm done remembering things.

We've just wrapped up for the night, all of us standing to

depart, when Sasha suddenly looks at Kayden, leans on the table toward him, but doesn't speak. I hold my breath, not sure what to expect, while Kayden seems to wait, giving her space to speak, which I admire in him, but he seems to decide she needs a firm nudge. "Say what you have to say, Hunter," Kayden orders.

"The other day—"

"Is done."

She gives him a three-second stare and then nods, turning and leaving. Adriel and Kayden lock stares, and I watch that exchange, aware then that Adriel objects to Sasha being a part of this mission, but I do not think he's spoken it aloud.

"Say what you have to say, Second," Kayden orders him.

"Are you sure she can handle this?"

"Yes," I answer without hesitation, and when both men look at me, I focus on Kayden, deciding the things on my mind must be said. "And if you doubt her, she'll doubt herself." I look at Adriel. "The best thing you can do for her right now, as the man closest to her, is not to put doubts in her head. Just like I can't tell Kayden to be careful every time he leaves here, or he'll think about me, not his job. If you can't do that, you need to back away from her. And you, Hawk, should tell her you chose her for the warrior she is. She'll want to live up to it. I see it in her eyes."

Neither man reacts, though Kayden's eyes warm with admiration I'm very pleased to see. Wordlessly, Adriel turns and exits the room, and then Kayden is standing in front of me, tall and broad, his body towering over mine. He cups my face and kisses me. "She needs to hear that I believe in her."

It's not really a question, but I answer, "Yes. She does."

"Very well, Lady Hawk. Then she will." He starts walking away and my lips curve as I realize his intentions, and as I have another moment to fall in love with him all over again. Yes, he will kill. Yes, he will destroy you if you betray him. But that is because he is loyal to the soul.

I follow in his wake, eager to watch the events unfold.

He is already at the stairs by the time I'm in the hallway, already down them when I reach the top step. I watch as he calls out to Sasha, then watch as she turns, her eyes going wide at his approach. And even at a distance as he speaks to her, I see her stand a little straighter, determination stiffening her spine. She is pleased. She is motivated, and they are now both safer.

Kayden returns to me, his longish brown hair always just a little wild, his jaw a little shadowed while his faded jeans, biker boots, and fitted white T-shirt somehow read like an invitation for sex to me right now. I savor every step he takes until he stops in front of me and motions me down the hallway to our left.

Curious about where we're going, I fall into step with him, past the room where Enzo died, and farther. We stop exactly where the War Room is on the other side of the castle and enter what turns out to be a giant gym, complete with mats, punching bags, and equipment.

"Okay, I'm impressed," I say, facing him.

"Take your shoes off, and let's go to the mats."

"What?" I ask. "Why? Do you have time for this now?"

"What you said about not telling me to be careful got me

thinking. We both need to know what the other one is capable of, what skills we each possess. We need to know that if the other one is in trouble alone, he or she can survive."

"You know I can fight, and I know—"

He throws a punch that stops right in front of my face, but instinct has my hand covering his fist by the time it does. His gaze meets mine, a challenge in their depths. I throw a punch and he captures my fist as well. "Game on, Hawk," I say.

He inclines his chin and we drop our hands, take off our shoes, and go to the mats. "Let's do this, Lady Hawk," he says, and so it begins.

An hour later, we're lying in the middle of the mats, staring at the high ceiling, both of us breathing hard. Kayden says, "A guy walks into a bar, and you glimpse a shoulder holster—"

"Wait. Is this a country song or a joke?"

"It's a situational exam," he says. "Like what your dad gave you."

I roll over and climb on top of him, straddling his hips and pulling my shirt over my head. "I take his gun. That's the answer."

His full, sexy lips, which I really want on mine right now, curve, and he turns me on my back, the heavy, delicious weight of him on top of me. "And I take the woman," he says, his mouth closing down on mine, and I decide that combat training and this man are my Happily Ever After.

CroCro

Too soon, and not soon enough, Saturday has arrived. One day before D-day. I am ready for this to be over and I really don't feel like making the shift to shopping from planning war.

Maybe that's why I've just taken yet another black T-shirt from a hanger and pulled it on. Wait. It's the same black T-shirt. Maybe I do need a little shopping. Just not today. Actually, today is exactly when I need to go shopping.

"Fuck you, Garner Neuville," I bite out, yanking up my pant leg and strapping on the ankle holster Kayden had delivered yesterday, before sliding my new backup firearm inside. "I'm going to go shopping and enjoy it."

I pull down my pant leg, grab my boots, and sit down on the bench, just about to stand when Kayden appears, his faded jeans paired with a light blue Jaguar F-TYPE shirt, reflective of how much he loves his cars. The look on his face, however, is not love. "What's wrong?"

"Gallo is testing me. He wants to meet with me and Chief Donati."

"Wait," I say, standing up, remembering Kayden's worries that Gallo was still trouble. "I thought he took the deal. Did he back out? Is he here in Rome?"

He rests a shoulder on the door frame. "He came home to pack up, but says before he leaves town he has information about The Jackals that both myself and Donati need to hear."

"And you think it's one last attempt to come at you?"

"Somehow, in some way, I assure you it is."

"When's the meeting?"

"Three hours from now. An interruption I really don't need today."

"Is everything else still on track?"

"Word is that Alessandro touched down in Paris. Carlo's

man met with Neuville this morning and told him that not only had Alessandro stolen from him, but he's in town and planning to steal the necklace right from underneath him. Everything is going as planned—at least on the Paris end of things."

"What does that mean? 'At least on the Paris end of things'?"

"Matteo caught wind of one of our guys doing a side deal with Alessandro. We're headed there now to find out what it's all about."

"Do you think it has something to do with what Gallo wants to talk about?"

"That's what we need to find out." He reaches behind him and pulls a leather wallet from his back pocket, closing the small space between us and flipping it open to display several credit cards and a healthy stack of euros. "These cards have my name on them, but I cleared them at the bank for you. Once we get married, I'll take you to the bank and get your name on everything."

"No, I don't need that. I don't need the cards."

"Of course you do. You're going shopping and you need money."

"You already gave me a credit card." I fold my arms in front of me. "I don't want your money, Kayden."

"Why the hell not?" he says, sounding baffled. "You can enjoy spending it."

"I'm not going to spend your money."

"Ella, sweetheart." He unfolds my arms and presses the wallet into my hands. "You're marrying me. It's our money."

"It's our life, not our money."

"I told you. I have money and I'm going to make a lot more money. We're going to make a lot more money. Enjoy it."

"But then you'll think I'm with you for your money, and that would feel horrible."

"I thought you were with me for my body," he teases.

"Well, that's true." I grin.

"All the more reason to spend a ridiculous amount of money on lingerie that I can look forward to when I get back Sunday night. The driver I lined up for your shopping trip should be here in the next forty-five minutes. A guy named Oliver. I'm thinking about moving him up in the ranks, so let me know what you think of him." He kisses me. "I'll call you after I find out what this is about, and we'll figure out dinner." He disappears into the bathroom, leaving me with his wallet, a smile on my face, and apparently an Italian named Oliver.

∞∞

Forty-five minutes later, I head downstairs to find Marabella and Giada waiting in the main foyer, both in long coats. Marabella wears a blue flowery dress under hers and Giada is in a daring emerald pantsuit.

"Ella!" she greets me, saying something in Italian before rushing to hug me, her long brown hair teasing my cheek. "Do you know what I said to you?" she asks as Marabella and I share a quick smile.

"I do not," I confirm.

"Then learn Italian. You're in Italy."

"Yes, ma'am," I say. "You're right and I will."

"And do you have anything but black in your closet?" she asks. "I swear we bought you some colors."

"She only wears the black," Marabella chimes in. "She ignores the colors."

We're laughing when we step onto the porch to find a black sedan waiting, only to have Matteo step out of the driver's door. "Should we go by my apartment now or later?" Giada asks. "I want you to see it, Ella."

"Let's do it now," I say, almost absently, rounding the car to meet Matteo while Giada and Marabella enter the near side.

"Are you driving us?" I ask, noting the tan leather jacket that I'm certain is worn to camouflage a shoulder holster he doesn't usually wear.

"I am, indeed, your driver for the day."

"Where's Oliver?" I ask.

"I had to pull him. He has a contact I needed him put to use for another job."

"Isn't this below your pay grade?"

"Since Kayden handpicked Oliver, I wasn't about to handpick wrong. Plus, I have an ulterior motive for joining you."

Now he has my attention. "Which is what?"

"I need a birthday gift for a woman. I have no idea what to get her."

"Oh," I say, the explanation seeming to explain much, but still not sitting exactly right. Yet not much will until Neuville is dead, I suspect. "I'm sure Giada will have ideas."

He opens my door for me and I slide inside, and unbidden, and perhaps because of the timing, Kayden's words play in my head: *If you face anyone who dares threaten you or one of our own, or even a civilian, you deliver the message that code requires.*

The car starts to move, and I answer that memory with a silent *Without hesitation*, before allowing myself to be drawn into the conversation. In only three minutes we're at Giada's apartment, which is small but adorable. It's also well furnished, thanks to Adriel. We hang out there for a half hour, and Matteo confesses the name of his secret girlfriend, Abella, and everyone laughs at how close her name is to Marabella. After hearing how head over heels he is for her, I make a mental note to ask Kayden how The Underground handles such things. Whatever the case, we head out to the Spanish Steps shopping area, with a few jewelry stores for Matteo's Abella on the "must do" list.

Two hours later, Giada has spent a ton of money on things for her apartment, and we've just exited a jewelry store where Matteo has purchased a necklace for his new woman. I'm enjoying myself for the most part, but Kayden's silence regarding his investigating a Hunter who met with Alessandro is weighing on me, and The Code keeps playing in my head. Loyalty and life first.

"I'll take the bags to the car," Matteo offers.

"Perfect," Giada says. "I'm so glad you came." She points at a store. "We'll be in there. We still need to get Ella something not black to wear."

Matteo gives her a tiny nod, but just before he turns, I

note this odd smile that has me frowning. My phone buzzes
with a text and I reach for it, glancing down at the message.

> Kayden: You okay?
> Me: Yes. Is all well?
> Kayden: Weird situation. Will tell you about it later.
> Walking into meeting with Donati and Gallo. Are we still
> good for an early dinner?
> Me: Yes.
> Kayden: Talk soon, sweetheart.

Feeling much better, I look up to find Giada looking at
me. "Everything okay?"

"Of course," I say.

"Not my feet," Marabella says, and I glance up to find her
motioning toward a bar, which means a coffee shop here. "I'll
be there. I need to sit."

"Are you okay?" I ask, giving her a critical inspection. "You
look a little pale."

"Just old," she says, giving me a tiny wink. "Nothing coffee
won't help me pretend isn't true. Go shop."

Giada lights up and links her arm with mine, and I suddenly
realize Marabella is just giving us some time alone. Glancing
over my shoulder, Marabella and I share a look before I'm
pulled along by Giada. "Did Kayden tell you about the coin?"

"Yes. He was honored, and I was proud of you."

"I really am trying to make changes," she says. "It feels a
little weird being away from the castle, but it's thrilling, too.
I'm starting a life. I'm going to college. I'm going to do something for me."

"And I can't wait to hear every detail."

She opens the door to the store. "Chanel," she says. "You know you love it."

I laugh and we enter, and before long, the attendant and Giada have pretty much put half the store in a dressing room for me. The attendant, a woman in her fifties who barely speaks English, looks at me and I catch, "Would you like . . ." And the rest just has me blinking.

Giada laughs. "You need to learn Italian," she reminds me. She motions to some sort of back garden. "They serve champagne on the patio. She wanted to know if you'd like a glass."

"Oh. No. Thank you. I prefer to stay sharp."

Giada laughs. "Tipsy is the best way to shop. You go home with more."

But your gun hand isn't steady, I think.

"Go," Giada motions. "Go get in that dressing room and try stuff on. I want to see."

I go down the hallway and step into the dressing room. Slipping off my coat, I inspect the clothes waiting on me, not sure I even want to attempt to try all this stuff. Nevertheless, I sit down and take off my boots. "Ella," Giada says at the door.

"Yes?"

"Matteo says Marabella wants him to drive her home. I need to make sure she's just giving us time alone, and nothing is wrong."

"Yes," I say. "Go see. Now I'm worried."

"I'll be right back."

Remembering how pale Marabella looked, I don't like this one bit, and I quickly pull my boots back on. That's when

something comes sliding under the door. I look down and my
blood runs cold, because I know what I'm looking at. One of
the missing pages from my journal. Adrenaline surges through
me, but that person I become at times, that deep down is really
me, kicks in. I unzip my purse and make sure Annie is handy,
and with her in reach, then, and only then, do I bend down
and open the folded piece of paper, sucking in air when the
writing belongs to Garner Neuville:

Bella. You should know I can get to you anywhere,
anytime. And I can get to anyone you care about
anywhere, anytime.

My phone rings, and I know, with gut-wrenching certainty, that it will be him.

I pull my cell from my coat pocket and glance at Unknown Number on the caller ID. Steeling myself to hear his
voice, I whisper, "Fuck you," to myself, but don't speak into
the phone.

"No hello, Ella? What kind of greeting is that?"

"What do you want, Neuville?"

"You and the necklace. So here's what's going to happen.
Listen carefully and do not speak. You're going to exit the
back door and Matteo will be waiting for you. Good man, by
the way. Very corruptible. I love that about him. Leave the
phone. We both know it can be tracked. If you make a phone
call or send a text after we hang up, Kayden and Adriel will
die. The two of them are sitting across from Gallo, who I have
on payroll. For how much, you ask? I paid him six million dollars, one million more than Kayden offered him to go away,

and he's been instructed to shoot Kayden and Adriel should either of their cell phones ring. I'm thinking that Gallo hopes it rings, aren't you? Oh, and sweet Marabella and Giada. It would be a shame to see them die today, wouldn't it? If you call anyone, someone dies. You have sixty seconds to make it to the back door or someone dies."

"I'm not dressed," I say quickly. "I need two minutes."

"Ninety seconds."

The line goes dead.

seventeen

Neuville will kill everyone I care about, just because I care about them.

That is the only thought I can afford right now, outside of how to warn Kayden before it's too late to save him, and everyone around him and us. I have no room for worry, fear, or anger. Just rapid decision and action. I need that two minutes I asked for, not ninety seconds, and I have no choice but to risk taking it. I toss my phone down, having no doubt Matteo is monitoring any movement it makes via the satellite tower. By the time it hits the floor, my gaze is already on the space under the door dividing me from another seemingly empty room, as a wild plan forms in my mind. I'm under the wall in a split second, squatting and finding exactly what I need in yet the next room over: a pair of legs under that wall, which means a purse and phone should be present as well.

I go to my knees and lower myself to my elbow, face to the carpet, and scan for the purse that is thankfully on the floor, but it's going to require me reaching deep into the room. The woman is dressing, her back to me, and I have no time to spare. I go all in, sliding my upper body under the wall and snagging the purse to drag it to me. The minute I have it, I dig for a phone, find it, and shove the purse back into the room, uncaring of where it lands. I'm already on my feet and dialing the one person I know isn't in danger at the moment or corruptible, like those bastards Gallo and Matteo, praying she answers an unknown number.

"Bonjour."

"Sasha, don't speak, just listen," I order. "This is life or death and if you're in a public place, take cover now."

"I'm not," she says. "Go on."

"Matteo's dirty. Gallo's dirty. Neuville's here. He's got guns on just about everyone, and *don't* call anyone. Gallo will shoot Kayden and Adriel if their phones ring, or he might just do it anyway. Get creative and save them. I have to go."

"You can't go with him, Ella. He'll kill you."

"He'll kill everyone else if I don't," I say. "You know him. You know I have to do this."

She hesitates, then says, "Yes. He'll kill everyone. We'll get to you. He has to go to the airport."

"I can handle myself," I say, anticipating my purse and gun being taken from me and digging out cash for survival when I escape, and credit cards to be traced, if I can manage to use one of them. "Save the others."

"Leave the phone on."

"Trace it after you save everyone else."

I end the call, turn the cell on vibrate, and stuff it in the opposite boot from my right now much appreciated backup gun. The money and credit cards get shoved deep in my sock, though I'd rather they be at the soles of my feet, where I know I won't be searched. I open the door, scanning the empty hallway, and walk down it. I'm out of time but I look right toward the store, and then left toward the back door. My hand goes inside my open purse, gripping Annie.

Inhaling, I shove open the door that takes me into a narrow road and shared sidewalk dividing us from yet another row of stores and restaurants. Matteo is parked to my right and doesn't get out, and I start to get into the backseat. My idea of pulling my gun on him is dashed when he faces me, holding his own. "Give me the gun and the purse," he orders. "And I know your skills, Ella. Don't think for a minute I won't shoot you."

"Neuville wouldn't like that," I say, slowly lifting my purse over my head. "He wouldn't get to rape me again first."

"Maybe he'd settle for Giada," he taunts.

"Sick bastard," I growl, handing him my purse.

He yanks it from me. "Get in—and I'm only giving you my back for two reasons. You aren't getting close to the wheel, and if we aren't standing in front of Neuville in ten minutes, he starts killing people." He glares at me a few moments. "Understand?"

"I understand he's going to kill you."

"Not before he has some fun with you." He races forward, turning the ignition and mumbling something in Italian while putting us in gear.

Ten minutes.

My mind races.

I still have a gun, but I won't for long if I don't use it.

Ten minutes.

That's all Sasha has to save everyone.

It's going to have to be enough, because Evil Eye applies here, and when I see Neuville I'm killing him. It's what Kayden would want me to do, and I don't let myself think about Gallo killing him the minute he saw him today. Kayden was nervous about him as it was, on edge, and ready for whatever came his way. He's alive and Neuville's about to be dead, right along with this piece of trash driving me.

"Why?" I ask, as he weaves through people walking the shared space, which buys time for Sasha to work her magic. "Kayden's a good man."

"Alessandro and I have something in common," he says. "We both stole from the wrong person."

"You stole from Neuville?"

"And Kayden," he says. "Neuville found out."

"You should have—"

"Gone to Kayden? He'd have sent me to Neuville anyway, but with no way to save myself."

"All you're doing is ensuring that Kayden kills you."

"He won't be alive to know I betrayed him."

My gut twists. "You underestimate him."

"But not Gallo's hatred."

Kayden won't underestimate that hate, I assure myself. I know he's alive, and he'll stay that way. But if I get found with this phone on me, Neuville will kill someone to punish me. I slip it out of my boot and under the seat, hoping they figure out where I am and where that means I'm going next. Or that

Matteo follows. Whatever the case, it ensures Matteo is found and pays for what he's done.

The car jolts to a stop as a group of walkers step in front of us. "It was you who took those journal pages, wasn't it?"

"You know the answer."

"You were watching us in our tower."

"*He* was watching you." The announcement turns my blood to ice. "I couldn't save you from that."

"Did you even try? How did you get in there?"

He scrubs a hand through his dark hair. "I was over my head, Ella. I'm still fucking over my head. Maybe I should have gone to Kayden, but I didn't."

"You can now."

"It's too late for that," he says, turning us around a corner that puts us in a pedestrian- and retail-free area, which means I'm running out of time. "I just need my payday and I'll disappear."

"From the necklace," I say.

"For delivering you."

I don't have time to let the spike of anger this creates in me take hold, because he cuts right and we're suddenly in an alleyway and then halting. "The party stops here, Ella."

He's right. It does, because my gun is already in my hand.

Matteo's cell phone rings and he listens before handing it to me. "Neuville wants to talk to you."

I inhale and take the phone. "So close," he says, his voice meant to be pure seduction, but it cuts like a rusty nail. "If we open the doors and you resist, even slightly, someone dies. Kayden dies. And just in case you doubt I'm going to do it, watch Matteo fall."

I suck in air and look up at the same moment a bullet pierces the front window and Matteo slumps forward. Dead, and he never saw it coming. "Party is over, Matteo," I whisper.

Neuville laughs, a nail-biting sound. "That sounds like enjoyment. I'd better pick someone else."

My heart races but my voice is calm, steady. "You made your point."

"I like insurance," he says. "You should know that, but you seem to need a reminder. Nathan's at the hospital right now, and his current patient has a syringe in her pocket that would kill him in thirty seconds. I suggest you leave whatever gun you have on your person that Matteo missed in the car. Understood?"

"Yes," I lie.

The doors to both sides of the backseat open almost instantly, and I react. I shoot the man to my left and then the one to my right, and step over him. But there are three more men, all pointing guns at me. And then there's him, in the center of them all, tall, dark, and striking in a fitted black suit, so close I can almost see the evil in his charcoal eyes.

And my gun is aimed at him. "I am many things you didn't realize I was," I say. "Including a perfect marksman. Tell them to put their guns down. Because if they shoot or move you'll be dead, even if I am, too."

"I knew everything you were," he says. "More than you did, and I could tell you things you burn to know—but not if I'm dead."

My father. Those words rip through me and I know in that moment that Neuville is connected to my father's death—and that's all I need to know. "You have nothing to say that I want to hear."

"Well, believe this," he says. "If I'm dead, Gaston, my second, who I'm sure you remember, has been instructed to visit our friend Sara, which won't upset him. He's quite fond of her. He's been watching her, you know."

My blood freezes with those game-changing words. Kayden will protect himself. Nathan is far more than just a doctor and can do the same. I trust Sasha to have protected Giada and Marabella. But Sara is an entirely different story.

"I can almost hear you thinking," he says. "Let me vocalize your thoughts. Is Sara safe? Are all those people protecting her as good as you are? The answer is no to both. She is not. They are not. Now, Kayden's men are good, but there's that layer of Americans between them and her, who all mean well, and are exceptional in their own country, but not in France. Paris. I own those places. Put the gun down or I'll have a bullet put in her body now, and let her suffer while she waits for you to get there."

"She is nothing to me," I say. "A girl I met while undercover."

He removes his phone from his pocket. "Then I'll tell Gaston to fuck her, shoot her, and get rid of her." His eyes meet mine, a brow arching, and evil radiates from him.

He isn't bluffing. He never bluffs. I lower my weapon and Bastile, a brawny man with a goatee, who's also Neuville's personal bodyguard, snaps his fingers at me, silently demanding my gun. I look at him, remembering the many times he smiled at Neuville's nastiness toward me, and his tall, muscular body looks like a mighty fine target for a bullet.

"The gun," he growls.

Grimacing, I hand him the damn thing, which earns me a stomach-churning "Good choice, little one" from Neuville, who I force myself to look at. He then steps aside, placing me in profile, and grandly waves me forward, inviting me back to his world, and my personal hell.

I walk forward, cold air biting at my bare arms, but I feel nothing. No physical reaction. No emotion. This is about survival for me and death for him, and I'll ride out whatever storm I have to in order to get there. One of his men opens the back door of a limousine for me and I slide inside. A moment later Neuville is across from me, the smell of him whiskey and cigars and bad memories. Almost instantly the vehicle is moving, and I know his urgency is all about escaping Kayden's city.

"Where's the necklace?" he asks.

"I don't know."

"You do know."

"I don't remember."

His lips thin. "So I hear." He studies me, his eyes heavy lidded, expression guarded. "Did you fuck my brother?"

"I never made it to your brother. Someone attacked me and I ended up in the hospital."

"And then in Kayden Wilkens's bed." Without warning he is next to me, and a huge chunk of my hair is in his hands. "I hate the brown hair. Did he like it? Did Kayden like it?"

"No," I say, my eyes meeting his. "I did this."

"I see the rebellion in your eyes," he says. "Good. That only makes me want to fuck you and punish you all the more.

And I will punish you on the plane." A needle jams into my neck—and everything goes dark.

⊱⎯⎯⎯⊰

I gasp for air and jolt to a sitting position to find myself on an airplane, engines humming, and Garner Neuville looming over me in his egotistical power-mongering way, a syringe in his hand. "They were right," he approves. "Woke you right up." He moves away, thank God, and sits in the leather seat across from me, the cold air chilling my bare arms, my fingers digging into the arms of the chair.

"Where's the necklace, Ella?"

"I don't know."

"That's what I hear. I'm not sure I believe you."

"Why would I lie?"

"Three hundred million dollars," he reminds me.

"That I don't need or care about."

"I wonder if Kayden would trade the necklace for you?"

"He doesn't have it either."

"But would he?"

I know he would, but I won't give Neuville the power over Kayden or me that he's looking for. "You're all greedy bastards. And if someone hadn't tried to take the damn thing from me, I wouldn't have lost my memory in the first place."

"Convenient that you remember me, but not that necklace."

"I'll tell you what I told your brother. Nothing about having everyone hunt me down for that necklace is convenient."

"When you were talking with my brother, or when you were *betraying* me with him?"

"He said he'd kill you," I lie. "I saved you."

"Is that right?"

"Yes."

"And you believed him?"

"Yes.

He stares at me, eternally it seems, as is his way. He tries to tear you down, unnerve you. He wants me to reply again because the silence rattles me, but I do not. I won't. I stare back at him, and while I can still see how I once saw his sculpted face, gray eyes, and thick, dark hair accented with a widow's peak as handsome, now all I see is a mask for the devil.

"Take your clothes off," he orders.

I don't gasp. I don't give him a reaction. That's what he wants, and it's not like I didn't know this was where I'd be headed the moment I found myself getting into that car.

But this isn't about me. This is about saving Sara, and living to kill this man. And the bottom line here is that I'm in a plane, in the air, going who knows where, and no one can rescue me. I have to get through this flight to ensure Neuville doesn't survive this night—if it's even the same night. I don't know how long I've been out. I don't know how long we've been in the air. And if I refuse his order, he'll enjoy making me do it. I'm not giving him that satisfaction. I take off my boots, cautious to keep the money and credit cards from his view. Those credit cards might be the only way I have to tell Kayden where I am.

Pushing to my feet, I don't give him the satisfaction that hesitating and looking awkward would reward him with, or the reluctance it would indicate. I simply take off my clothes and I'm naked, calm, and composed on the outside in only seconds.

On the inside I'm angry, and feeling other things as well. Humiliation. Dread. Vulnerability. Fear. I hate that one the most. But training in mental fortitude saves me from their destructive influences, and I package them up into a tight mental ball and set them aside.

Neuville looks me up and down, lingering at places I know he will touch me, but that ball I set aside is not in the mix. I am my father's daughter, a CIA agent, a survivor, and Lady Hawk—and a Lady Hawk cannot, will not, cower. I will think of my Hawk. I will remember that surviving this means he will replace every memory of this man with new ones of him. Good things that overcome the way this man rapes me with his eyes and leaves me standing under the cold air that makes my nipples too damn pointed, his eyes too damn pointed as he lusts over them, and me.

It's at least ten minutes before he stands, placing himself almost directly in front of me, and grabs a chunk of my hair. Again, it's no surprise, but it bites. It always bites.

"You will change your hair back to red tomorrow," he orders. "You will be nothing you were with him." He lets go of my hair and grabs my wrist, showing me the hawk tattoo. "Did he threaten to kill you if you didn't get this?"

"It's a tattoo," I argue.

"That's a no, and the wrong answer. I will not fuck you with this on your body. I will burn it off before this night is through, and make sure you suffer as a punishment for making me do it."

And I will kill you before you ever get the chance, I silently vow. I just need to get to Sara. The minute I'm in the same room with her—

He backs me up and sets me down in the chair. "Hands on the armrests," he orders, and when I do it without question, I get the reaction I want: irritation. He wants me to resist. He wants to punish me. It turns him on. And I won't give him the triggers he seeks.

I have to remind myself of this when he reaches inside his pocket. At the sight of the rope he produces, I know my mental resistance to being tied up is something not easily fought, and it comes at me fast and fierce, and I have to deep breathe to calm myself. You don't kill a mob boss on a plane, with his men on it, and live.

I let him tie me up.

When he tugs my head back this time and leans over me, forcing me to look at him, he all but yanks the hair from my scalp. "You are mine, and so is the necklace." He kisses me, and it's all I can do not to bite his damn tongue off. But he bites me instead, damn near taking a chunk of my lip, his teeth creating a sharp, intense pain that radiates into my jaw and leaves me oozing blood I cannot wipe away.

He kneels in front of me, spreading my legs and resting his hands on my thighs. "Your father knew where it was, and he wouldn't tell me either."

"What does that mean?" I demand, the mention of my father like another bite that radiates through me and becomes a ball of unnamed emotions in my chest.

"He had the necklace, like you do. He was undercover in

my father's operation, and his boss, now your figurehead of a boss, stole the necklace from him. And like you, your father refused to return it to my father. Only your boss, your father's old partner, was working with me, about to hand that necklace over, when your father intervened and took it. At that point France and Italy were ruled by Niccolo's mother and my father, who'd married. That necklace was key to my plan to take over the empire when I killed them."

"You say that like killing your parents is nothing."

"They *were nothing*," he says. "And why, you might ask, do I feel that way? None of your fucking business. What matters is that I waited years for that necklace to show up in order to act on my plans. Years of nothing, in which I had to share the power with Niccolo and turn to you for a solution."

"I was never a solution. I knew nothing about the necklace."

"But I knew your father had trained you all your life. I knew if anyone could find that necklace, it was you."

My world starts to spin.

"I created your covert team," he continues. "You aren't really CIA, though even the agency has whispers of your secret unit. It's really quite comical. *I paid* for your college education. *I paid* for your training. *I made sure* you questioned your father's death and had the skills to figure out where the necklace was, and finally you gave it to me. Dane Owen Daniels, 'DOD,' was the link, an old friend of your father's who helped him hide the necklace. But we didn't know who he was until you gave us a way to find him and the necklace."

My gut knots with my stupidity, for allowing myself to be a

token in a game my father lost, and which I am close to losing as well. "And then you had me transport it across the border."

"It seemed profoundly appropriate. If you fucked it up and got caught, you'd be the thief. I made you. I erased you. I even killed your 'boss' at the fictitious CIA operation when I brought you here, to ensure no one could track you. So you see, you work for me. You've always worked for me. You belong to me. And *you will* bring me the necklace."

"Did you—"

"Order the murder of your father? Of course I did. My only regret," he adds, his hands sliding up my thighs, "is that I didn't keep him alive and force him to watch me fuck his beautiful daughter." His thumbs are now stroking my inner thighs just below my sex, and it is all I can do not to lean forward and smash my head against his, kick him away, and finally live out that fantasy of snapping his neck.

I'm trembling, visualizing that fantasy, and he laughs, low and dirty, a sound that crawls over my skin like slimy, disgusting worms. "I should force you to have an orgasm right now," he says, "just to prove I can despite all the hate you're throwing my way, but that would be a pleasure you don't deserve right now. Instead, you get to spend the rest of the trip thinking about what I'm going to do to you. How many ways I'm going to fuck you when we're alone."

I decide I'm done playing submissive with this man. The game starts and ends tonight. "I'm going to kill you," I promise him.

"I hope for Sara's sake you don't," he says, "because I might not survive to enjoy you, but then, neither would she survive another day." He squeezes my legs, thumbs digging into my flesh with brutal force. "Keep them open."

He backs up and sits in his seat, pulling out his phone and snapping a picture. "When the time is right, when I can send this without him tracking our location, Kayden is going to enjoy that one, I think, don't you?"

I don't focus on the horrific knowledge that at some point he's sending that shot to Kayden. I focus on the one positive confirmation he's given me. Kayden is alive; be it by design or not, Kayden survived Gallo. But Neuville can't let him live. Not after he defied Evil Eye. He's setting Kayden up, planning to kill him, and no doubt thinks he has some plan to justify it and escape retaliation. That picture is bait and we're headed to Paris. Where Sara is right now. But more so, in that moment, I remember everything. I know why I was blocking the location of the necklace, and my hiding place is both brilliant and almost sadistic on my part, when I think about it now.

It's in his house. I hid it in his house, and some part of me couldn't bear the idea of ever stepping foot in that place again.

eighteen

sara

Saturday, the evening of the Louvre charity event

I know I should have some profound words to write tonight. That's what kept me reading Rebecca's journal after I found it. I hung on every word. Everything felt impactful. For me, though, it feels rather simple. These days, after so much tragedy has swept our lives, I've been working on that. Simple. Keeping it simple. I'm not sure it's working. I mean, I'm in love with Chris Merit. There is nothing simple about that man. But here's simple tonight:

1) Yes. Ella could still be in danger, but she is safe with a man who seems to care about her. I know from personal experience that one thing, one very special person, changes everything.

2) Yes. Garner Neuville is looking for Ella, but we've known this and it sounds like his operation is about to be taken down. We don't have details, just that after this weekend, he won't be a problem. Then I can hug Ella in person.

3) Yes. The extra security tonight for the charity event, just in case Neuville suddenly targets me, is unsettling, but why would he target me now after months of ignoring me? And even if he did, we've taken very serious precautions. Not only is Blake Walker here, but so is Jacob. And Jacob might be part of Walker Security now, but he was security for Chris's building back home, and then for us, before he even knew the Walkers.

So that's my version of simple. The not-so-simple part of all of this is how Chris is affected by the idea of me being in danger. Especially considering we're fresh off the loss of his ex right here in Paris, which is why it's time for me to go be with him. More later . . .

✑✑✑

I shut the journal and stand up, giving my silver knee-length a quick once-over, smiling at the idea of walking downstairs and showing it to Chris. I picked it for Chris, because he's been all about silver on his canvas lately, and it seems *I'm* always his canvas lately. The idea has me smiling through tiny splintery nerves I can't show. If I'm nervous Chris will be a hundred times more on edge, and as it is, he only tolerates public events for one reason: to help the kids and families dealing with the tragedy of cancer.

I slip the strap of the heart-shaped jeweled purse I bought for the night over my shoulder and head for the door, hurrying down the hallway. Reaching the top of the stairs, I find Blake and Chris standing at the base, both incredibly sexy in tuxedos. As I start down the stairs both men turn toward me and Blake, who is tall, dark, and hopefully deadly if we need him to be, waves and heads toward the garage. Chris, my blond, hot artist, simply watches me walk down the stairs, and I swear I will never get over the impact of this man looking at me like there's nothing else in the world but me, and us.

The moment I'm in front of him, his hands settle at my waist, branding me, owning me.

"I love this dress on you, but it's going to make me spend the night thinking of how to get you out of it."

My lips curve, warmth radiating through me. "I love you in the tuxedo," I say, my hands flattening on his lapels, "even if you hate them. But there's something about knowing your dragon sleeve is underneath it that drives me a little wild."

Those green eyes of his burn with amber flecks. "Show me tonight."

"I will," I promise, smiling, my hand brushing his scruffy jaw. "The rebel in you just won't shave for these events. It's like you want to remind them you're not this guy."

"We're ready now."

I turn to find Blake motioning us forward, and we head downstairs to our private garage. It's not long before we've ignored the two Porsche 911s and are loaded in the back of a black, nondescript sedan, with Jacob in the driver's seat. "Hi, Jacob," I say. "We got you in a tuxedo too, I see."

"You did," he says, glancing over his shoulder, his brown hair trimmed to his scalp. "It appears," he says dryly, "that Paris isn't romantic after all."

"I take it you enjoy a monkey suit as much as I do." Chris laughs.

"It's obligation, never choice," he says. "But you two are good obligations."

"Well," I say, "I assure you that plenty of women are going to think you are their perfect romance tonight."

"Let's roll," Blake says, climbing in the front seat and looking at us. "Kayden has three of his men inside the event and three on the exterior, backing us up. Our tech guy's already hacked the security feed and is watching from a not-so-remote location. There's not a reason you two can't enjoy your night."

"We appreciate all you and your team are doing," Chris assures him, his hand sliding to my bare knee.

"You just go make some money for some sick kids," Blake says. "Always a cause we want to help with."

"Amen to that," Jacob says, and we are officially moving. But as everyone focuses on our travels, the mood shifts, almost as if we have some odd sense of wrong tunneling into the center of everything being right. Not even Chris's hand on my bare knee warms me where I've suddenly become chilled.

⋙∾⋘

This event is being attended by politicians, actors and actresses, and high-profile businesspeople, but Chris is a rock star in the art world, and the minute we step out of the car cameras are flashing. This part of the event is Chris's least favorite, but once we're inside, with the towering glass ceilings and art-lined rooms everywhere, we're in our element. We both love this place. And I love seeing how people respond to Chris. And more so, how he responds to them. He's a billionaire by inheritance and a millionaire from his art, all of which he donates, but you'd never know it. He's the most down-to-earth person, never hurrying anyone away. Never acting like he's above anyone.

We make our way to the main event room, with scattered tables of desserts featuring different types of chocolate delights, Jacob shadowing us and Blake overseeing the bigger picture, somewhere out of our sight. I forget about the earlier tension and I can sense Chris relaxing as well, our hands, and our gazes, touch often. And finally I can understand, if not speak, enough French that I understand what people are saying to us, even managing to make contacts for a few purchases I want for the gallery in San Francisco, which Chris and I are helping a friend reopen.

Finally it's time for Chris to head to a table in the corner, where he signs paintbrushes, and there will be an auction for several pieces he created for the event. As usual, I stand by his table and chat with people, which they seem to really like, and so does he. The line is exceptionally long tonight, but I know Chris. We won't leave until everyone who wants to talk to him has had the chance.

About an hour into the signing, I catch Chris's gaze and whisper, "Bathroom," then find Jacob to escort me. Feeling happy we didn't cancel the event, considering the turnout, I weave through the crowd and we reach the restroom a guard pointed us to so we can avoid a long line. Sure enough, there is an empty stall and I enter. Once I'm done, I'm about to open the door when a piece of paper slides under it. I laugh, because this has to be one of Chris's crazy fans.

Bending down, I pick up the paper and unfold it:

Do as you're instructed or your famous husband will be your dead famous husband.

My stomach rolls and my fist balls over my now racing heart. Inhaling sharply, I force air into my lungs and keep reading:

There are several people in his line, and in the crowd, carrying syringes. One quick jab and he will never paint, let alone breathe, again. Go to the parking garage and make sure you are not followed. Tell someone, and your husband dies. Take your phone with you, or use it, and your husband dies. If you try to warn him and we can't get to him, we'll start injecting random, innocent people. If you arrive in the garage and do not have this note in your hand, the results will be the same. At any moment, if we think you have warned someone, the results will be the same. We're watching.

You have five minutes. Ready, set, go.

This can't be happening. It can't be. But it is. There must be a way out of this.

Think, Sara. Think!

People will die. Chris will die. If I leave and they take me,

Chris will lose his mind. But what can I do? I close my hand around the piece of paper and open my purse. They say they'll know if I use my phone, but an unsent text message isn't using it. It shouldn't register in any electronic monitoring being done.

> Chris. They were going to kill you and innocent people if I don't go with them. They say they have syringes of poison. They told me to go to the garage. I have to go. I wouldn't be the person you love if I didn't go and I let innocent people die. I can't let you die. I love you too much, and no matter what happens, you were my safe place. My only place.

I'm shaking when I exit the stall and set my phone on the sink. A woman walks in and I want to hand it to her and tell her to take it to Chris, but she could be one of them. I exit the bathroom and Jacob is waiting. We start weaving through the crowd, and even from ten feet away, I can see Blake huddled with Chris at the table. And my gut tells me that Blake just got some kind of heads-up about what's happening. That gives me hope of a rescue that I cling to, but nothing more.

I turn to Jacob. "I forgot my phone in the bathroom. I need to get it. I had a text message I don't want read on it."

His brow furrows. "Let's go."

"Oh, wait." I point to a woman only a few steps away that I don't even know. "Can you grab her? I need her. She's a big donor. Please, Jacob. I need to talk to her first."

He gives me an odd look but says, "Ma'am," and turns a moment, and I weave in between several people and repeat this move several times. I never stop walking, and I don't let myself look back toward Chris. I enter the elevator to head to the garage, and a dark-haired man in a dark suit enters after me. When the doors shut, he turns to me, his lips twisting evilly.

"Good work, Sara. Garner Neuville will be proud of you."

✑ *ella* ✑

He meant it when he said he wouldn't touch me with the hawk tattoo on my arm, and though his manipulative personality, combined with my tattoo, an extension of Kayden, saves me from his touch, no such thing is true of his attention. He watches me the entire flight, which I estimate to be two hours thus far. And while his eyes are all over my naked body, intent on taunting me and promising me punishment, I tune him out. I see him but do not see him, nor do I allow myself to feel him. Surviving him is a practiced skill that I do well, and my mind is not on Garner Neuville, or my naked body, or even the chill of the air blowing on my skin. I disappear into a mental zone that's all about calculating, plotting, and tallying what the voices and movement in the plane tell me, which equate to four men and a pilot, in addition to us. The real question becomes how many will be on the ground when we land, and how many will travel with us to our new destination. Certainly his bodyguard Bastile and a driver, and if it stands there, my odds are good.

Time ticks by and each minute takes me farther from Rome, but I hope not Europe, where Kayden's best resources exist. Finally, less than three hours since I awoke, I'm certain, the engines' hums shift, our altitude with them, and we begin to descend to the ground. Neuville changes as well, a sense of urgency in his energy showing in his gray devil eyes. He unties me, the cigar-and-whisky scent of him turning my stomach. His hands on top of my arms, which are positioned on the armrests, and his body close to mine jerk me fully back into the present, where I'm naked and his breath is hot on my face.

"Get dressed, but don't get used to those clothes," he orders. He sits back down and watches me struggle through a bumpy descent I should be strapped in for.

His gaze goes to my nipples and for a moment I feel disgust at his inspection, but I shove it aside, cursing that part of me that remains ever so human, and thanks to this man, at moments fragile in a way I despise with every part of my being. Humanity is a luxury, or curse, a demon even, that I can't afford. I'll wrestle that part of me later, with Kayden.

"I need to go to the bathroom," I say once I'm dressed, which is true. That human thing wins again, but it also gives me a chance to exit this plane with anything I might use as a weapon.

He looks irritated. "I'll go with you." He stands and motions me to the back of the plane.

And I know what's coming. He'll keep the door open and watch me, but I don't have a choice. I have to be 100 percent on my game when we land, so I can assess what's really happening with Sara and Kayden. When I have the chance to kill and not be killed.

I turn and walk to the back, looking for any small weapon

I can discreetly latch on to. But the walk is short and there's not even a pen or pencil I could jab in his neck or better yet, his groin.

Instead, I endure the bumps and shifts of the plane as I go to the bathroom with Neuville watching, absolute sadistic enjoyment in his expression as I do. That bothers me more than him looking at me naked, but by the time I'm back in my seat, strapped in, with him directly in front of me, I'm just ready to be out of this steel prison and on the ground. The sensation of the wheels hitting the pavement promises me that he's one step closer to dead, and I have to bite back a smile.

He does smile, those brutal lips of his curving, and I know the look on his face. It's the prelude to an attack, be it mental or physical, that he is savoring before it even happens. And it's not a bluff, and nothing he does has limits one would expect from others, thus you never know how bad the bad he will deliver might be. And that look on his face is crystal clear, no words required. He's planned a surprise for me when we land, which he will like and I will not. But I can't let myself think about who, or what, that might be—I must be focused on a way to escape.

The plane halts and the doors open. He grabs my arm and forgets I'm buckled in, cursing. "Take the damn thing off."

I unhook the seat belt and I'm instantly yanked to my feet. I let him drag me in front of him, me facing forward, him at my back. I step into the aisle and I move forward, while one of his men gives me an up-and-down glance that I ignore for a view of my own. The gun holstered at his rib cage is like chocolate on a bad day. I want it. I could take it if the moment were right, savor its delicious promises. *If only the moment were right*, but I want more than Neuville dead, I remind myself. I want to see Kayden again. I want to save Sara. And my father's words play in my head. *Discipline. Patience. Timing. You're a small package. Strike like a cobra, not like a four-hundred-pound bear.*

"Keep going," Neuville orders, his damn hand at my hip. Maybe I'll chop it off instead of killing him, but that would be a dirty job. There are other things I could chop off, and they could be worth the bloody aftermath, an idea that speeds my steps and leads me to the end of the walkway, where Neuville of course shoves me.

Getting the idea he's intended, I more than happily step to the open door, and aside from the SUV limo awaiting us on some remote runway in who knows where, there are a good half dozen extra men and three black sedans. *Wonderful. A convoy.* If I kill the mob boss and our car stops, they kill me. Which means if I make that decision, I have to overpower our driver and the car while we're still moving.

Neuville nudges me toward the stairs. "Move. Get going." He's irritated, obviously eager to get on the road, and I hope that means we're in Kayden's territory—my territory now, where escape will come with easy-to-find assistance.

As I hurry down the stairs, the sun is quickly sliding into the horizon, and the barely existent landing strip is void of any landmarks I can use to pinpoint our location. "Where are we?"

"A place we're now leaving," he replies predictably, his hand gripping my arm, tugging me toward the black SUV limo where Bastile waits for us by the back door, his holster just beneath his jacket and his big, tall body an easy target to hit when I eventually take his gun. "Get in," he commands, as if I don't get the point of the open door.

I climb inside the vehicle, and that's when his gloating look on the plane comes back to haunt me, shock radiating through me as I find myself staring at Sara, who is wearing a stunning silver party dress.

"Ella," she breathes out, a hint of relief in her shock that I'm not sure she should feel.

Recovering my initial jolt quickly, I give her a quick nod and mouth, "No emotion."

She narrows her eyes and nods back, and the solidness of her chin, the determination to survive in her eyes, reminds me of the strength that I've always sensed in her, even when at times I didn't think she knew it to be true. And while, no, I am not happy that she is here, the one good thing about Neuville putting us in the same place at the same time is that now I can kill him. Maybe not in this car, where she could end up in the crossfire of whatever action I take, but soon. Really soon.

Neuville slides into the car next to me, across from Sara, while Bastile joins the driver in the front seat. By my count that puts at least four men in two other cars, plus a driver in each, if I assume only those on the plane join us, and I can't assume that at all. There were more men on the ground, many of whom could remain with the plane for our later departure, but they could also ride in the additional cars. The odds are not in my favor. This is not that right moment.

The minute the doors are shut we begin to move, and Neuville turns his attention on Sara. "Well, now," he says, giving her an inspection, and though I can't see his eyes from where I sit, I see hers. He's already imagining her naked. "You really are a pretty little thing, aren't you?" he says. "Chris Merit does know how to pick a woman. And that's a 'fuck me' dress if I ever saw one. So yes, I think I will. Fuck you."

To Sara's credit, she listens to me. She shows no emotion. Instead, she looks at me and I silently tell her to hold her ground. *Don't react.* "Should I fuck her now, Ella? I mean"—he grabs my arm, turning my wrist upward for his viewing and mine—"I've been staring at your naked body for hours, but I can't fuck you with this trash on your skin."

"I was naked for hours and your men knew it," I say, goading him and turning the attention on me, and away from Sara. "That big one with the goatee looked at me like he wanted to fuck me. Is that what you wanted?"

He doesn't take the bait. His lips curve sardonically. "I'm sure they all want to fuck you, Ella. I liked that they knew you were naked on the plane, and also that they couldn't have you." He holds up the picture he took of me. "And I like that Kayden is about to see you like this and know that I'm about to have you. He'll think I already have, though, won't he? But we won't send it to him until we're ready for him to find you. He'll trace the data source when I hit Send, and I'm not foolish enough to use my regular phone line with The Underground involved."

I face him. "You downplay Evil Eye too easily. You will pay for this."

"I have recordings of you and Kayden plotting to kill me," he says. "Evil Eye will be voided." He looks to Sara. "Come to me. On this side of the car. I want both beautiful women by my side."

"It will not be voided," I say, determined to keep Sara away from him, no matter what that means for me. "You kill a Hawk, you die." I shove my wrist at him. "You hurt a Hawk's woman, you die."

He grabs my hair and yanks me to him, and this time Sara reacts. "Let her go!"

"I'm fine, Sara," I say quickly, worried she'll try to help me and get hurt. "Stay where you are."

"Should I give her a lesson on obedience now, or later?" he asks me, his mouth close to mine, breath hot and disgusting, lips so close I could bite a hole in them to match mine with one hard slice of my teeth.

"You want me, and you're just pissed that you can't have me. You never had me. You never broke me."

"I own you," he promises. "And Hawk will be tied up for the show. He will watch the pain you feel when I burn his mark from your arm, then watch you endure suffering while I fuck your friend and punish her for all of your sins. And then I'll punish you and fuck you. Over and over and over again. And then, and only then, will I let him die." He shoves me away from him so hard, I hit the car door.

His phone rings and he answers it, and Sara and I make eye contact. "I'm sorry," I mouth.

"It's not your fault," she silently replies, her response gutting me. "He's a monster."

But it *is* my fault. Like my father, I couldn't help forming an attachment with a civilian; I pulled her into this by becoming friends with her. I am not someone who can have friends. Yet I love this woman, and I have to save her.

I lift a finger, letting her know I'm listening to Neuville's conversation. We'll be at the location in five minutes. His people don't know if "he" is in the city, but the plane they sent as a decoy in Neuville's name should have ensured that "he" followed. I assume they're talking about Kayden. The rest of the conversation provides little information. The car begins to slow and Neuville ends the call.

We pull into a driveway, and Sara looks out of the window as motion detectors illuminate the property we've entered. "No," she whispers, her voice lifting more and more as she repeats, "No. No. No."

"What is it, Sara?"

She whirls on Neuville. "You will not do this here." Her voice trembles not with fear, but anger. "If you want to rape me or kill me or whatever, you will *not* do it here."

"What is this place?" I ask, looking for the game-changing confirmation that we're in France and not far from the city. "Sara, talk to me."

"It's sacred," she says, looking at me. "It *can't* be here."

"It's Chris Merit's chateau," Neuville says, and he holds up the naked photo of me again. "It's really perfect. Lots of rooms for play. A dungeon where I can chain Kayden."

"A studio for Chris's work," she snaps. "This is his escape from the city." She looks at me, desperation in her voice and eyes. "There are reasons he can't lose this place, and me, Ella."

"It's too late to turn back in the name of fine art, though he is quite talented. I have one of his pieces in my den. But at this point"—Neuville holds up the phone and the photo of me naked in the airplane seat—"once we're inside and my men have secured the property, we'll send some photos to Kayden and have him join us, alone of course. His noncompliance will come with a price for you ladies."

"Paris?" I ask, seeking complete confirmation in a way that won't make him suspicious. "You dared to come back to Paris?"

"The countryside outside of Paris," Sara says, her finger-nails digging into her palms. "I will do anything you want. Just not here."

Neuville gives her an amused look and then glances at me. "She gives me what I want too easily. Don't you think?"

"I'll take you to the necklace," I say, setting my trap, and getting the intense reaction I expect.

His expression instantly turns explosive and he pulls me hard against him. "Where is it?"

"In the city, not far from your house. But if we go there, she's free the minute I hand it to you."

"Tell me where it is."

I shake my head. "I get it myself, and she goes free right now. Leave her here."

He glares at me, anger crackling off him, and then he re-leases me. "She goes with us." He looks to the front of the car and calls out, "To the city."

One of his men doesn't like this idea, warning him of the dangers, but as I expect, Neuville's jaw sets. "To the city," he orders again.

The man doesn't give up, suggesting that part of the convoy take me and return with both his prizes. But again, Neuville is predictable. He's not going to let me or that necklace out of his reach. He barks an order and the car starts to move. Neuville then moves, sitting across from me, next to Sara, grabbing her leg and aligning it with his, his fingers at her knee. He stares at me and I stare back, a challenge between us. Sara for the necklace.

nineteen

The entire hour-long ride, Neuville holds onto Sara and stares at me. Sara shuts her eyes, enduring the devil at her side in her own way, and it works. It won't get her beaten or killed. It's calm. It's not panicky. It's the kind of reaction that intrigues Neuville enough to make him want to fuck you, not kill you. Which is still torturous, but at least it's not dead.

Unfortunately, the convoy follows us. Fortunately, Neuville's arrogant need for a huge SUV limo makes us stand out like a sore thumb that Kayden will surely notice. When we reach the city, I direct them to the Champs-Élysées. Sara's eyes light with the name that places us close to her home, and the many people looking for her and us. Greed, like his arrogance, has led Neuville down the wrong path. My path. The one that ends in death.

"Where now?" Neuville demands.

I call out the address to his driver, as well as the name of the chocolate shop.

"A chocolate shop? This had better not be a game. You know how I feel about games that I don't start," Neuville warns.

"Would you have ever thought to look there?" I ask. "And this is the last place I remember having it. I hid it there the night David died. But I can't promise I didn't move it. If I did, though, I'm close to remembering everything. I'll find it for you."

"Who else knows about this chocolate shop?"

"No one," I say. "I remembered it on the plane."

His eyes glint like hot coals. "Are you lying?"

"Matteo told you about my amnesia. You watched me on the castle cameras. I didn't know until I saw you again. You were my trigger."

He leans forward, grabbing my legs now instead of Sara's. "You and that necklace are mine. Sara, I will release. But you aren't leaving me again. Understood?"

"You'll never have me," I promise him. "Even if I'm with you."

His lips curve. "Ah, Ella. I do so enjoy the way you challenge me." The car begins to slow and he leans back, releasing my legs, the driver telling him in French that we've arrived. "Is that the place?" he demands.

I look outside. We're stopped in front of the row of stores and businesses where the chocolate shop is nestled, and thankfully it's still open. "That's it," I say, my senses tingling in ways I understand but couldn't explain to someone else. This is it. Everything ends here.

"Pull around back," he orders the driver, a directive I

revel in. The odds that Kayden will be here or have someone here are more than 50 percent, and the back of the building gives him room to take action. Or me. I'm no princess waiting to be rescued by her prince; the back door works for me as well. Especially since Neuville is concerned about a surprise attack and instructs the other two vehicles to take up strategic positions near the store. He's worried about Kayden and that works for me. Fewer men for me to kill at one time.

"Where will I find the necklace?" he demands as we claim a chunk of the tiny lot, which seems to be for employees, not oversized limos.

"I hid it inside a certain display box," I say, but in my mind's eye, I see myself in a hallway by the bathroom, burying it under the foliage of a fake plant. "I'll need to go in myself."

He considers me a moment. "Bastile," he calls out, ordering him to escort me into the store in French, at the same time that he grabs a chunk of Sara's hair. He yanks her to him, leaning in to speak beside her ear. "Tell her if she calls for help, I'll kill you. Choke you to death, one breath at a time. Right here in this car." Sara doesn't comply and he jerks her head backward. "Tell her."

"He'll kill me," she repeats, squeezing her eyes shut.

"I'll choke you," he says, disgustingly licking her ear. "*Tell her.*"

"He'll choke me," Sara repeats and now her eyes are open, the look I find there resolved to whatever comes next. Not panicked, just . . . resolved.

What comes next is Neuville dying and her going free.

"No phone calls," he says. "No conversations with strangers." He reaches up and attempts to rip down the front of Sara's dress. Luckily the lining defeats him, but he acts as if it hasn't. "Her dress comes off if you are one minute over ten."

I inhale, but I don't look at Sara again. I can't. I don't want to think of the two of them in the car alone when I need to think about how to ensure she gets out of it alone and unharmed. The door opens and I exit into the dark parking lot to stand in front of Bastile, whose close proximity allows me a better look at his shoulder holster with only one gun, resting at his rib cage. It's almost time. I'll be taking that from him soon. Just not now. Not until I ensure that I send Kayden a message that I'm here in the city, just in case this location isn't on his radar, as I expect it to be.

We walk toward the store, going to the front door, which pleases me. And then I get more of those tingling sensations that have become a part of my missions. They tell me when I'm on target. They tell me that my people are watching. And my unrushed pace gives Kayden or his Hunters a chance to confirm that the limo equates to my presence. We round the building and I continue walking slowly. Bastile doesn't like this. He grabs my arm and yanks me forward. Another plus in my favor; it tells the right people the tone of my situation. But no matter what, much of what comes next must be dictated by me. Those watching, and I feel that they are, won't know how much danger Sara is in, or even myself. There could be a gun pointed at my head, or hers, that they can't see.

"I'll be inside the exit, watching you," Bastile warns before opening the door, and I walk inside the decently spacious store, considering this is Paris and all things come in petite.

Wasting no time, I immediately walk to the opposite side of the store, knock over a box, and use that for camouflage as I yank the credit card from my boot that, thankfully, slides out easily. I think I've been found, but I'm going to make sure. Next, I walk to a table with a packaged gift and motion to the attendant. She hurries over to me and I put my back to Bastile and face her, slipping her my card and speaking in French. "I'll take two of these, please. Charge them. It's a gift for the man by the door and his wife, so please be discreet? I want to surprise them over dinner tonight for their anniversary."

"Oh, yes, of course. I'll be right back."

"Wait, please. If he comes over here, can you say, 'I'm sorry, I don't have that item'? Tell him that you're checking the other store and can I check back in an hour? That will give me an excuse to sneak back here in a few minutes and get my card and package, while they shop elsewhere."

"Of course," she agrees, thankfully quite sweet. "I love secret gifts. They are so fun!"

She hurries off and I turn to find Bastile charging toward me. "What was that about?"

"The display I was looking for is missing. She's trying to find out if it's still in the building." I cross my arms in front of me. "We just have to wait for her and pray. Otherwise—"

"You said nothing else?"

"Wait with me. She'll be right back. Or do you need to hold up the door?"

The attendant hurries back to me and sticks to the plan. "I'm sorry. It's just not available here. I'm checking another store. Will you be in the area awhile? Can you check back in an hour?"

"I will," I say. "And I'll come back."

"Excellent," she confirms. "I'll try to have good news."

I give her a tiny nod. "Thank you," I say, and then turn to face Bastile, who's scowling at me.

"Are you about to tell me that you don't have what we came here for?" he demands.

"I'm telling you we've hit a bump in the road. The display is in one of the other locations. I hid it in a drawer attached to it. We'll find it."

"He is not going to be pleased."

Like I don't know that, but I hold my tongue. We head back to the door, but once we're there, he holds the handle and looks down at me. "Should you contemplate putting those CIA skills to use, and try to save your friend, know this: We trained you. We planned for you. We have a man with a gun following your every step back to the car."

But I know Neuville won't kill me.

"And if you just thought Neuville won't kill you, he gave us permission to hurt you. Badly. He seems to like the idea of you trapped in bed indefinitely. He said to tell you he thought that might finally break you."

Damn. "I was thinking about how to find the display," I say blandly.

He smirks. "Of course you were," he says, and then opens the door.

I exit into the chilly night air I hadn't even noticed before now, my mind racing. My plan had been to take his gun, open the car door and shoot Neuville, then shoot his driver and save Sara. I can't be sure Kayden's people, even if watching me, know about a sniper, who may or may not exist. And I don't plan on being in anyone's bed but Kayden's. The tricky part of getting in that car is having no gun. If I snap Neuville's neck, the driver can turn a gun on me, and it will be hard to take away from him with the seats between us.

My mind firm now that I've told Kayden where I am, I just need to get us to the next chocolate shop location. I'll grab Bastile's gun when I'm about to exit, and immediately claim shelter back inside the car. Plan decided upon, now I need to convince Neuville to go to another store.

Bastile opens the door and I climb inside the limo, finding Sara smashed to Neuville's side while he strokes her hair. *Sick bastard.*

"Where is my necklace?" he demands, the door sealing me inside.

"It's in a display drawer, and that display was shipped to another store. We need to go to the location by the Notre Dame cathedral."

He calls over the seat for the driver to get Bastile. The driver rolls down the window and calls for Bastile. The next instant, a challenging development occurs. Bastile opens the door and gets in beside me. He repeats what I've said, in French. "The woman said to check in with her in an hour."

Neuville's eyes turn hot and sharp on me. "What game are you playing, Ella?"

"This is not a game. You know what Matteo told you. You know what was on the security feed you watched."

"I know you know where that necklace is. I see it in your eyes. In the defiance you think I don't understand. But I did break you in ways you don't wish to accept. And I will break you now."

He looks at Bastile and spits out a command, and Bastile pulls his gun and points it at Sara. "Here's what going to happen," Neuville says, yanking Sara across his lap. "I'm going to fuck her while you watch unless you tell me where it's at. If you try to stop me from fucking her, Bastile will shoot her."

"No," Sara says. "No." She shoves against him and he laughs.

"I'm going to enjoy this." He grabs her hair and there's a struggle.

I go to the place where I find control and calm, because this is the moment I've waited months for. Bastile's management of his weapon is pathetic, his supposed respect for my skills lacking. He thinks I'm small. He thinks he's strong. He's right, but those things don't matter.

I count to three in my mind, and then act. I take Bastile's gun and I'm in his lap, straddling him, the gun at his chest and trigger pulled before he even knows what happened. The next second, I rotate, and I'm sitting in the lap of a dead man.

The driver rotates, a gun in his hand he intends to use on me, and thankfully I have a clear shot. I hit him between the eyes and my gun is now on Neuville, who has Sara's dress to her waist.

"Let her go," I order, and slowly, too slowly, he eases his grip on her.

Sara scrambles out of his lap and as soon as she's against the door, she slams her foot in his face. He growls and reaches for her and I land a foot in his groin, doubling him over. His phone is on the seat and I grab it, dialing Kayden and moving off of Bastile, who I shove against the door.

He answers quickly. "Who is this?" and just the sound of his voice, knowing he's absolutely alive, sends a rush of relief though me.

"Kayden."

"Ella," he breathes out. "I'm here, sweetheart. I'm at the chocolate shop."

"Is it safe to send Sara out to you?"

"Yes, and I'm coming to you."

I end the call. "Get out of the car, Sara."

"Not without you."

"Get out of the car, Sara, so I can kill the bastard."

Neuville straightens. "You think Evil Eye is bad? Kill me, and the wrath I have planned for Kayden will make him wish he were dead."

The door opens to my right and Kayden slides in beside me, the smell of him so masculine and safe and him, and the feel of his presence is like a breath of air I didn't think I'd ever take in again.

"Your husband says to get out of the damn car, Sara," he tells her.

"Chris," she whispers, and she's out of the car.

"Why is he still alive, sweetheart?" Kayden asks.

"Because she knows killing me comes with a price," Neuville replies.

"Is there a plan we need to follow?" I ask.

"The plan includes hurrying the fuck up. He's your prize. Do it and let's move."

Neuville has gone quiet, his eyes meeting mine, and I see in their depths that he knows what's coming. He accepts it. He even challenges me to do it.

"This seems too easy, too humane. I thought we'd punish him."

"And as much as I love how you think, we just need him gone, and to deal with the logistics." Kayden raises his gun. "You or me? Let's just do it."

I point my gun at Neuville's groin and shoot him, his scream radiating through the air. I let him feel the pain, just for a few seconds. I just have to let him feel it. And then I lift my weapon and shoot him in the head. He's dead. The monster lives no more. Kayden grabs my arm and helps me out of the car, and Adriel is there waiting. "Where's Sara?"

"We just put her and Chris in a car on the way to the airport," he says. "I've got this mess."

"We'll meet Chris and Sara there," Kayden tells me, and another car pulls up. "That's our ride."

We climb into the backseat, and I don't know the driver nor do I care who he is. Not when Kayden's taken my gun and is now cupping my face. "Ella," he whispers, his mouth closing down on mine, in a deep, passionate, drink-me-in kiss that I return with all that I am. And when we come up for a breather, we linger there, breathing together, and for me, finally breathing again, I realize.

"I thought I'd lost you," he confesses, a tormented quality in his voice that I feel straight to my soul, an echo of exactly what I'd felt. "Are you okay?"

"He's dead. That makes me absolutely fucking fabulous." My hand flattens on Kayden's chest, and I can feel his heart thundering under my palm. "He just . . . and I . . ."

"Tell me he didn't—"

"No," I say, saving the part about the tattoo for later, when we're alone. "He didn't." I lean back to look at him, focus on the things that won't take me places I can't go right now. "Matteo's dead. Neuville had him killed."

"We found him, and my only regret was that I didn't get to do it myself."

"What about Gallo? Did you kill him?"

"Gallo came clean. Like I said, he's a good cop and that part of him won over the hate. Especially when Neuville threatened the lives of his sister and other civilians. He was afraid to warn me on the phone, or I would have gotten to you sooner to prevent this."

"I was rooting for him," I say. "I'm glad he wasn't one of the bad guys."

We turn down the street where Neuville lives, or rather *lived*, and I stiffen, sucking in air as memories assail me, flying through my mind as if I'm skimming pages in a book.

"I'll go in," Kayden says, his hand squeezing my leg, and I blink to realize we're already in front of Neuville's insanely expensive home, a black stone building in one of the most expensive areas of the city.

"No," I say. "He's dead. His ghost isn't going to haunt me. We came for the necklace, and I know where I put it."

Our driver opens the gates, clearly possessing the code, and it's not long before I'm in the marbled foyer, with many people, including Blake, in my path.

"Holy fuck, woman!" He charges forward and hugs me. "Thank you for saving her." He leans back and looks at me. "I've gotten fond of those two, and had no idea just how deep this shit really was."

"I'm the reason she needed to be saved," I say, the words rasping out of my suddenly raw throat.

He gives me a probing stare. "That sounds like ten years of therapy that you won't get, so just talk to her. She still loves you, I promise you." He glances at Kayden. "Chris is another story. He's going to want to hurt someone."

"I'm sure it will be a fun plane ride to Italy."

I glance at Kayden. "They're coming with us?"

"Just until the dust settles and Blake finishes up here," he says, his hand settling possessively on my back.

"Since when are you doing Underground cleanup?" I ask Blake.

"Since it makes damn sure my clients, who I also consider friends, aren't attached," he explains.

Kayden's fingers flex at my back. "Let's get this done and get out of here."

I nod and hurry forward, making a beeline for the kitchen, a stunning room of navy, green, and white, pausing at the table where I find three dead men posed.

"Meet Neuville's second and third, as well as Alessandro. He's the one with the goatee," Kayden says.

"Something tells me Neuville's promise to make your life hell if he died isn't going to go so well," I say.

"The only thing the French mob is going to be thinking about right now is saving themselves from Niccolo, and dealing with law enforcement," he says. "The police will find these three, and Neuville, in a few hours, after receiving reports of gunfire."

"That works," is all I say, and that's all the thought I give them. They're monsters better removed from this world, and I'm here for a reason. I go to the navy-tiled island and point to the silver, rectangular light fixture running the length of it. "It should be there, on this side."

"You can't even reach up there," Kayden points out.

"That was the idea," I say. "I had to climb up to put it there."

He reaches over the top of the light and lo and behold, he produces the necklace. I let out a sigh. "Three hundred million dollars. There it is."

"There it is."

He sets it on the counter and opens a drawer underneath, removing a jewelry case. "This is our little special touch to the crime scene, which I put here for safekeeping until we're ready to leave." He opens the box to display a second butterfly necklace. "A five-million-dollar perfect replica," he explains. "Adriel will place it in Alessandro's pocket. The British government is going to pick it up and put it in their protective care. We'll keep the real necklace. Our goal was to protect the real necklace when we found it, and we completed that process today. Now, if the fake is stolen, this won't start all over again."

"Where will we keep it?"

"We have a private vault under the castle," he says. "No one but me, and now you, knows about it." He places the fake necklace back in the drawer. "Adriel will make it all come together."

Then he picks up the real necklace. "Let's go back home, Ella."

"Yes. Home."

And for the first time in perhaps my entire adult life, and in the face of such horrible events, I feel like I *have* a home. And that home is Kayden.

We arrive at the airport, parking in a private hangar, and I've never wanted time to talk to Kayden and be with him more. I want every detail about this day's happenings, as he does from me, but even more, I just want him.

"Time to go take whatever blows Chris Merit has for me," he says, reaching for the car door.

"This is on me, not you. And I fear that Sara now hates me, which guts me, but how can I blame her?"

He kisses me. "She won't hate you. I promise. Let's go prove me right."

We leave the car and cross the pavement, and we're at the

top of the steps to the plane when he says, "Let me deal with Chris first."

I nod and he enters, with me following, and sure enough, the two men huddle up, voices deep and a bit rough.

Sara steps into the aisle, her dress torn, her hair and makeup a mess, but the minute we make eye contact, I know I haven't lost her. She tears up and so do I, and then we're hugging. "I'm so sorry," I say, cupping her head.

"Just tell me you killed him."

"I did." I lean back and look at her. "I shot him in the groin first. Then I killed him."

She nods. "Good. You're so badass! I thought you were—"

"I know, and I'll explain everything later. Just know this: I'm sorry for the lies, but I love you. I know I'm not what I seem, but I love you. I can explain."

Chris appears above her shoulder with no anger in his face, just relief. "Thank you for risking your life to save her," he shocks me by saying, his hands settling on her shoulders.

"I just . . . I know I can't be around Sara and keep her safe, but don't shut me out completely. There are ways—"

"We'll figure it out," Chris says. "Right now, Kayden needs you as much as I need her."

"Yes." Sara and I hug again, and I move down the aisle to where Kayden waits. "How bad was it?" I ask as we buckle in.

"He's a good man," he says. "And he knows Sara loves you, but he's worried about her safety."

"Of course he is."

Kayden's phone rings. He takes the call and manages some details on the ground, and by the time he's done we're taxiing onto the runway. And then we're in the air, the ride smooth when the day has been anything but that, and a surreal feeling comes over me.

"It's done," I say. "It's really done."

"Yes. It is." He unbuckles his seat belt and goes down on a knee in front of me to unbuckle me as well. "Ella. What you did today was nothing shy of incredible. You are the most amazing person. You're brave. Passionate. Caring. I am so lucky to have found you. You are a Lady Hawk like no other could ever be."

"And the same is true of you, my Hawk."

"I can't give you complete safety. Today proved that, and you proved you can handle that."

"I can. I just hate that we can't trust everyone around us."

"We'll find a way to never have another Matteo. Together."

"I was afraid you'd—"

"Shut you out? I can't. You're in my heart and soul, Ella." He reaches to his seat and produces a velvet box. "Will you marry me?"

I smile. "I already said yes."

"Not with a ring." He opens the lid, and I gasp at the perfect circle of a pale pink diamond.

"Pink," I whisper, smiling at him. "Like my ballet slippers?"

"Yes. Because that Hawk on your arm is the warrior in you, and the ballet slippers are the woman. I want you to be both. I want you to feel you can be both with me, and as much as I want to protect you, I vow to let you be both."

I start crying. "I think this warrior has shut down for the day."

"She deserves a break," he says, taking the ring out of the case and slipping it on my finger. And it's a perfect fit, like the man, The Hawk. My future husband.

∽∽∽∽∽∽

Kayden and I talk the entire flight, and it's early morning when we approach the Rome airport. We've just hit the runway when his phone rings, and he quickly pulls up the news on his iPad, playing a video story:

> In a scandalous and shocking breaking story, French and British officials are at the home of Garner Neuville, long known to be the head of the French mob. He and two of his highest-ranking members were found dead, along with a man name Alessandro Abate, an Italian national who is known to run a notorious treasure-hunting operation. At the center of the dispute is a necklace worth three hundred million dollars, stolen more than a decade ago from the British government.

"And now," Kayden says, "it's over."

"What about Niccolo?"

"He'll hyper-focus on trying to take over the French mob until he dies. But Neuville's fourth won't let that happen."

A few minutes later the doors of the plane are open, and Kayden pulls a leather jacket on to cover his shoulder holster and weapon, then reaches into the overhead bin and offers me my purse. "Annie is still intact."

"Oh, Annie," I say, opening the purse to stroke my gun. "How I missed you."

He laughs and so do I as we head up front to chat with Chris and Sara, who seem much more relaxed now. We exit the plane before them for safety reasons, heading down the stairs inside a private hangar.

Sasha is waiting on us at the bottom of the steps and she wastes no time throwing her arms around me. "You did it. You brave bitch, you! Damn, you scared me." She fights tears, and my chest tightens because I know what Neuville put her through. I know what *I* put her through with that phone call.

Seconds tick by and she gives me a nod, the emotion scrubbed from her face moments later. "I'm going to play shotgun to the driver escorting Sara to the castle." She glances over my shoulder as Sara and Chris exit, whistling, and proving she's officially pushed aside Neuville, at least for now, as she adds, "And apparently her really hot husband. Holy hell, she has good taste. I like her already." She hands Kayden the keys to one of the F-TYPEs. "Sweet ride, boss," she says, motioning to the ice-blue Jag waiting a short distance away.

Kayden and I laugh, and then get Chris and Sara introduced to Sasha and into the car. We follow them, and they've just entered the gates of the castle, with us about to as well, eager to lock up the necklace, when a limo pulls up right next to us.

"Niccolo," Kayden says, shutting the gate with us and him on the outside, and placing the car in park. "At least we'll get this over with right away." He glances over at me. "Ready?"

I nod and we both open our doors, finding him standing

only a few feet from us. "You lost the necklace?" he snaps. "How did you lose the necklace?"

"We didn't know what happened until we landed here," Kayden says. "We watched it on the news."

"That necklace was worth three hundred million dollars," he bites out. "How does a Hawk and his Lady Hawk lose it?"

"Your brother's dead," I say. "There's your prize."

Kayden adds, "And maybe you'll even live to enjoy his death. You do have that new cancer therapy."

Niccolo locks eyes with Kayden. "I am going to live, Hawk. There will be many more years for you to hate me. You'd be advised not to forget that." He walks away, pausing at the door of his limo to add, "And I hear his fourth is now in charge." His lips quirk and he climbs into the vehicle.

"Why did that make him smile?" I ask.

"Never let the enemy see you blink," Kayden says. "And make no mistake, we're still the enemy. Win at all costs or die forgotten."

It's the saying that connects to the tattoo on his arm, the same one etched into the War Room table, and I know now why it's so familiar. Kayden is a warrior, as was my father. As am I now, and perhaps have been every moment of my life, even before I understood that was who, and what, I am. And warriors always win at all costs or die forgotten.

"What about The Jackals?" I ask, my mind looking for any loose ends. "Any bumps there?"

"Disbandment is effectively under way," he confirms. "In three months that organization will be gone and forgotten."

He motions to the car and we climb back in, and it's not

long afterward that Chris and Sara are tucked away in our spare bedroom. After we watch their door shut, Kayden motions toward ours. "Now we lock away the necklace."

He leads me into the bedroom closet, where he pushes aside his clothes and presses a button. The wall moves, and a door opens.

"It's like in the movies," I say.

"Better than the movies, because it's ours."

He flips on a light and we walk down a long set of winding stairs that ends in a huge stone room lined with wine bottles in racks. "A wine cellar?" I ask.

"By design." He hits another button, and one of the wine racks lowers into the floor and a safe emerges in its place. "Each wine case has a safe. That way if someone finds one, they won't find them all. Or so we hope." He presses his finger to the steel door and it opens. He then removes a velvet box and sets the necklace inside it. We both stare down at the butterfly.

"It's really gorgeous, isn't it?" I ask. "But three hundred million dollars? That's insanity."

"It creates insanity." He closes the box and places it in the safe, sealing it away along with a chapter of our lives. The safe is then lowered and the wine rack returned to its prior position. "Now, it's really done."

He steps to me, his hands framing my face. "But we're just beginning, and I plan to live every day with you like we're dying. And to kiss you like I will never kiss you again."

And so he does. He kisses me, and it feels like a kiss from a dying man. A kiss to last forever, whatever our forever may be.

Dear Readers:

I can't believe it's over! I'm already imagining the wedding, and a chance for Ella and Sara to sit and talk for hours. They need to talk about those journals! And about the wedding . . . well, you know Ella might need to have a gun strapped under her dress, and actually have to use it. That would be so fun and pretty sexy, too. And you know Niccolo would have to show up with a gift, and a problem. Oh yes, he would. Maybe that follow-up story will happen. I'd like it to happen. If not, perhaps I've now sparked your ideas for what comes next—and a reader's imagination and excitement are the best compliments a writer can have. I already miss Ella and Kayden and I hope you will, as well. And then there's Sasha and Adriel—those two need a story! Whatever happens, thank you for taking this journey with me.

And if you haven't read Chris and Sara's story, and even want more Blake Walker, you can find them all in the Inside Out series.

xoxo
Lisa

Can't get enough of the sizzlingly sexy and provocative adventures from *New York Times* bestselling author Lisa Renee Jones? Keep reading for an excerpt from the first novel in her bestselling Inside Out series.

if i were you

On sale now!

I am still standing in the middle of Chris Merit's display, in stunned disbelief, when something snaps inside me. I am hot and confused and feeling like the world is spinning around me. I've spent money I don't have on the ticket for the night, but I can't get out of this gallery fast enough. I run for the door, not literally, but I might as well be running. This heat I feel is unexplainable, considering the gallery is chilly, and I need air desperately. I need to think. I need to figure out what is going on inside me, because it is nothing I know as familiar.

Exiting to the street, I welcome the cool night air washing over me. I turn quickly to my left, intending to head for my car, when the strap of my purse catches and snags on the brick of the building and somehow it snaps open. The contents spill to the ground. With exasperation, I squat, trying to retrieve my items. This is so my life, and there is a tiny part of me comforted by my familiar clumsiness, by something that feels like me. I mean, who else can manage to catch her purse on a wall, of all things?

"Need some help?"

My gaze shoots upward to find Chris Merit at eye level, and for a rare moment in time, I can't find the words to ramble with my nerves. While I'd felt comfortable with him inside the gallery, I am dumbstruck now that I know who he is. He is brilliant. He is also incredibly good-looking and he's squatting down on the ground with me, which somehow feels wrong. This night has me feeling as if I am in the Twilight Zone. There is no other explanation for how bizarre it is.

"I . . . ah . . . no," I manage. "Thank you. I got it. It's a little purse. Doesn't hold much." I scoop up my lipstick and a tiny wallet, and slide them back inside the bag before pushing to my feet.

He grabs my keys and stands, towering over my five feet four inches by a good foot. I hadn't realized how tall he is when he'd been sitting beside me at the Ricco event, or how earthy and deliciously male he smells, but the wind lifts and the scent tickles my nose. He is different from Mark, not so sophisticated and debonair, more raw, and yes, like his scent, earthy.

He gives me another one of those devastating smiles he'd used on me in the gallery and dangles my keys in the air. "You might need these to go wherever you're going so fast."

"Thank you," I say, and accept them. His fingers brush mine, and electricity charges up my arm, across my chest, and steals my breath. My eyes meet his, and I see awareness in the deep green depths of his stare. Only I'm not sure if it's the same kind of awareness I feel. Maybe it's simply that I hide my feelings horribly and he now knows I'm reacting to him, and it amuses him.

"You're leaving early," he comments, his hands going to his hips, which pushes back his blazer enough for me to see the stretch of his black T-shirt across his impressive chest. I approve, as I'm sure the rest of the female population does.

"Yes," I say, and jerk my attention to his face, to a full mouth that has me a bit breathless, but then everything has me breathless tonight, it seems. "I need to get home."

"Why don't I walk you to your car?"

He wants to walk me to my car. I'm not sure why he would

want to do that. He doesn't even know me. Is it possible that he felt that same electricity I did, or do I amuse him and he wants to continue the entertainment? Mark did say he has a strange sense of humor. "Why didn't you tell me who you are?" I blurt, not liking the idea of being a joke.

His lips quirk. "Because then you would have told me you loved my work even if you hated it."

My brows dip. I'm not sure how I feel about that. "That's sneaky."

"It spared you the awkwardness of pretending to like my work."

"There wouldn't have been any awkwardness. I like your work."

"And I like that you like my work," he approves, a warm glow in his eyes. "So . . . shall I walk you to your car?"

My escape has been further waylaid, but I'm not sure that is a bad thing anymore. "Okay," I squeak, appalled at my lack of voice. There is a reason I don't date much: I'm horrible at it. I get shy and I pick the wrong men, who use both of those very things against me. Dominant, controlling men, who seem to turn me on in the bedroom and off in real life. It's genetic. I'm quite certain that had I a sister, she would have been just as foolish about men as myself and as my mother had been. And while Chris, at first impression, doesn't strike me as arrogant or controlling, his failure to tell me who he was earlier in the evening was in fact a way of controlling my reaction. Not that I think he is interested in me. I'm overanalyzing and I know it. Chris Merit could have his choice of women and, in fact, probably has. He doesn't need to add little ol' me to the list.

"You know my name," he says, pulling me from my reverie. "It's only fair I know yours."

"Sara. Sara McMillan."

"Nice to meet you, Sara."

"I should be the one saying that to you," I say. "I wasn't joking when I said I love your art. I studied your work in college."

"Now you're making me feel old."

"Hardly," I say. "You started painting when you were a teen."

He cast me a sideways look. "You weren't joking when you said you studied my work."

"Art major."

"And what do you do now?"

I feel a little punch to my gut. "Schoolteacher."

"Art?"

"No," I say. "High school English."

"So why study art?"

"Because I love art."

"Yet you're an English teacher?"

"What's wrong with being an English teacher?" I ask, unable to curb the defensiveness in my tone.

He stops walking and turns to me. "Nothing is wrong with it at all, except that I don't think that's what you want to do."

"You don't know me well enough to say that. You don't know me at all."

"I know the excitement I saw in your eyes when you were in the gallery."

"I don't deny that." A gust of wind rushes over us and

goose bumps lift on my skin. I don't want to be scrutinized. This man sees too much. "We should walk."

He shrugs out of his jacket, and before I know what's happening, it's wrapped around my shoulders and that earthy raw scent of his is surrounding me. I'm wearing Chris Merit's coat and I am dumbstruck all over again. His hands are on the lapels and he is staring down at me. My gaze catches on the brilliant colorful tattoo that covers every inch of his right arm. I've never been with a man with tattoos and never thought I liked them, but I find myself wondering where else he might have them.

"I saw you talking to Mark," he says. "Did you buy something tonight?"

"I wish," I say with a snort, and my embarrassment at the unladylike sound that comes too naturally only drives home reality to me. We are from two different worlds, this man and I. His is one of dreams fulfilled, and mine is one of impossible dreams. "I doubt I could afford one of your brushes, let alone a completed piece."

His eyes narrow. "You shouldn't walk away from something that intrigues you." His voice is a soft rasp of sandpaper that still manages to be velvet on my nerve endings.

Suddenly, I'm not sure we are talking about art, and my throat is dry. I swallow hard and though I hadn't decided I was really going through with it, I blurt, "I'm taking a summer job at the gallery."

His light blond brow arches. "Are you now?"

"Yes." I know it is the truth as I say the word. I know I've already decided I am going to take the job. "I'm filling in for

Rebecca until her return." I search his face for a reaction, but I see none. He is unreadable—or am I just too affected by his nearness to see one?

His hands are still on the lapels and he doesn't move for a long moment. I don't want him to move. I want him to . . . I don't know . . . but then again, yes I do. I want him to kiss me. It's a silly, fantastical moment—no doubt brought on by the journals—that has me blushing. I cut my gaze, feeling as if the heat in his will scorch me inside out. I motion to my car, shocked to realize it's only one parking meter down. "That's me."

Slowly, his hands loosen on my—or rather his—jacket. I immediately walk to my car, willing myself not to dump my purse again. I click the locks open and I stop by the curb before opening my door. I turn to find him close, so very wonderfully close. And that scent of his is driving me wild, pooling heat low in my belly.

"Thanks for the walk and the jacket." I shrug out of it.

He reaches for the jacket and takes it, and I hope he will touch me and fear that he will, at the same moment. I am so out of control and confused.

His green eyes burn hot like fire before he softly says, "It's been my pleasure . . . Sara." And then he just turns and starts walking, without another word.

about the author

An award-winning *New York Times* and *USA Today* bestsell-ing author, Lisa Renee Jones has published more than forty novels spanning many romance genres: contemporary, romantic suspense, dark paranormal, and erotic fiction. In each book the hero is dark, dangerous, and sexy. You can find Lisa on Twitter @LisaReneeJones, Facebook.com/AuthorLisaReneeJones, and her blog LisaReneeJones.com for regular updates.